Laura Beatty is the author of *Darkling* and *Pollard*, which was shortlisted for the Ondaatje Prize. She has also written two biographies, the first about Lillie Langtry and the second about Anne Boleyn.

Also by Laura Beatty

Fiction
Pollard
Darkling

Non-fiction
Lillie Langtry: Manner, Masks and Morals
Anne Boleyn: The Wife Who Lost Her Head

Lost Property
Laura Beatty

atlantic·fiction

First published in hardback in Great Britain in 2019 by
Atlantic Books, an imprint of Atlantic Books Ltd.

This paperback edition published in 2020.

10 9 8 7 6 5 4 3 2 1

A CIP catalogue record for this book is available from
the British Library.

Paperback ISBN: 978 1 78649 740 6
E-book ISBN: 978 1 78649 739 0

Printed in

Atlantic Books
An imprint of Atlantic Books Ltd
Ormond House
26–27 Boswell Street
London WC1N 3JZ

www.atlantic-books.co.uk

'The brain is a metaphor of the world…
[It] can be seen as something like a huge country:
as a nested structure, of villages and towns, then
districts, gathered into countries, regions and even
partly autonomous states or lands.'

The Master and his Emissary, Iain McGilchrist

'The Russia of our books and kitchens never existed.
It was all in our heads.'

Second-Hand Time, Svetlana Alexievich

Before

At the midpoint of my life, I found myself in a dark wood.

Dark as a blanket.

I think, I did not want this.

The woman who lounges on a nearby step as if on a sofa, her carrier bags bunched round her like scatter cushions, looks up as I pass and says with surprising lucidity, 'I can relate to that.'

She is always here. I have often hurriedly, as if doing something I shouldn't, dropped a few coins in her cup but without eye contact. Once, in the early days, I did greet her. She looked so familiar. She looked like someone from a book I once wrote. It doesn't matter whether she is or not. Books are not real. But still, I thought, she looks unsettlingly familiar.

'Do I know you?' I asked, stepping into the fog of her smell. I clattered my coins in her cup and she sparked a lighter and held it up in response, its flame almost touching my nose. She opened her mouth, with its dark interior and its teeth like solitaire pegs. She said something incoherent about waves and slaves and her voice was grating and several passers-by stopped to watch. I turned quickly away. Their attention made me somehow complicit and I didn't want that. I must have been mistaken. I didn't know her after all. Of course I didn't; a bag-lady, out on a doorstep.

'Never. Never Ne-ver,' she shouted behind me, as I scuttled away, head down.

I haven't addressed her since. I hurry past, trying not to look. But out of the corner of my eye, last week, I noticed she now has a little sign, propped up like a birthday card in front of her. It says 'BritAnnia' in wonky writing.

Day after day, like everyone else, I pass with my head turned away; all these people heaped like trash on the streets of our cities with their bags and their lighters and their various sad and private madness, we just pretend they don't exist. But she is hard to ignore. She is always there. And now today, wearing something on her head like an upturned coal-scuttle, she has a road-sweeper's broom in her hand and for a moment she is lucid. It is the lucidity, not the fancy dress, that makes me stop a second time.

Then, because I am looking, I read the names on her bags. Oh, I wish I hadn't done that. They say Boots and Boots and Mothercare. Mothercare,

Mothercare, Boots, just as I once wrote when I first started out, when I invented my Anne, my Everyman.

You what?

I steady myself with one hand against the wall. The woman on the step: did I, or didn't I make all this up? I mean, am I in my head, or out of it? We need to sort this out. Because we've made so many copies of life, all meant to be useful. We've written so many books and drawn so many pictures and made so many films and taken so many photographs that we've got confused. I can't tell any more what's true and what's not. Where exactly is it we are all living?

I check no one is looking and lean in to ask her, 'Look, who are you and what exactly are you doing?'

'BritAnnia!' she says, hissing through the solitaire pegs.

I put my face in close. 'You're not Britannia,' I hiss back. 'You are plain Anne. I know. I made you up.'

Maybe her condition is catching.

'That's enough,' my rational self says to my other, my heart panicking into close quiet. But I don't know now whether she is herself, or just more me. At the midpoint of my life. Out in the street on the way to the shop to buy something as innocent as milk. Dark as a blanket.

I go on again, as if with purpose but it's lonely not knowing. 'Hello?' I put my hand out unsteadily, as if hoping for a rail. I need to sit down for a minute. 'Can anyone see a step?' I think I need a guide. I look round for the little flare of BritAnnia's lighter. 'Show me a light, can't you? I know you've got one.'

'Hello?' Into the darkness. 'Hello? Is anybody there?' And while I wait for an answer, I stand still.

Where am I? Because I can't see. The dark is crowding at me now. Is it universal – this dark – or just mine? Have you noticed? I stand still and I look up and, looking up, I find trees – are they trees? Or are they tower blocks, the light only barely making it through – hemming me in, pushing skywards, casting their obliterating shadow. No air to breathe, no light. This savage city – or is it a forest? – that we have wandered into by mistake. This make-or-break place of wolves and cut-throats. So the stories are true, or have taken over, because this is how it happens. This is how you get lost. Where the shit is the path? You know, the path we were all on together? I thought we were in this together. Because the path was so clear when we set off – remember? – when we made our promises and took our places and set things up for life, booming with confidence in the thoughtless certainty of morning.

Idiots.

Nothing in response. Just the rustle of paper blowing, or leaves, a noise so small I might have imagined it, just something dropping unnoticed to the floor. I hold my hand out in front of me, my writing hand. It is dimly visible – as, at my feet, are birds: pigeons, hobbling, and little, brittle, fume-caked sparrows. All of these seem solid.

Is my writing hand to blame? Because this is a place I didn't intend. I thought writing was there to throw light on the way we are, so that the way we are could change. But the change hasn't happened, or something else has taken over, because look, our dystopias seem to be coming true and now our eyes are too tired, or too dark with imagined disaster, to protest. 'Yes,' we say sagely, with told-you-so voices, 'we knew it would be like this.'

'Keep going,' tradition booms, or is it only the blood in our own ears? 'Push on. Put your best foot forward.' Tradition always speaks in clichés. 'Don't rock the boat,' it says. 'Chin up. Keep moving.'

'But which way?' you scream into the shut mouth of the wood, or the city. 'Which way? I have children to think of. Quick, we are desperate.' Forward or back? To the Left? Or Right? All look equally wrong. Things are worsening so fast and I really don't think there is time.

Now there is only a crawling, bent-double passageway anywhere you look: under things, over things, rotten logs – or are they really people? Is this a wood or not? Everything has gone feral. Sour buddleia growing in cracks. There are drains and bogs and sump-holes you could break an ankle in. We've been over it all before. It's all so fucking wearisome.

Luckily we are a resilient and hopeful species. We don't give up, thinking it out till the last – you too – trying a new angle, speeding up brightly along what looks like a possible pathway. Somewhere there are settled people who function thoughtfully together. I am sure of it.

Somewhere there are societies where the world and its image communicate usefully; where the image's authority is only borrowed because the world is still solid and pre-eminent, and where real things don't get stared through or denied just because we have addressed the reality of their problems in our imaginations.

But the track that looked so promising founders again, in the quiet. Just the sound of your own breath faster and faster, and your own shuffling footfall among these mouldering generations of litter, of wrappers, of leaves. It's so dark. We're lost. This time I think we are really lost.

Tradition is dumb. It assumes progress is linear. It takes no account of the fact that life is full of spirals and arcs. Circles exist as a definite possibility. We might, if we aren't careful, make a wide parabola, skirting the edge of whatever this is and turning inwards again, away from the light. We learn nothing, as it turns out, from books, from history, from thought, or from art. After all this time, it is possible that out of exhaustion and disillusionment we might just give up. We might just end up sitting down on a log, or a person, in the unending filthy shadow, in this tacit submission of all things to forgetting, ignoring the warnings of what happened before. We might just shrug and let ourselves be consumed by stillness till we crumble and sift down, to be scurried over by those mice that appear so dangerously on the rails when you wait for the Underground. If we don't fight, it is possible that we might never come out again.

'So are you saying we should fight?' my one self says to my other, desperate enough for anything. Turning my head back and forth, straining for advice. 'Is that what you advise?' Because it's true, there is always revolt, both private and public. You can take up an axe, you can hack yourself a clear-way back to the sea. That at least would be energetic. It would be something to do, other than talk, and blood-letting can be cathartic.

Hesitating in the moment of decision, because revolt has its own life and you have to have the stomach for it; revolt turns things so that the earth replaces the sky. We know this. We cut our own king's head off once upon a time. It's hard not to get lost inside violence. It will push itself up, blooming like a giant mushroom, bigger, deadlier than we could ever remember, or ever have imagined. It will topple the trees – or the towers, it doesn't care which – while the people who released it cry and run for cover. It will grow until its canopy, just like the wood in the first place, umbrellas itself above our heads, and our sky, from horizon to horizon, is just gills the colour of decay.

As the trees come skittling down – as the sky mushrooms and darkens and the bedrock is revealed – what do you suggest that we do?

I SAID, WHAT DO YOU SUGGEST WE SHOULD DO?

God has gone very quiet.

1

Let's start again, more calmly.

In the world of poems or stories intractable problems find their solutions in some sideways step to a parallel reality, a place that is elsewhere but companionably alongside. Think of Dante and Gulliver and Gilgamesh. Think of the fairy tales you were told as a child. You take a journey by foot or ship, or you open a door in a wardrobe, or you take the proffered magic cloak, or the proffered hand of Virgil. Whichever way it is, you slip round the back of the wind, or down through the circles of Hell, and if you pay attention, and you don't drop it or give it accidentally away, you come out holding the answer. Often the answer you hold is simply acceptance. So you could say there aren't any answers. There isn't even understanding a lot of the time, but still parallels can be a comfort – they offer connection between things that will always be separate and they allow, in fact they thrive on, difference. That used to be the point of books. They provided the parallel.

Something is lost and I can see now that it may be me. The world, both human and planetary, seems to me to be broken and instead of fixing it we have simply removed our lives into some other, better, curated reality – inside screens, in the printed text, to a world we have made, like children, out of words and pictures. And I have fallen into the gap between the two.

If my condition is normal for my time of life, if it has a name and a little pill to match, then I don't want to know it. I feel as though it's the world that is sick – just that no one except me has noticed. Cassandritis, you could call it, and as I do so I can't help hearing, with a shiver of rightness, the name hidden in that second syllable.

So I'm packing up and making a change. Nothing unusual about that; it is quite normal to take a sabbatical. I'll just go for a year and come back wiser, or quieter, or more calm. I don't expect, in midlife, to be offered any cloaks and I don't think Virgil will stir himself for less than an epic poet, but I could put my faith in parallels. I'm not expecting things to be better anywhere else. I don't know what I'm looking for. Hope perhaps.

Now that I have made the decision, now that I have resisted the pull to give in to the madness of it all, as if in reward, in these wide and graceful streets the sun is shining. London can be a lovely city when you are leaving it. Brisk light and shadow on the grand nineteenth-century buildings, and I am going to buy storage boxes, to put my life into.

The trees are in their autumn beauty and many people are out, holding hands, talking languages, walking. Nothing looks especially wrong. The homeless have been tidied, as far as possible, out of sight; swept into dust-heaps on every corner under the humps of their nonetheless stinking blankets. The newspapers, as on most days, cry outrage as though innocent, but everyone still has a hand to hold.

'Don't look at the down and outs. Don't look at the hoardings,' my one self says. 'It may not be as bad as it looks and there are reasons for everything in life.'

Shops are reassuring places; I am immediately distracted.

I could buy a laundry basket that folds away, a peg box, a desk tidy in leaf print, an elephant-foot waste basket. The solutions are all here. Here you can look better, live better, improve your cars, kitchens, skin, hair, partner, clothes, desks, waste management, character. Everything is new. Nothing yet has failed or been spoilt. Nothing has betrayed its initial promise and there is everywhere so much well-lit space and so much choice. The swing doors open and shut continually, wafting the smell of factory-newness out into the street to tempt those outside to come in. Come in. Come in. And in and out again floods the obedient crowd, hurrying home to be better.

I start grazing, gathering up armfuls of new stuff before I've even reached the department where I will buy the storage boxes to put the old stuff in. This is exactly what I've always been looking for! And it is beautiful! And this! And look at this!

I come to my senses in the home-storage department, glazed with picking things up that I don't need. 'Put it down,' my one self says to my other. 'Put it all down. This too is madness.' I reluctantly put away the desk tidy. I put away the elephant's foot and the peg bag. Instead, I buy plain see-through plastic boxes with lids, for ten pounds a throw. I go home and put my clothes into them, folded carefully. They are pitifully visible through the sides of the box. I also put in my knick-knacks, pencils, notebooks, all my other belongings. I look at them too. The process is oddly ceremonial, like a burial, but 'Nevertheless,' I say to myself, 'go on.'

The mansion flat where I live has an outside balcony with, at the back, a little room that used to be a privy, now a walk-in cupboard. The stuff that will fit will go in there. Someone else will have my room. The flat isn't mine; it belongs to my aunt who is away in St Petersburg. So now I have no fixings, no place at all in this country of my birth, and this is a hard thing. I am sweeping myself from the surface of my life. Nevertheless, I go on. I carry the boxes out and stand them in a stack in the cupboard.

Down on the street, the woman with the carrier-bag three-piece suite, who thinks she is Britannia, hasn't moved. I can see her out of the window each time I pass. She is still sitting among her belongings on her step. So I stop my packing, pull my phone from my pocket and look up 'belongings' and 'belong'. The word has such emotional charge in English. I look up French, Spanish, Italian, German, Bosnian, Bulgarian, Greek. Only the Bulgarians have a word that has the same root for both. Most differentiate between possessions and people. They use two separate words. None of them use one that contains within it an equivalent of longing. Being and longing and belonging.

'Belongings,' my one self says, with authority, to my other. I like to pontificate. 'Belongings don't matter, whereas belonging does.' But there's no comfort here. My other self is hurled abruptly into mourning, among the drifts of possessions, and the see-through containers. Belongings do matter. They are little weights that tie us to our lives in time and place. These vases with frogs and flowers were given to me as a child. This pot with a cow on it my son made when he was seven. This picture I bought with my first earnings. These things are hooked and weighted like anchors, holding me moored to the fact of my life, my past. Who will I be when I've cast off?

When the van arrives and the rest of my furnishings, my pictures and all my books are driven off into storage I stand at the traffic lights, a lone figure, stationary among a flood of movement, while the people and the traffic pour relentlessly past, either side. I watch the van out of sight. And BritAnnia snug among her bags, on her doorstep, watches me. Now I have nothing. I feel lightly giddy, as though whatever force holds my feet to their print on the ground might slacken suddenly, as though I might unmoor and float away. My belongings were so solid, such tangible proof of my life in reality, of myself. Without them there is no evidence; nothing left but the finite mess of body that I am, and my waning life which floats constantly in front of me, lit like a moon.

Normally, under these conditions, there would be a guide to take me by the hand, to lead me somewhere enlightening, show me things, explain. Quest literature is full of gods made into pillars of salt, or cloud; of sorcerers or genies, or, as I said before, epic poets returned from the grave. No one has yet come forward.

I am sitting on a railway bench, thinking about this, on a day when the sky has pulled itself down as far as my feet, thick as a duvet. I am waiting for a delayed train. Around me and away down the tracks whitish shadows bulk dim into the distance, even the most solid things reduced to suggestion. Little red tail-lights of trains to elsewhere swallowed in fog. Stillness. Foundering. On the digital board the estimated time of my train recedes into the future as if things had started running backwards. I'm not surprised.

I should say 'we'. *We* are sitting on a railway bench, because I'm not in fact alone. I don't have a guide, as such, but I have the man I share my life with. We are doing this together, although of the two of us I am the only one in extremis, the only one looking for answers. He isn't bothered by the intractability of the world. He is never in one place for long enough to feel implicated by its failure.

'The thing is,' I tell him, 'I was hoping for a guide to point us in the right direction.'

'What do you mean?' he says quickly. 'I *am* a guide.' It's true. He is. He has a small travel business. He takes people round archaeological sites. He's an expert on the ancient world – Greece and Rome in particular. 'Won't I do?' He sounds mildly aggrieved.

'I know, of course,' I say, before correcting myself. 'I mean, perfect.' Although it isn't. I had promised myself the obliterating gravitas of Virgil.

There is nothing heavy about Rupert, his four decades of knowledge so lightly worn. To cover my confusion and to apologize, I say, 'I was hoping you could do something like Virgil does for Dante; slap me in the face with the nature of man, show me the heart of life.'

He leans forward, his beard beaded with mist. 'How often would you like slapping – daily? Or just once a week?' He has his eyebrows lightly raised, his head ironically tilted. He knows if he slaps me I will slap him back. I look at him as he sits beside me. He doesn't have the nose to be Virgil. Sideways on, his nose and his forehead make one line and his eyes, all the time, have the look of somewhere else. Also he has a kind of detachedness. He looks a bit like Hermes. It wouldn't be hard to imagine…

'Can't you just pretend?' he says, as if he'd read my thoughts. 'If I was a god in disguise, you wouldn't be able to tell.' Now it is my turn to look ironic. He isn't a god but it's true: if he was, I wouldn't know. He pulls a filled baguette out of the pocket of his old leather coat and begins wolfing through it as though it needed killing first.

'What did Hermes do?' I ask.

'Well, his official title is the Psychopomp,' he says between mouthfuls. 'He's a guide, traditionally of animals as well as people. He deals in dreams and cattle and technology. He is a trickster and a thief, and he guides souls on their final journey to the Underworld.' I think on what he's said. Some of it is OK.

'Either way I will have to put you into my account,' I say to him, half apologetic. I know he doesn't like to be pinned down. 'I mean, it wouldn't be honest to leave you out. I'm not the sort of person who would just set off on a major journey by myself.'

He looks at me in silence, his mouth very full. After a while he swallows. 'You can't put someone called Rupert into a book,' he replies, and goes back to eating.

He is right, though not for the reason he would have given. When I write his name down he drains out of it, as if the loops of the letters were holes in a sieve. Empty.

What shall I do – call him something else? Nothing else works.

Everything I try feels false. I ask him what he thinks. He is silent again. Then he puts up one hand in front of his very full mouth to act as a shield. He always talks with his mouth full.

'If you put me in, it won't really be me. It will be someone else.' Little flecks of something like pickle spray from his lips.

'No,' I say, hesitating, 'it won't… True.' It is an odd paradox that for the sake of truth I have to use his real name, but that the result will be someone invented.

That seems to be the end of the conversation.

We need a vehicle. We are on our way to test-drive a second-hand campervan in which to make our journey. The dealership is in a hinterland of scrub outside Pangbourne, gorse mostly, being picked round by ponies in a cat's cradle of electric fencing. We rock our way, by taxi, a little hopeless, up a track in and out of potholes to a concrete yard. The driver says he is happy to wait; lots to look at here. He says it like it's the greatest joke ever made. It's true, it's a sorry set-up. There is a litter of forgotten-looking vans too big for what we want and a Portakabin, tilted as if standing on one leg ashamed, and well it might be. Out of it, as we pull up, comes someone blazing with reddish hair, part boy, part fox, with several sets of keys jingling in his hand and a cocky little terrier trotting behind him. His clothes look as though he had slept in them not just last night but for the whole of last week. But he is impossibly, almost embarrassingly handsome. I have to make myself look away. Instinctively I try pulling myself together. How have I got so old, so invisible? I look brightly round at the collapsed vehicles. The one we are trying out is very small. Rupert and the fox boy sit in the front seats, their shoulders touching and their heads hunched forward, and I, sitting sideways on one of the benches, can't see out of the back windows unless I fold myself in half. When the boy turns the key there is complete silence. The van is dead. Unfazed, he hops out and jump-leads it back to life.

'It's not the fastest,' he says as we move at a slow running pace, back down the track. 'But once it's going, it'll go forever.' In the rear-view mirror I can't help noticing that my mouth is open. I shut it and look at the needle of the speedometer. We are on the open road. It is trembling with effort, trying to hold itself at sixty.

'Thanks,' Rupert says over the rattle of the engine. 'We'll have a think.' He says it in a way that means 'we are not interested' and 'you'll never hear from us again' and I find myself surprised because, despite the jump-leads, despite the junkyard hopelessness of the outfit, I am not able to see past the fox boy's patter, the power of his blazing looks. Obviously, or so I thought, we were going to buy it.

Finally, days later, we settle on a second-hand Romahome. It is fifteen feet by five, more or less, made of yachting fibreglass on the Isle of Wight, an upside-down boat on wheels. A good vessel for an upside-down time. I like the fact that its name is that of a tribe of outsiders, and I like the fact that, read backwards, it spells amor. Let's hope that will be some protection.

London to Greece overland, to the island of Syros, is where we are going. You can fly the distance in a few hours and one change. It isn't what people consider 'a journey'. But we are going by parallel. We plan on taking months.

We provision ourselves for the trip. We buy a fold-up colander to save space, teabags for a continent devoted to coffee, a fold-up steamer so we can cook two things in one pot, a fold-up shovel for latrine digging, a camping shower that can be hung from a tree. Or rather, Rupert buys. The wood has closed about me again and I am in a different place. In this savage and extreme world, why are we busying ourselves buying kettles? I walk round the shops very carefully, newly aware that my body, which is all I have, is very soft, very puncturable.

Rupert considers torches, maps, e-guide books. He makes lists and crosses things off. Sometimes he asks me, sometimes he just looks at me as if to ask and then carries on. The closer the deadline comes, the worse it gets. I leave my purse in a shop in Richmond and he travels the two-hour round-trip to retrieve it for me as a matter of course. I am aware all the time that I am being very gently carried. I don't feel bad. It is a matter of practicality. I haven't actually checked but it feels now as though I have no skin at all, as though the complex networks of vein and muscle, the wet mesh of my capillaries, are directly exposed to London's air. I worry briefly about grit.

Meanwhile, on the floor in the flat's sitting room we make piles of books, among them *The New Penguin Book of English Verse* which is as heavy as an anchor chain and I hope will do the same job. This is the oddest thing – the side by side of normality and crisis. A flayed person carrying out mundanities. Rupert, who isn't flayed, walks endlessly about the streets buying, organizing, clicking his fingers. He likes clicking. He clicks his fingers all the time; not the ones I would use – the first and second – but the fourth. He can do both hands. He's very popular. I have known him since I was eighteen but it seems as if I am seeing these things for the first time. Did I notice before? I honestly can't remember. Everywhere we go we bump into people who seem to know him. He greets them all ecstatically; someone he knew from New York, someone who worked in a restaurant he once owned.

'Hey, Steve!' he says in response to a shout of delight in the Portobello Road.

'Steve? What Steve? Don't you Steve me!' says Steve, whose name is Tom. Rupert laughs but afterwards, ashamed, he says to me, 'That was terrible, poor Tom. I just didn't remember.' I say nothing because I think I'm not there.

In the final week we make a farewell tour of various friends, parking in their driveways and serving them tea in the van. 'Hilarious,' they keep on saying. But I, as always, am serious.

On the evening of our departure my brother comes to the flat with celebratory food and drink. Both my selves are reduced to a kind of stunned silence but I eat and talk banalities nonetheless. Questing takes a certain type of courage, or so it seems, sloughing the familiar and accepting what will come. That's why, in books, it is done by heroes, or by those who have nothing to lose. For a long time now I have doubted my resilience.

After supper we load the van into the small hours, cramming into the tiny lift, up and down from the third floor with armfuls of luggage. In the van my brother and I stow things into overhead cupboards until they are rammed. He is cheerful and tender. He hopes I will have an exciting time. I am to send him regular updates on where I am and what I see. He doesn't say anything about whether or not my skin is still in place. But then, he isn't looking for damage. Why would he? This looks like a normal thing I am doing; going away on an extended trip because my three children are now grown up.

Rupert is nonchalantly still packing. Weighed down with bags and rucksacks, my brother and I wait again by the lift. The pressure which has been building all day breaks in a bomb-blast of thunder. We stop and listen. Uninterrupted drown-fall. My brother and I look at each other. 'Portent,' he says.

Outside on the balcony, when we go to see, water-sheets are hanging in the dark. And in the flat the rain pours into my aunt's bedroom through the ceiling. We run to and fro with trays and saucepans. We move the furniture aside. Everything is dissolving. There is the sound of drumming. 'This is not apocalypse', my one self tells my wide-eyed other. 'It's just a violent weather pattern.'

When the rain ends we pack a final load into the creaking van and go to bed. This is the last night, but I don't sleep. I lie in my bed listening to Rupert's untroubled breathing, and the night city. Nothing has drowned; the traffic, the people on the streets, all the great machinery of global society still turning. I lie on my back looking at the ceiling that I now know is permeable. I clench my hands under the covers. 'What are you so afraid of?' my one self says to my other. In my head, it is D.H. Lawrence who answers.

'Sometimes,' he says, his consonants clattering like little slips of shale on the hard hills of his native landscape. 'Sometimes, snakes can't slough. They can't burst their old skin. Then they go sick and die inside the old skin, and nobody ever sees the new pattern. It needs a real desperate recklessness to burst your old skin at last. You simply don't care what happens to you, if you rip yourself in two, so long as you do get out. It also needs a real belief in the new skin. Otherwise you are likely never to make the effort. Then you gradually sicken and go rotten and die in the old skin.'

Maybe I'm not flayed after all. Maybe I'm just rotting. I may be sick already. We all may be. 'I'm frightened of change,' my one self whispers to my other, 'for myself and for everything else. I can't tell where I stop and where the world starts and I don't want either one to burst.'

My other self has no answer. Everything seems so shifting, so uncertain as if our civilization or even our whole species has found itself failing

Lawrence's test. The rising chatter of opinion, escapism in all our art forms, while violence of every kind runs riot in a dying world. Everywhere, the old, the comfortable bonds are loosening. The people I saw in the London streets, on the day I went out to buy boxes, holding hands, talking languages in the sun and the flying wind, are drifting unconsciously apart. Soon we will all be out of reach.

Departure. England has decided to look its best, washed luminous by the last night's rain, but I harden my heart. I have fallen out of love with my country. In the London Underground recently they have been handing out badges encouraging conversation. Tube Chat, the badges say. A cosy attempt to lessen our cultural isolation, our horror at breaking the silence of strangers. But it is very difficult for an island not to be isolated – its nature is right there, rooted in its own name.

We drive slowly out of London, past places I've never been before. The lighthouse at Trinity Buoy, which has lost its purpose and is the size of a toy, and the towering City, which is taking its place. Where new towers have yet to rise, cranes rest against the sky. They look delicate, unaware of what they are creating; this mouth crammed with glass fangs.

'All the better to eat you with, my dear,' the City says to itself as we pass.

Rupert is driving. The radio is on and his telephone rings incessantly – each time he has to answer it with one hand and turn down the music with the other. He bobs up his knees to steady the steering wheel. He drives sometimes for quite a distance like this, using his knees to steer. I should care but it seems I don't. I just let myself be carried, my two selves sunk like stones to an inaccessible bottom, as if it had happened and I were actually dead already, carried to the afterlife with my few necessaries around me. This is Hermes' job, guiding souls down to the edge of the Underworld. Maybe Rupert is Hermes after all.

'Yep,' he is saying into his phone, 'yep, I can do that... Send me the details and we can discuss it all when I've got them in front of me... No problem.'

'A lot of people seem to need your services,' I say when he finishes the latest call.

He nods. 'I am much in demand.'

Even above the telephone and the music the van clatters constantly, the gas-cooker fittings, the crockery and glasses in the cupboards. As on a boat, you know you are travelling. I can't help glancing into the back every now and then, until I get used to the noise, to check that everything is still safely stowed.

Outside, the countryside is caught in the current of autumn. Woods crowd to the horizon either side. Kent dressed to the skyline for departure, under a patchwork sky. And everything, it seems, is lit with leaving, my thoughts shedding and drifting as if they too were seasonal.

'Are you OK, England?' I ask it only now that I'm leaving, half surprised to find I mind. As if in answer, up ahead, smoke billows in the distance. On the hard shoulder a police car is in Hollywood flames. Everyone speeds by as if it was normal. Bizarre. I blink and swivel round to check I'm not dreaming. I am not. We continue.

Now, on our right, there is the sea, dotted with ferries going different ways, and a castle squatting dour on its hill with a matching town down below. We have got as far as Dover.

The town, when we enter it, seems forgotten, turning its back and facing landward as if the port didn't matter, the few inhabitants who happen to be out wind-blown along its streets with lowered heads. Everything looks ill-assorted, as though no one had cared or thought it through. Once elegant houses in streets that have either lost track of where they were going or just given up in the face of a one-way system, cower in the shadow of giant ferries.

We buy porridge oats in the supermarket and food for supper, one lemon, some pasta and a head of broccoli. I had almost hoped we wouldn't be able to go but the boat is not full. We can cross at 18.20.

Goodbye then, England. I have no idea what you are. Are you the books that I read, or the language I still love?

It is evening. There is no one on the quay. The windows of the houses appear blank as we pull away. I look at these famous chalk cliffs and the rising hills behind. I look at the single trees in outline on their ridges, and their woods of oak and ash. I think of the stubborn ground and its weeds and of all the bodies of water up and down the country; the ponds and the quick rivers, the ones clear to their pebbled beds, or the ones still with silt; and I think of the man-made fields and little hedges and I roll them all up together. Is that what you are, England – just the landscape I know in my bones?

Nothing answers of course, and it is late in the day to be asking, but that doesn't stop me. It seems an urgent question. I lean out as if to make England hear. It seems I have to know before I leave.

Or are you maybe something else?

Something more shifting, like the tiny woman that I saw once passing, bolt upright and alone, in the back of an enormous car; or the long lines of her people, generations of them, stubbornly shelved in classes? Or tea, or pubs, or football? It is getting more difficult to see. I don't know in the end what England is or ever was. I don't know if it is much different from anywhere else.

We stand at the rail, watching. Everything is opalescent, palest grey. Pink and gold and pale blue. One or two birds wheeling. All at once, as we wait, little lights spring on everywhere at the same time and the darkness comes, like a seepage, not down but through; the world turning itself inside out like a trick. Or England removing itself quietly, leaving nothing behind. Gone. Just the lights sparkling on a black ground, a second night sky mirroring the coming stars.

Noise and juddering until Calais. From white cliffs to white fences. Miles of them, under harsh lighting, high and doubled, with coils of barbed wire at the top. The Jungle. Another bigger and worse forest to get lost in. 'Think yourself lucky.' It seems my one self has perspective, at least.

'Give it a rest,' my other self says, but still, as the fence unrolls its length, I look. There are up to ten thousand people here we are told, landless, in transition, in a rigged-up horror of tents and pallets. None of them are visible as we pass. In fact there seems to be nothing at all either side until further on black police vans solidify out of the dark, driving fast with lights flashing. I count six that scream by and a little knot of them later, stationary by the white fences. Police in riot gear with their backs to the road, looking in. I can't see any opposition, only darkness.

We drive slowly through the outskirts of Calais, peering at street signs. France looks immediately different. Low buildings of a larger landmass. Wider apart. Quiet streets. Place Crèvecoeur. We are not going on the motorway. We are taking the coastal road, which winds among dunes with the lights of England constantly in view to our right.

We stop short of Boulogne, at a campsite. It seems strange and vaguely unwelcoming. In the van's headlights as we look for our pitch, caravans and campers, their windows dark as if abandoned, stand about in little plots of exhausted grass. It is a curious no-place to arrive at and it isn't home. We can plug into the power if we want. The showers and toilets are a walk away. It seems too far and too complicated. I settle wearily into the feeling of travel-grime. Maybe I won't bother to wash until we get to Greece. I decide to read the campervan manual. 'Continental power is often reversed so live and neutral change places. You should check first as it will override all safety devices.' I have no idea how to check. I stare at the page. 'It will no longer be possible to prevent electric shocks and may permanently damage equipment.' There are thinly drawn diagrams of the electric circuits in the van. They don't seem to translate to any of the switches in view. It is in English but still I feel I have entered a community whose language I do not speak. Both our phones are dead. This never happens in the modern world. We are cut off.

It rains all night. I listen to it drumming on the roof of the van. But my one self was right. Thank God it isn't a tent. Thank God it isn't a tent.

On the way to the showers in the morning I pass a pétanque court under water.

The campsite is next to the beach. Marram grass and a few pines and a grey sea whose waves jerk as if tied to each other, tugging and pulling in different directions. Horizontal rain still. The showers don't work. I run to the campsite office to ask about hot water and am hurled through the door by a gust of wind, so that the rain arrives ahead of me at the reception desk.

'Lovely weather I see, just like in England.'

'That's because we are neighbours.'

Two women with coiffed hair, despite the weather. They are sensibly wearing anoraks at the desk. Neither of them seems insulted by my nationality. Still, I can feel the components of apology rolling separately, as if they were ball-bearings, to the tip of my tongue. It is a new condition I've developed, a form of Tourettes, connected to the coldness of elective insularity. I look at the ladies behind the desk. Who am I apologizing to? They don't obviously mind. I close my mouth to stop anything unnecessary rolling out. Their manners are pleasant as though they have been polite for centuries. Courtesy, from the Old French courteis, so they must have been. They don't over-smile or tell me their names or ask if I have found everything to my liking. I think I have perhaps arrived in the land of the grown-ups. I take two little bronze jetons to put into the shower slot.

I thought the French were supposed to be rude. Rude also comes from Old French, although originally Latin. I can still see England across the water, a low, tussocky outline, stupidly close. Maybe if I didn't know I was in France, I wouldn't be looking for difference.

But it is different. You would have to be stupid not to notice.

The windows, when we drive into Boulogne later, are different; the height of the roofs; the dormers with space above the window as though their eyebrows were raised. The slim buildings that look taller than ours, the wide streets, the giant church, cavernous, smelling of stone and scented dust. The language. The supermarket, where there is no fresh milk. We look up and down the aisles. Just banks of UHT. We buy instead a chipped glass lid for the saucepan we already have. At the checkout Rupert points to the chip. Might there be a reduction? The girl passes the question on to her superior. Again no over-smile, in fact this time the reverse. Her superior says dismissively, and without looking at us, 'It is bought as seen.' Good, a rude French person.

As if someone had simply wiped the sky clean, the weather lifts. Windy and blue. Later, off a cobbled street so quaint it looks like something from a film set, we have fish soup and WiFi for lunch, served to us by a man whose face and voice are made out of ash. He has an elaborate and worn routine. 'Oui Madame', rolling his eyes and emphasizing the madame at every request. Through the window I can see him handing out dishes and repeating his patter. Gales of laughter blow through to the back where we sit in the half dark, sucking up soup and electricity. Something has lifted inside me. Maybe it's crossing the Channel and leaving England. Maybe it's the different buildings. Or maybe it's just the sky – as if I too had been wiped clean, or is this my new skin? Whatever it is, I feel different.

'So?' I say to Rupert.

'Yes?' He doesn't look up.

'Well… How do you feel? I mean, nothing has really happened yet.'

Rupert is looking at his computer screen, his face lit with its underworld light. 'How do *I* feel?' He is busy doing I don't know what. I can hear him clicking on links, travelling sideways in some other, internet dimension. 'What exactly were you expecting?' He speaks slowly because he's only half concentrating and without taking his eyes off what he is doing. What *is* he doing?

'I don't know,' I say. I look at my surroundings, at the fakeness of the real cobbles, this dark café, with its ashy owner. This, now I come to notice it, inedible viscous soup. 'I don't know. Something.'

'What something?' Rupert looks up. 'We've only just started.'

'I said I don't know. I mean, what am I supposed to be looking for?' My voice is barely above a whisper. The emptiness of the restaurant is making me self-conscious. Even so, it sounds urgent, impatient. 'I just don't want to miss anything.'

Rupert is engrossed again in his screen. 'Mhmm.' It isn't much of an answer.

'What are you looking at? Are you gaming?'

'Gaming?' He looks up again. 'I'm researching campsites.' But when I get up to go to the toilet I can't help noticing he is watching pratfalls on YouTube.

It's a bit disappointing. In the journeys I have in mind, the travellers throw themselves energetically upon chance and are met as they go by hungry old men asking to share their lunch, or by talking animals. They are tested at every turn or they are offered advice and, if they pass the test or heed the advice, they are given things that will help on the journey; a magic key, an amulet, an always-full porridge bowl. I push the soup away from me and Rupert looks up at last. 'Alright,' he says, snapping shut his computer. 'Let's go and look at the church and the museum.'

I jump up. The ashy waiter's chauvinism extends as far as bill-paying so I hurry out, leaving Rupert to settle. I look up and down the street. Maybe a test will present itself. But Boulogne is disappointingly empty. There are no people and I see no animals, let alone ones gifted with speech. We are approached only once on our way, diagonally across the street, by a heavy-looking man with a soft, ingratiating voice. He is already talking by the time he comes level. His tongue is large and very pink and he speaks to us in ornate English.

'Excuse me, sir and madam, could you give me some money? I need to eat.' He has been eating a great deal, that much is obvious, but he is asking strangers for money and I am not, or not yet. Besides, I know this test. You must share what you have with an open heart or you won't make it to the next level. We give him money, only one of us with a vested interest. The stories don't say if it is enough for one person to have an open heart.

There is nothing much to look at in the church, just its scoured interior, bare stone, and dust suspended in stillness. Empty as a shell. Only, at intervals along the walls, there are commemorative plaques so, for want of anything else to do, we set ourselves to read them. I stop, for no particular reason, in front of one to Eustace II, Count of Boulogne.

The second Count. Who's counting? I ask him in my head. Whoever you were, you are long gone now. Rupert catches up with me. 'Find anything?' he asks.

'Nothing.'

Turning, as we leave, at the sound of a footfall, I look back up the aisle. Someone else, it seems, was in the church all along. Towards the gloom of its interior, a man with long and silken moustaches scissors away on impatient legs.

Later, sitting in the van in the Boulogne campsite, I search the internet for information about Eustace II. He was a Norman knight whose moustaches were so flowing and so noticeable that he was familiarly known as Eustace aux Gernons (Eustace of the Moustaches). He was married to Edward the Confessor's sister, Godgifu, a good marriage, good for advancement, his tricky heart so fluid it might have been made of mercury.

I don't know yet what it has of significance to tell me, but this is the story of Eustace aux Gernons, as I find it out. He sailed, in 1051, across the Channel to visit his brother-in-law, the King, in England. At the end of his stay, riding away with his company to take ship again at Dover, he stopped to eat supper at Canterbury, where Edward had installed a much-hated Norman Archbishop, Robert of Jumièges. After supper he and his knights went on to Dover where they planned to stay before sailing for France the next morning. Just short of Dover, in sight of the sea, they stopped again and put on their byrnies.

What is a byrnie? I have only a vague idea so I look that up too, moving crabwise across tabs and links.

It is a long tunic of chain mail. If you want to get free lodgings, try wearing armour. So the company armed and then legged up onto their horses again, to bully the town into hospitality.

They fanned out, each one selecting which house he liked best. One of Eustace's men, as the Anglo-Saxon Chronicle tells it, 'came wishing to lodge at a householder's without his consent, wounded the householder, and the householder killed him'. The record doesn't give the homeowner a name. Who was he, this man who seeing a shadow cross the window went fatally to the door? Was he always intemperate, or had he past experience of Normans helping themselves to what he considered his?

I look up Normans, Norse-men, the descendants of the Vikings who, before they took England, or parts of it, had first taken France from the mouth of the Seine as far as Rouen. They were only three generations from their origins in Eustace's time. Edward the Confessor, half Norman himself, replaced a line of Viking kings from Sweyn Forkbeard to the hopeless sons of Canute. So by 1051 there would have been plenty of Norse-men already in England, both from their homeland and more recently from Normandy itself, pushed like pegs into positions of power. They were the old enemy.

So a Norseman, then, drew his sword on a Dover doorstep while, in the dimness, at the back of the room, perhaps a wife was watching. Her pleading voice, which knew already. 'Don't lose your temper. Let him in. Give him what he wants.' But the householder didn't or couldn't listen. Once struck, he fought back and, although the man was in mail with a long Norman sword, the householder killed him outright. What now? Silence. In dread he must have lugged the body aside while, in the back of the room, the woman leaned into the silence between her life and its change. It's done now. It's done, and what will happen to me? Listening no doubt for the sickening sound of hoofbeats.

Eustace of Boulogne, hearing the news, wasted no time. He 'got on his horse, and his companions on theirs, went to the householder and killed him on his own hearth, then went up to the town and killed, inside and out, more than twenty men, went back to the King, and told him only a part of what had happened'. You lied, Eustace, I say under my breath as I read the account. You must have lied, because you didn't tell the King that your company had been the aggressors. Poor Dover. The King's response was angry and unfair. He ordered Godwin of Wessex, whose fiefdom Dover was, to punish the townspeople for the insult. When Godwin refused, he was exiled.

But the following year Godwin came back to England, from Flanders, at the head of an army. Terms were agreed to avoid civil war. Among them the removal of Robert of Jumièges, the hated Norman Archbishop. His dismissal, like the death of the householder, had its consequences. It angered the Pope and it was one among other justifications later used by William the Conqueror for invasion.

'You can't keep a good man down,' Eustace's voice floats back to me, cold, across the sea of time. When the Normans did invade, Eustace came with them. He appears in the Bayeux Tapestry, along with his moustaches, riding beside William, arms spread wide. He looks heroic although, as it actually happened, he was on the point of fleeing. William, mounted on a black horse, so the account goes, 'with a harsh voice… called to Eustace of Boulogne, who with fifty knights was turning in flight and was about to give the signal for retreat'.

'Where are you going, Eustace?'

'It isn't myself I fear for; I am only thinking of you, my lord.' I am fairly sure his voice was sibilant. 'But at the very moment when he uttered the words, Eustace was struck between the shoulders with such force that blood gushed out from his mouth and nose and, half dead, he only made his escape with the aid of his followers.'

Half of me is pleased. 'That served you right, you liar,' my one self says, although he's long dead. 'Liar and coward.'

But my other self looks away, remembering the church and the man I might have seen vanishing on his long thin legs, where the stone nave, hollow like a shell, disappeared into darkness. 'That isn't how the world works,' my other self says, quietly considering.

William's response, heroic rather than accusatory, was not to flee but to lift his helmet and show his knights his face. 'Fight on. Fight on,' as Eustace was carried screaming from the field. And so he won.

Eustace is one of the likely patrons of the Bayeux Tapestry. Attempting through embroidered flattery to adjust the account, just as he did at Dover, recording for posterity the King's heroism with himself, flank to flank in battle-line, not fleeing but urging the King's safety. Maybe William was persuaded, maybe not. Either way, Eustace, following his own interests, can't help changing the face of England as he passes. After all, his brutality and his manipulation of Edward flicked the line of dominoes that set in motion the invasion that gave us many things by which we now define ourselves. 'Thank you, Eustace,' half of me grudgingly says, 'for our Norman monuments, for our questionable land-ownership system, for the Domesday Book, the Tower of London, the cathedrals of Ely and Durham, and for our shaded and subtle language.'

'What exactly *are* you looking for?' Rupert asks, glancing up from his own reading.

I snap the laptop closed and carefully stow the tiny scrap of paper with password numbers for the campsite WiFi. A magic key if ever there was one. 'I don't know really.' My selves are sunk back into quiet. 'Help, I suppose.'

'Help with?'

'Everything.' Am I glaring? 'Everything,' I say in a more controlled voice. 'I mean, not just with what England is, or might be, and how to fit and what to do, but with what anything is. Everything's got so hard to differentiate, not just places themselves from each other, but also our representations of them. Nothing we write or make has any use any more – and I always lived by assuming that it did – it just seems to be a parallel place to live, where you don't need to bother with the mess that's been made of the real world. If the real world is still real. See?' Rupert looks patient. 'I just don't know how I'm supposed to be, or what I'm supposed to do. I don't even know if there's anything I *can* do.'

'Live?'

I go back to glaring. 'Or even what the point of it all is.'

'There isn't a point,' Rupert says, the full force of his elsewhere eyes tipping themselves into mine. He says it lightly but he means to help. 'Just so you know.'

'OK.' I seem to be angry. I don't know yet if I agree, or not. I only know I don't want to.

In the evening we are friends again and we take a walk. The owner of the campsite tells us it is not advisable to walk into the forest, which had been our first thought. The ash trees all have a disease and are being felled. They are dropping their branches. The forest is dying. The owner recommends we walk instead to the local site of interest, the Cultural Centre of the Entente-Cordiale, through the outskirts of the village of Condette. The Centre is at the Château Hardelot, a stage-set reconstruction of a nineteenth-century pastiche, built originally by an Englishman among the ruins of a thirteenth-century original. There is a newly built wooden Elizabethan theatre in its grounds. Nothing is showing tonight but they have a full programme of events every summer and cream teas, incongruously, are offered in the castle tearoom.

From the battlements, against a stormy sky, a flag is flying – the Tricolour which shades, halfway across, into the Union Jack. It is prettier than either flag and looks in the light of Eustace more ethnographically honest. And Eustace is here too, at least in spirit, because this place was originally built by the Counts of Boulogne, his descendants.

Castles are mostly museums now. It is difficult to think of them as anything other than giant fortified storage boxes for belongings. This one, taken and retaken over the years, was finally ruined on purpose by Richelieu, who thought the Counts too powerful. It has long-established connections with England. Henry VIII stayed here with Anne Boleyn, his public mistress, while his wife Katharine was kept prisoner in a damp castle at home, where it was hoped she might catch cold and not recover. In case she didn't, they were here, titupping across the marshes, to persuade François I, King of France, to intercede on his behalf and ask the Pope for a divorce.

Then in the nineteenth century, after Richelieu had had his tantrum, the castle was bought by a series of unconnected Englishmen who one after another tried to restore the sprawl of ruins and ended up building something new instead, a turreted nonsense that sits up, gamely parvenu, inside the old walls. The latest of these landlords, John Robinson Whitley, established it as a resort in 1899. Golf, tennis, hunting and fishing were all on offer. Edward VII was a frequent visitor, he and his guests teeing off from the turrets. Mostly this doesn't seem relevant. It seems like clutter. But I'm trying to be thorough. As I said to Rupert at lunch, I don't want to miss anything. Around us and beyond the castle the Marais de Condette nature reserve, with its reedy waters and its birds, stretches out, unnoticing.

We head back to the van through the village, its widely spaced buildings sunk in suburban quiet. Little houses with dormer windows. Wood-stacks, very tidy. It looks nothing like an English village and I am still collecting difference. Different street-lighting. Different building materials, smooth plaster or stone, oval bricks that look like bathroom tiles. Tiled roofs that come low over the doors, and look like fringes. On the village pitch, football practice is taking place under floodlights. Men make little dashes round coloured cones. The ball pops up as if on springs. And on the other pavement, in wide lapels, his hair and his beard frizzed out in disorder and his eyes glittering, steps a Victorian-looking man with a lady on his arm. Even in the dusk, they seem closed in on themselves, the bubble of intimacy. The lady in particular has the glazed look of someone in love.

As soon as we wake up, one of us is outside. With the bed down, there is only room in the van for one person to dress at a time. We have been unable to fill up the water tank because we can't open the cap – it just rotates maddeningly inside its hole. We both try separately, exerting different amounts of pressure, thoughtfully, as though cracking a safe. Nothing. The threads to the screw, if there are any, refuse to engage. For this reason I wash up in cold water and a coat at the communal washing-up stand, although at first, as if in sympathy with the water-tank cap, when I unload the plates and pan into the sink, not even cold water will come out of the tap. There is no mechanism, nothing obvious to open or twist. I have to ask a German boy, standing in front of a big veteran-looking camper opposite, how to turn it on. He shows me the small panel on the wall, at which you wave your hand and water pours in response, but for too short a time to manage anything other than the most perfunctory rinse. I wash up one-handed, the other waving continuously in front of the small panel. We ask the campsite owner as we leave if he has any ideas about opening the water tank. It is new, we explain. He too is polite, but he speaks to us slowly as though we are a pair of donkeys come braying into his office by mistake, burrs in our ears and our mouths full of thistles. 'With the key?'

We have much to learn about the practicalities of our new life but it doesn't seem to matter. The weather is exhilarating, sunny and with a little ruffling wind. We drive, after breakfast, back into town to look at the archaeological museum, closed the day before. I, at least, have made a discovery and its name is Boulogne; the ramparts, the arched entrance to the old town, and the houses with their painted shutters, bunting fluttering in between across the steep main street. I have never seen any town so lovely. I clatter up and down on my new hooves, braying in amazement.

Charles Dickens is in town. That is who we saw last night near the floodlit playing field. Not with his mistress this time but with his family, in a rented house full of striking clocks, writing bits of *Bleak House* and comparing the French favourably with the English. 'As to the boarding-houses of our French watering-place,' he writes, 'they are Legion, and would require a distinct treatise. It is not without a sentiment of national pride that we believe them to contain more bores from the shores of Albion than all the clubs in London.' He dips his pen, cocks his head briefly like a bird. 'As you walk timidly in their neighbourhood, the very neckcloths and hats of your elderly compatriots cry to you from the stones of the streets, "We are Bores – avoid us!" We have never overheard at street corners such lunatic scraps of political and social discussion as among these dear countrymen of ours. They believe everything that is impossible and nothing that is true. They carry rumours, and ask questions, and make corrections and improvements on one another, staggering to the human intellect.'

In case he is not at his desk but out enjoying the market, freshening under the wind, I keep my head down until I am safely inside the walls of the museum. I don't want to attract attention. I know already what his judgement of me will be.

The museum is housed in the town castle, also built by Eustace's descendants. We cross the moat, round which school children are running, urged on by a teacher handsome in a beard and sports clothes. 'Allez! Allez! Regardez-devant. Soufflez.' It is the girls in the class who are running, pink-cheeked and puffing, struggling to obey instructions. 'Soufflez! Soufflez bien!'

To one side, the watching boys add their own encouragement. 'Allez, Marie,' they shout as the girls run past. Some of them jump up and down in their desire for Marie to win. 'Allez, allez, Marie!' I look for Marie but I can't tell which one she might be. At the back several girls just walk, ignoring all instruction, one pair with their arms around each other in conversation.

We pass through the arch and into the surprise of a lopsided courtyard, an irregular octagon enclosed by buildings of varying lengths. For a long time we just stand delighting in its oddness.

At the far side is the entrance to the museum which contains, of course, belongings: Greek and Roman antiquities, the Egyptian collection of Boulogne's famous Egyptologist, Auguste Mariette, an exhibition of Native American masks and some nineteenth- and twentieth-century paintings of local historical interest.

Just inside the entrance I am stopped short by a mummy lying on its back in folded white linen, as if sleeping. Its mouth has a full set of teeth,

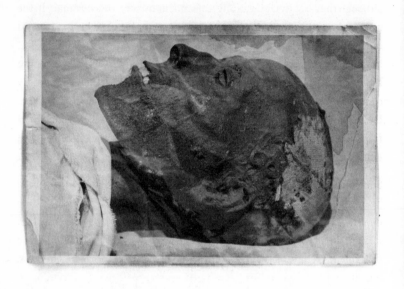

just slightly open, its profile fine. Sharp jawline, slender neck, tendrils of hair remaining curled about precise ears. Small, very perfect.

'Hello,' I can't help saying.

I've never seen anyone from the distant past so clearly. Its legend says that it arrived at the museum inside the sarcophagus exhibited alongside, although the sarcophagus was originally not its own. It was customary in the nineteenth century to swap mummies around, putting the best-preserved ones into the best sarcophagi in order to charge collectors a higher price. Neither the name, nor the origin, nor the date of the Mummy here are known, but still it is so clearly a person; its slim, piano-key teeth oddly characterizing. 'Who are you?' I can't tell whether it is a man or a woman. It can't answer. It is dead. It just goes on lying on its back, anonymous, so far in time and miles from whatever in life it might have been – its worth, which is only financial now, increased through dislocation.

Someone else is looking at the Mummy. A young man with a strong face, a beard that goes only under, not over his jaw so that it is possible to see the determination in his chin, hair that curls like the Mummy's own, only on him it is live, luxuriant. He looks like one of Dickens's much-admired Boulogne fishermen, picturesque, strong, independent. 'Auguste Mariette,' he says, 'Egyptologist.' I don't choose the things we see. I'm leaving everything to chance, so I'm not expecting any of it to join up or make sense. But still, Egyptology doesn't seem immediately relevant. 'I am sorry,' I tell Mariette, a little stiffly. 'I'm ashamed to say I haven't heard of you till now.'

Mariette is a native. He was born here in Boulogne in 1821, but at eighteen, unable to continue at school because of his father's remarriage, he travelled to England where he first taught French and drawing at Stratford-upon-Avon, before moving to Coventry to work in the ribbon industry. It is hard to picture him in a Midlands factory office, so young, his eyes so full of mental energy, his broad, adventurer's shoulders, his bounding legs, cramped by deskwork. He must have looked oddly out of place. 'What can you do, Mariette?'

But he can do so many things; which to choose? He hesitates.

'Can you draw?'

'Of course.'

Coventry was famous then, among other things, for its ribbons. Not the simple coloured ribbons of nowadays but woven silk ribbons of complex design, cascades of flowers so well drawn as to be botanically distinct. Lilies of the valley, roses, blue convolvulus, complicated sprays of grasses and berries. They were made on looms still at that time, mostly by pieceworkers, and they presumably needed designers. He found the town a familiar enough mix of medieval and modern, only built in sandstone and red brick. Mariette applied himself to his new life, tried to settle into Coventry's fog-muffled, industrial grind. He hurried, energetic, with his drawings under his arm through cobbled streets, under air that was thickened with soot. He admired the buildings and felt restless. He worked harder, trying to settle himself. But even as he arrived, the ribbon business was teetering on the edge of collapse. Steam factories were being built and the market was soon to be swamped by cheap imports from the Continent. In the end there wasn't much of a living to be made for an ambitious young man. False start. He gave it up and came back to France.

In Boulogne he completed his studies and set up as a schoolteacher. 'Did you watch your children run, Mariette?' I would like to ask. 'Did they too run at your encouragement round these walls?' He looks nonplussed. Internally pacing the confines of his career, he is distracted, unhappy. Boulogne is so small. His movements about the town, or on the high stool in the airless classroom, are always restless. He has the look of something confined, a wind caught and kept in a bottle.

Mariette wasn't any better suited to teaching than he was to ribbons. He kept thinking there must be something more. Then in 1842 a cousin, who had been on Champollion's archaeological expedition to Egypt, died and his papers were sent back to the family in Boulogne. Something had to be done with them. They needed ordering at the very least, and possibly offering to some local archive. The family called for Mariette. He was clever. He could do it. So here, at last and quite by accident, was the something he had been waiting for. Now in his spare time after school, Mariette would sit late into the night, reading through his cousin's accounts, and on days off he visited the castle museum, looking at its Egyptian finds in the new light of archaeological discovery.

So this is how it is that I find him here, stooped, as I am, over the Mummy, peering into the case, whispering to himself with incredulity. 'These things from the very distant past, from the outposts of our civilization, these have just been discovered,' he says. 'Only months ago they were under Egyptian sand, waiting, forgotten.' Something is happening inside Mariette. A new fierce light is dawning; the light of the Egyptian desert and its hidden contents. It is adventure and scholarship and travel all in one.

The duck of Egypt, in his own words, has infected him: 'un coup de bec, il vous inocule le venin et vous êtes égyptologue pour la vie'. For the last time Mariette changes course. He learns Coptic and applies for a humdrum post at the Louvre transcribing inscriptions. Just under ten years later he sets off, on the Louvre's behalf, to Egypt to buy manuscripts.

By the mid-nineteenth century the market for antiquities was already a racket, dominated at the time by the English buyers. Mariette, going out for the first time, was hopelessly inexperienced. So, in order to avoid coming home empty-handed, he set off instead with a Bedouin tribe to explore the temples in the Egyptian deserts. At Saqqara, as yet unexcavated, he saw amid a desolation of dunes and stone a single carved head sticking up from the sand. He had read Strabo, the ancient geographer, and he remembered enough to know this was roughly the right area for the ancient Serapeum. As Strabo had described it – close to Memphis, and in so sandy and so exposed a place that many of them were already, even in his time, half buried – there was an avenue of over a hundred sphinxes. Could it be? Mariette decided to excavate. He didn't bother asking anyone's permission; there wasn't time for that. The Louvre's unspent manuscript fund was put to use and the Bedouin were persuaded to dig. His hunch was rewarded with finds so astonishing that Mariette was immediately accused of stealing. Beyond the national prestige or the importance for scholarship, finds were commercial. No matter that you couldn't ship or sell an avenue, if the French laid claim to the dig then there would no doubt be plenty that would be transportable. Mariette's discovery was big. Besides Strabo's lost avenue, there was also an underground tomb complex and the famous stepped pyramid. The English and German archaeologists elsewhere in Egypt complained to the government. Mariette was an amateur. He didn't know what he was doing. Not only was he stealing, he was damaging things. Hurriedly he had to shovel the sand back over his finds until the French government was able to formalize the dig by sending money.

After four years he came briefly back to France but, announcing that he would 'either die or go mad' if he didn't return immediately to Egypt, he took his family and settled in Cairo, continuing his excavations for the rest of his life. A strong supporter of Egypt retaining the artefacts of its own history, he set up the Cairo Museum, which (while admittedly shipping much to the Louvre) he filled with his finds. Having absorbed the lesson of his first encounter, that digging was a competitive business, he struck a deal with the Khedive that gave him the monopoly. To the fury of the English and German archaeologists, all digs except his own were outlawed. Here was a true vent for his energies. In one year alone he opened and oversaw the excavation of thirty-five new sites. Egypt in return honoured him with the titles of Bey and Pasha.

But in 1880, when Mariette knew he was dying, he appointed a Frenchman as his successor at the Cairo Museum in order to ensure that France retained the pre-eminence he had won for it in the world of Egyptology. The alternative would have been either an Englishman or a German – an Egyptian was not even considered. So even after a lifetime given in passion to a foreign culture, Mariette still thought of himself as French. Why? This is so odd, so inconsistent. What is this Frenchness that is more powerful than a life-long love for somewhere else? Is identity something decided topographically, at birth?

I leave Mariette brooding over the Mummy and go on to find Rupert. I pass through rooms of Greek and Roman antiquities; a room of First Nation masks, including a beautiful feathered moon, half dark, half bright; collections of medieval instruments, things made of whalebone, curious wicker snow-shoes from Siberia – there is everything here, but no Rupert. I find him outside, sunning himself in front of a statue. A bronze man in

a fez cap, standing on top of a pyramid, his hand absent-mindedly leaned on an Egyptian head. It is Mariette. He is looking away, out over the city roofs, elsewhere to Cairo perhaps, where he is buried, in a sarcophagus presumably belonging to someone else – maybe even to the Mummy where we met, both of us so intent. 'Je suis entré dans l'Egypte,' he was to say when he was famous, 'par la momie du musée de Boulogne'.

Outside the bells of the town are ringing as if enumerating echoes. People and places intertwine while remaining distinct, like the design on a piece of Coventry ribbon. As if displacement worked to strengthen origin, distilling it into some kind of essence. I feel I am beginning at least to see a pattern. Eustace of Boulogne goes to Dover where he brawls the Norman invasion into existence and, being rewarded with English land, settles for a while in England. Dickens, born not much further along the coast, loves French places and French manners, leaves England and comes back and forth to Boulogne, to write, to holiday, and later to be with his mistress. Mariette, who is born in Boulogne, falls for Egypt where he spends his life uncovering ruins. And a ruin who is unnamed and has no choice is sent back from Egypt to Boulogne to lie in a glass museum case, staring up at strip-lighting forever.

On our way back to the van we are accosted by the same man as yesterday, rolling towards us, fat and aggrieved. Again he is halfway through his patter before we get near enough to speak. He doesn't appear to recognize us.

'We gave you money yesterday.'

He looks outraged. 'But one must eat every day.'

We are hungry ourselves so we shop. Everything looks delicious. 'Of course it does,' we say to each other as we go in and out of the greengrocer's, the pâtisserie, the mini-market, 'it's France.' We arrive at the van, laden with ambitious ingredients. I look at the two-ring cooker in something like despair. What was I thinking?

It doesn't matter. We climb in and head off, cramming little tarts and quiches into our mouths as we go, sitting happily in a welter of pastry flakes. We leave the town, driving out through suburbs, past a wooden sign for McDonald's with a makeshift yellow arrow stuck against a wall on a side street; the McDonald's itself looks slovenly and almost apologetically small a bit further on, as if it knew it shouldn't be here. Beyond it, France unfolds its long and open distances as if yawning and stretching. Even if it isn't visible, the size of the landmass makes itself felt. It is as though there were simply more time. More time for fields not to bother with fences just yet, for trees to extend themselves into woods, for roads to unfurl straight for miles, uninterrupted by buildings. More time for the sky to go on and on to a horizon that is hazed as if it might never be reached. The surrounding fields have turned into plains full of sugar beet, now being harvested. The air smells curiously sweet. On every side beet is piled at the field boundaries into gigantic Toblerone pyramids. Everywhere there are lorries, turning, carting, stacking, unearthing.

Every now and again we dive sideways into small villages and climb out of the van, to wander around these places that think they are normal. This one, for instance, empty of people at midday. All its houses quietly sufficient. Its church with a great tiled dome, which bulges outwards from its top and then, as though changing its mind, narrows upwards into a needle spire. The whole roof is covered with tiles that fit together so tightly they seem to flow, down over its timbers almost to the floor, as if they had been poured. At its entrance, above the door there is a carving in high relief of Adam and Eve, showing their expulsion from Eden, and their life of spinning and digging afterwards. In one corner Cain is chopping at Abel and in the middle sits a slim and benign Christ. It is not polished like the art of the ancient Egyptians, thousands of years before, but alive, quirky, exuberant even. And its little figures look recognizably western medieval. They match the village in their extraordinary ordinariness. Up in the top right-hand corner workmen in medieval clothes and with real faces squirrel up and down ladders with sacks on their backs, or stand with their heads popped up above battlements. As if the Tom, Dick and Harry – say, Jean, Jacques and Godelot – who might have carved the relief, made a bid for immortality and put themselves into it, teetering on ladders like the ones they were standing on, building forever a substitute for Eden. Well, if you were carving whose face would you use? Adam looks solidly handsome. Eve with her buttery looks and her heavy-lidded eyes might be anyone. Anés from the dairy, with her long flat hair. 'She's pretty. Use her.'

Rupert goes back to the van for his big camera. 'Well,' he says as he passes me, 'this is what you wanted, isn't it? A time when art was able to change the world?' So I look again – is it? I crane my neck backwards. What does he mean? Am I missing something?

And then I think I see it. I see what he means. I see how we make our representations of reality, in text or in image, and then, seduced by their design, or their insistence, we start to invest in the truth that the copy tells. A switch takes place: now when we look for truth, we don't go to the world, we go to poetry, or art, or philosophy, or literature, or we go to religion. I look around me in panic. 'What if I've changed my mind? What if that's not what I want?' I ask Rupert when he returns. He is busy with light meters and white balance. He takes no notice.

Above my head, set in stone in every sense, is the consensus, for instance, about how we depict our religion. Because Christianity is immigrant. It wasn't ours originally. It came to us in our isolation from the outside. You are wrong, you islanders, its proponents told us, worshipping your nine herbs and your trees and brooks. You should change. This story about foreigners, which was a greater truth than anything we'd found at home, would surely have looked threateningly alien. Take the fourth-century Irish poet, for instance, who stopped in his doorway and glanced up on a normal day at something that caught his eye – what's that? The little boat in the middle distance, now on the waves' crest, now in the trough, pushing relentlessly on towards the shores of Ireland. To him the Christians, with their weird voluntary baldness and their hooded cloaks and their insistence, were fanatics. What were they doing, and why did they need to do it here? Because they kept coming back. And why Ireland, which was just how he liked it? With its blowing bog cotton and its ancient gods striding across the hills under a patched light.

But whatever the poet thinks or wants, on and still on comes the boat, persisting through the waves until it turns in under the lea, because there is no stopping what is going to happen. Out step the monks, whoever they are, lifting their habits clear of their ankles, to tell this country, which has its settled structure and its literary tradition and its established religion, that it is wrong.

And why did some people have to listen? Why did it have to change? To soothe himself, in sadness he writes his poem.

> He is coming, Adzed-Head,
> On the wild-headed sea
> His cloak hollow-headed
> His staff bent-headed
>
> He will chant false religion
> At a bench facing East
> And his people will answer
> 'Amen, amen.'

That was a long time ago and Christianity has bedded itself so deep in our culture now that we think of it as our own, as we do the Norman Tower of London or the Mummy's compatriots in the British Museum. Christ often has fair hair and he looks a little bit like Eustace aux Gernons. Even if individually we no longer believe, Christianity is where we have come from. It is deeply who we are.

I'm trying to formulate my thoughts so I can ask Rupert what he thinks. 'What?'

'Nothing.' We are back in the van, driving to the usual accompaniment of telephone calls and music and clattering of pans. Rupert is steering again with his knees, while authoritatively describing a tailor-made tour of Armenia. I wonder if the client has any idea what is happening at the other end of the line. I wonder if he can hear in the background the pots and pans.

We aren't travelling fast. The van labours up the shallowest incline but I can see that the noise levels compensate somehow. There is a certain drama to it – the racket, I mean – that might in Rupert's eyes be the next best thing to speed.

'I've changed my mind,' I tell him when his call is over. 'I think it might all be art's fault. Those carvings…' I almost have to shout.

'What about them?'

'I think the damage is worse than I thought. I mean, we've been at it for so long.'

'Sorry?' Rupert says, reaching down for the music dial.

'I… I was hating London,' I say too loudly into the sudden quiet.

Rupert lifted his hand from the wheel and turned my chin towards him. 'I know, sweetheart. I think I'd spotted that.'

'But the thing I really hated was the fact that its culture seemed to have lifted loose from how things are. You know, it just all seemed to be about itself. So when I was looking at the carvings I was noticing the faces. They were so interesting. They were beautifully real – I mean like portraits – but that was just it: they were local. They were a sideways slip from the truth they were meant to be expressing. And I was thinking maybe that's where it starts – with that first dislocation. The next thing that's made is a reference or response to the thing that came before, and so on. Is that all there is? A copy of a copy of a copy?'

'Probably,' Rupert says, 'if you're human. Or if you can only be one person at a time. How many languages do you speak?'

'A bit of a few. What's that got to do with it?'

'Well, it's to do with point of view, isn't it? Each expression is local to a time and a place and a person but they all refer back to an original impulse. You just have to get to a point where you can see more than just one.'

'I still don't get it.'

'Well, think about it. The wider the view is, the more encompassing the communication will be. Languages are distinct. The differences between them are a sort of cumulative breadth of experience and time is a sort of cumulative depth. I suppose you could sort of use history.'

'A kind of reading between the lines, you mean?'

'More a kind of looking beyond, or through. If you use the analogy of photography, for instance, it means focusing on the deep background, not on what is in front of you.'

'OK. Interesting. Thanks.' He's clever.

I watch the landscape pass and I think of the deep background. The figures over the church door, in their western medieval clothes, sitting spinning under oak trees, should have had other faces. They are the unfocused foreground. If they were truthful, they should have had the stop-and-search, almond eyes and beaked noses of the East. They should have been sitting on parched rock under olive trees. I have seen a recent reconstruction made by the medical artist Richard Neave, using forensic and archaeological evidence, of a first-century Judaean that looks exactly like a Fayum mummy portrait.

So I put them side by side – why not? – these first finds of my travels, since they are already less different than I'd thought: Christ and the Boulogne Mummy, inching towards each other across the millennia between them, one with no face, one with no name. The Boulogne Mummy is older than either Christ or the Fayum portraits, which are more or less contemporaneous, but it isn't age that is the difference between them. The Mummy is problematically real, problematically strange. You are yourself, I tell it in my mind, despite your appropriation. I can't know you, and what is more, your culture is coldly alien, with its glass-smooth statues and its animal-faced gods. Out of the bare bones accounts of his life, Christ, by contrast, steps as recognizable as Robin Hood despite his floating features. If you had a story like Christ, I ask the Mummy, instead of a fixed and definite face, would you feel more familiar?

Mariette with his fresh-air energy is suddenly at my elbow. 'Come. Let me show you something.' He is stern and Rupert is on his phone again, so I go obediently where I went years ago, into a place made as flat as a picture by unrelenting sun, the Valley of the Kings, where Mariette excavated.

In the hot dust, on the sides of the mountains, men are sitting hunkered between their own knees, watching as we duck through the entrance to a tomb. Down into the ground, we descend, nose to tail, among an unending supply of tourists. Conditions similar to a journey to Hell. I shuffle forward, pressed between other bodies in asphyxiating heat which seems to billow up at me from underground. It's like having a blanket wrapped over your face. I can't breathe properly. There are too many people and the space is too enclosed. I don't want to go. I need to go back up to where there is proper air, but Mariette's bulk is filling the passage behind me.

A long way down, in a square stone chamber, where the light can't reach to fade their colours, stand – as they have done for the past several millennia – statues of painted gods. They have human bodies and the heads of dogs, birds, beetles, baboons. They are silent and utterly inscrutable, but in the heat and the half dark, looking at their ancient faces, I find what is most frightening about them is that they are true.

I follow Mariette back up to the light.

> But if cattle and horses and lions had hands
> or could paint with their hands and create works such as men do,
> horses like horses and cattle like cattle
> also would depict the gods' shapes and make their bodies
> of such a sort as the form they themselves have.

So said Xenophanes of Colophon, a pre-Socratic philosopher, bridging the gap between the Mummy and Christ. My point exactly. 'I'm impressed by your religion,' I tell the Mummy. 'It is braver for the fact that it isn't in your own image.' Perhaps it is easier to get at truth that way, or at any rate this truth: that these forms of life which are so different from our own are nonetheless both incontrovertible and mysterious. The Mummy's religion seems to offer a world differently ordered, where the human and the animal are held in equal and sacred balance. 'Your religion seems more modern than mine,' I say to it. But the Mummy doesn't answer. It is never going to answer. It just holds its mouth in the same half-open position, its piano-key teeth in rows, in silence.

Text and image are distortions. I owe Mariette an apology for thinking Egyptology had nothing to do with me. It's very relevant. If you want to identify the truths underneath the expression of their various stories, you have to practise a delicate kind of archaeology. Whether a god has a western face or a blue one; or whether Moses, for example, did or didn't go up Mount Sinai on his old man's legs in his leather sandals, whether he did or didn't come gasping down again, straining his back, carrying in his old man's arms two stone tablets inscribed by God, isn't the point. It doesn't matter whether he is black or white; it doesn't even matter if he is a dog or a cat. The commandments he brought back remain basic rules for peaceful co-existence, including – or maybe even especially – the ones, like the third, that look at first glance immaterial. 'Thou shalt not make unto thee any graven image' is read mostly as an instruction against idolatry, against horrors like the Mummy's half-animal gods. Religions are uncannily socially practical at their roots and we are uncannily good both at narrowing their ancient dictats and then disseminating them as dogma. Something happens between foundation and dissemination through the narrowing agency of art. Forgetting that religions arose out of our need to explain the world and our place in it, we read them backwards, as a proof of our own worth: we are the ones who are chosen.

No, *we* are.

Maybe if we could dig down, if we could comb the various layers impartially, and with a forensic eye, we might find something more universal. Maybe in the forgotten foundations of the graven image ban, for instance, there is an anxiety about over-particularizing, about fixing the floating face of God, that might, had we listened, have protected us from religious exclusivity.

Occasionally as we drive along, and when I think they are ready, I try out these or other thoughts on Rupert. 'Down there among the Mummy's gods I think I saw something,' I tell him. 'Maybe like Mariette we should all become archaeologists.'

'Mhmm,' is all he says this time.

Beyond the windows, meanwhile, something else is happening. The flat surfaces of the French fields pucker and heave and break open as if spilling their insides. Muck and stones and puddled liquids spout upwards. Shreds of men and animals and trees are hurled into the sky and fall huddled back, mingled in an equality of destruction. These splinters that fly at the windscreen, for instance, I can't tell whether they are bone or wood and the

49

people here are all too busy being frightened for me to ask. We are driving through the First World War.

All around us the land has rucked itself up in a mess, on which confused village boys from every country slide about at the orders of others, offering up their lives for reasons they have forgotten or never in the first place fully understood. Here is a horror. Odd that we find it culturally more acceptable than a god-faced animal.

But blink and the battlefields have zipped themselves up with green. They have tucked up the mix of mud and limbs under a coverlet of grass, as if it had never been. And now, from their re-smoothed surface, rises a memorial.

Lutyens designed it in memory, not of the dead, but of those who went missing at the Somme. It's a vast assembly of triumphal arches of different sizes and it sits on a hill above the village of Thiepval. The height of forty tall men, stacked on top of each other, it is visible for miles around, crouched massively over the low-lying quiet of its surroundings.

It is a triumphal arch. Triumphal arches were built by the Romans first, spanning the roads they'd conquered and wide enough for their armies to pass under them in procession with their captives led in chains behind. They were designed to express the unstoppable march of the Empire's power. Now they look massy and disappointed. Little human vauntings, as if Time might one day throw his hands up and say, OK, you win. You won the war. You made an arch. You will last forever.

At Thiepval the arch is made of brick, such a workaday, man-made material, with white stone trimmings. The quantity of brick. Its steady effort, one on top of another on top of another. I couldn't understand it at first. Why choose that? Stone would have made a grander monument. Brick is so suburban; so parochial and so red.

Rupert looks round with his eyebrows lightly raised. 'Isn't that exactly the point?'

The arch stands on a small rise. There is no road up to or away from it and to pass through it you have to walk up flights of steps as if into a church. So no self-aggrandizement. No triumphant processing. And at the top of the steps, when you arrive, just air. Just a high-roofed quantity of sky. You can see the farmland stretching away between the sides of the arch without interruption. You can see the great banks of clouds on the horizon that even from a distance fill its emptiness. There is nothing there. Nothing at all.

Clever to have a monument that contains emptiness. Because that is what it is. It commemorates only the people who were blown to pieces so small that they disappeared altogether.

And how could you make anything big enough to express what is our childish fear – that we be reduced to nothing? We need our bodies and the idiosyncrasies of our faces, our own and even more so those of the people we love. They are our only proof of all that matters, that we are alive, that we are individual. On the walls, the names of the missing are recorded: 72,194 men, quick or slow, scrawny or thickset, who left home with skin that was either clammy or dry; 72,194 who worried that their feet smelled or their hair was thinning; in short, with bodies that were solid and distinctive and precious. All of these left home and were atomized on the battlefield. Gone. Nothing found of them, not even a thinning hair. You are lucky, Boulogne Mummy. You have both a face and a body.

So many people were destroyed here. Standing up for a brief moment in silhouette, only to fall down, often before they had even started running. Again and again. Waves of them; 19,240 on the first day alone. So it is extraordinary, in fact, that we have found and accounted for so many. Below the arch is a little field of graves, those who were identified late, of whom some fragment was finally found, turned up by the plough maybe years after. It looks like a hospital ward, or a dormitory; the French in beds one side and the English the other, 'side by side', as an inscription records, 'in eternal comradeship'. Their memorials are of two kinds, rectangular headstones for the English, crosses for the French, determinedly preserving the only subset that we still allow to matter, that of nationality. Look, Mariette, just as you would have wanted.

The wind is blowing very cold as we get back in the van. Halfway out of town, Rupert says, 'Bugger.'

'What?'

He is leaning forward, looking at the dashboard. 'We need some bloody hills.'

'Hills? What for?'

'For freewheeling.' He says it as if I was really stupid.

'Do you mean we've run out of petrol?' I could be angry. He is a guide after all. He arranges trips for a living. I'm just incredulous. I look at him. How is it even possible? There are petrol stations every couple of miles. There is a dashboard with a needle and lights and a pointer. No one runs out of petrol these days.

'No,' he says, 'not yet.' He looks at me. 'It's not a problem.' He is humming, as if happy, but there is also a note of this-conversation-is-over. We won't make it to the next village so we turn about and go back. Round several roundabouts and we roll up to the pump.

Could we move up to the next one, the attendant asks. 'This one doesn't work.' Rupert turns the key in the ignition but nothing happens. A cloud crosses his face. It seems we ran out just in time. We have to push the van onto the pump. Emptiness of a more prosaic kind I think, and I say so to Rupert. But he is concentrating because even after the tank is filled, still the van won't start. He fiddles, hunched over the wheel listening. He tries again and the engine fires.

'No,' he says, his face radiant, 'it wasn't empty – just something locked the starter motor. I think I must have activated the alarm by mistake.'

We spend the night in a motorway truck stop. There are trees and a toilet block with canned music that comes on as soon as you open the door. I clean my teeth, listening to Mozart. As I walk back across the parking lot with my toothbrush in my hand the van, among the trucks, looks like a fish resting up among a pod of whales.

In the morning, thick fog. We drive in silence, as though we too were fog-muffled. Giant turbines, their heads hidden in mist and their spider-leg blades only visible on the down-stroke, sweep at the sky as we pass, otherwise nothing. We could be anywhere. I swivel in my seat to try to see. What am I missing? Although, later, when the fog has lifted, the landscape is unchanged. The fields are still flat as far as the horizon and the crop is still sugar beet, or perhaps turbines, or in some cases both. At intervals, giant pylons stride, overseeing their crop, as though the fields were their own, passing electric cables to each other with their arms held wide.

We don't have much idea of where we are going. Years ago, I thought I wanted to see Troyes, although I have now forgotten why, so we make for that. Its outskirts, low, built on ground as flat as a tennis court, are unpromising. Perhaps it wasn't Troyes I wanted to see after all. Miles of suburbs, logistics parks, factory outlets and business parks, designed with only speed and economy in mind. Roundabout. Roundabout. Roundabout. Or perhaps we have reached Kettering by mistake.

In the very middle of the town we stumble on the kernel of old Troyes. Half-timbered shops in pastel colours lean crazily towards each other across narrow streets, as if whispering gossip. Here commerce seems to have been forgotten. All the shops are shut although it is past nine thirty. We just want a croissant and a cup of coffee. After an hour we accept that we have to forget breakfast, and we go instead into the cathedral. It is made of towering stone on a scale that would accommodate the pylons should they ever choose to go to Mass. More accident-prone than most, it has been built and rebuilt and finally, as if in defeat, left unfinished. The original ninth-century cathedral was smashed by the Normans after successful invasion. Its replacement was destroyed by fire in 1188. In about 1200 building started again on the same scale. Twenty-eight years later the choir, or part of it, was destroyed by a hurricane. It was replaced. In 1389 the roof burned in a lightning strike. Meanwhile, its steeple, which was 360 feet high, had been hit by a tornado in 1365, and then later struck by lightning in 1700. At this point Troyes' bishops must have lost heart because things came to a halt. The steeple was not replaced and the building of a projected pair to the tower on its west façade was never undertaken. So despite its height, it looks now as if it were lying down. Its single tower, as knotted with decoration as a piece of coral, points skyward as if in angry remonstration.

The cathedral's history, no less than its fabric, is vivid, as if lit in flashes. You could pick any number of examples, but I pick Henry V, who wanted to join France to England and make it one kingdom, and who nearly did so. In the summer of 1420, he walked down this aisle with Catherine of Valois on his arm. She was beautiful and he was smitten. It was not in any way unusual for an English king to marry the daughter of a king of France, but this marriage was not just personal preference, it was a desperate bid by a battered France to end the Hundred Years' War. By the terms of the peace treaty – the Treaty of Troyes – Catherine was to be married to Henry, and her brother, the French Dauphin, passed over in Henry's favour. The Dauphin was effectively being disinherited by his own parents. On his father-in-law's death, Henry would become joint king of France and England, as would his sons and heirs in perpetuity. That was Henry's aim as he walked down this aisle.

'Isn't England big enough for you?' as he brushes past me.

But you can't ask kings questions, least of all when they are in the middle of getting married. It isn't a question of size, apparently. It is a question of property. The throne of France is Henry's by inheritance, through his grandfather Edward III, grandson of Charles IV of France. In addition, through conquest, at Crécy and Poitiers among other places, Edward III had established ownership of much of France.

Nor is his ambition a question of nationality, or if it is, then nationality isn't yet identified or defined through language. Henry, whose father is the first king since William the Conqueror to have English rather than

French as his mother tongue, thinks of himself as English although, like all nobility, he speaks French. Ever since the Norman Conquest the English court and its aristocracy have spoken French so exclusively that from time to time it has been necessary to legislate in favour of English. Parliaments are opened and conducted in French, as are legal proceedings, which still use French law. So, although Chaucer and Langland and others have made a start, England is still evolving its language, flicking backwards and forwards between different tongues in a way that is hard to imagine now. There is fashionable continental French, there is its rougher cousin Anglo-Norman, there is medieval Latin which is used as the language of scholarship, and there are the countless different English dialects, many of which are as foreign to each other as if they were separate languages altogether.

If language is not yet an indicator of nationality, then neither is territory: English kings spend much of their time living in France, either fighting for their French territories, or simply administering and enjoying them. The fact that from Henry III's time they hold these in complex vassalage to the French king is a politesse that they sometimes fail to observe. To them the English Channel is a link, not a barrier to divide, and the French kings are family.

So here he is, Henry V, Norman-looking, long-nosed, his dark hair cut in a bowl that runs high above his ears and forehead, as though he were wearing a beret. He has a hard and challenging look. At first I don't see why. In his portrait, he is shown in profile, flawless and to the left. But when he turns, in the light from these high windows I see it, the scar over one side of his face. Daring me to look, watching, as the scarred do, for a reaction. A man back from the dead.

And it is horrible his scar. When Owen Glendower rose to challenge the throne, Henry went to the Welsh Marches to fight at his father's side. He was sixteen and this was his first taste of action. At some point, an arrow struck the boy just under his eye with such force that it passed through his face to lodge in the back of his skull. He was carried off the field screaming, his life hanging in the balance; so too did the outcome of the battle.

Under the black mass of the hills on England's wild edge the English line wavered, hesitating in superstition. Because the heir to England's throne, the

Prince, was hit. God must be against them. And surely it was impossible to survive an arrow piercing the brain right through to the other side.

But the arrow was extracted, without anaesthetic, by fitting a specially designed screw into the broken shaft. The wound was treated with honey for disinfectant and in time it healed, but it left Henry disfigured, inside as well as out.

By 1420 Henry was known for his brutality. He had fought his way as far as the walls of Paris with unusual ruthlessness. He had massacred his prisoners at Agincourt in 1415, ostensibly for strategic reasons, including many of those nobles who would, under the normal terms of war, have been protected and exchanged for ransom. And then four years later, he had laid siege to Rouen. When the women and children were thrust out of the city gates in the hope that they might pass to safety, Henry had denied them passage. He had watched them starve to death instead, in the ditches around the city.

Was Henry really brutal? It is difficult to see clearly by lightning flash let alone to practise archaeology. These were extreme times and France in the fifteenth century was in political turmoil, but people are still and always people. So, an arrow wound is an arrow wound with all its effects, whatever the time, although attitudes to war and behaviour in war itself are cultural and therefore vary.

France, in fact, was in a hopeless way. Henry's enemy and future father-in-law, poor Charles VI, was mad. Here he is, for instance, in a miniature, eight years earlier, pallid on an overdressed bed. His eyes look jittery and too wide and he is waiting, propped on one elbow, for iron rods to be sewn into his clothes in case he breaks. He thinks he is made of glass. He feels tired all the time, his nerves at violin pitch. He has manic episodes in which on at least one occasion he has killed his own followers. He doesn't know when it will come again, the fog of paranoia that makes him lash out against imagined enemies. Around him, his courtiers are twitchy.

Under the instability of Charles's rule France split into factions and embroiled itself in a civil war over succession. Power shifted constantly between the different parties. Queen Isabeau tried desperately to stay on the winning side, but even so she found herself repeatedly wrong-footed.

Even within the family it was impossible to know whom to trust. Her two eldest sons both died while under the care of their uncle, John the Fearless, Duke of Burgundy. The younger son, now Dauphin, married Marie of Anjou whose father, blaming Isabeau for her own sons' deaths, had her imprisoned at Tours, dismantled her household, and took away her remaining children. And in more direct revenge, in 1419 just before Henry took Paris, the Dauphin himself invited John the Fearless to peace talks and had him hacked to death on the bridge at Montereau.

Given these conditions, perhaps disinheriting your own son in favour of a foreign monarch was less surprising. Perhaps to Isabeau and the fragile Charles this scarred and steely English king looked strong enough to end the eight weary decades of war, and afterwards both to unite and to hold his kingdom.

But it wasn't to be: Henry died of dysentery, two years before his father-in-law, when he was only thirty-six, and the war carried on for another twenty years.

And now the cathedral doors open and another couple enters, two men this time – or are they men? It seems that the second is in fact a girl – a girl in full armour – the seventeen-year-old Joan of Arc. She is escorting her Dauphin, the disinherited son of Charles and Isabeau, to his coronation. He has a hunted look, a thin yellowish man lost inside his vast clothes, such a weight of fabric, so much cloth of gold, and the padding on his shoulders extending improbably wide. Just as well he is wearing it all, or you might wonder who exactly it is who is royalty here.

Look at her, though. So glowing with her visions, so vigorous, so young, trying to adapt her thumping stride to the anxious steps of her cloth-burdened sovereign. *She* knows what a nation is. She is busy inventing one, with just the combination of fanaticism and startling simplicity that making nations takes. Round her, wherever she goes, the people press and kiss her hands, her clothes, touch the bridle of her horse, her feet, her stirrups. Bless us, they ask her. Baptize my baby. She is already a saint in their eyes. I would like to question her myself but the crowd is so huge I can't get anywhere near. 'What is she like? I can't see.'

'The Maid?' Sir Perceval Boulainvilliers has heard my question. 'She is an elegant figure, of satisfying grace, of a virile bearing.'

'But in herself, I mean, what is she like?' Is she mad, I would like to say, but I can see he is partisan.

'In her conversation she displays wondrous good sense. Her voice has a womanly charm; she eats little, partakes even more sparingly of wine. She delights in beautiful horses and armour, and greatly admires armed and noble men.' The crowd is jostling us apart. Faintly, above the hubbub, the litany continues. 'She avoids contact and converse with the many, sheds tears freely, her expression is cheerful and she has great capacity for work. Of such endurance is she in handling and bearing of arms that she remained for six days and nights in full armour.'

So she has the sense and robustness of the working class she was born into. She is industrious, healthy and strong and she likes power and nobility – she sounds modern. She has grown up in a countryside ravaged and reduced by war and spent her childhood witnessing the depredations of roving bands of English or their Burgundian allies, on the loose up and down the country, pillaging, burning, killing. Sometimes the intervals between raids were so frequent that there wasn't time for the farms to re-establish. Places fell into disuse. The forests came back with the English, as the saying goes. Several times Joan has had to drive her animals into an old fortress that the village, at her father's suggestion, had bought to use as a stronghold. Several times she has driven them out again to find the village wrecked, houses looted, fires lit inside the church. She hates the Burgundians. She hates the English.

You can write her down as lucky, as a fanatic, but still it is hard to picture finding in oneself the strength of purpose, the resilience, the physical courage she has at only seventeen. There are questions I would like to ask her because I have walked away from England. I don't know if I feel English – or even want to. How do you feel so French, I would like to ask her, when France in your time wasn't even properly a nation? And how did you find the conviction – was it just God?

I know how she would answer. But it is different for me – this I say quickly in my own defence. The oppression was more disguised. There wasn't an identifiable enemy. There wasn't God. I don't want to start all that again – doubting myself, thinking I'm mad. I don't want to start thinking again that I'm the only one who can see.

Did I walk out on my country?

Even if I had voices that came to me from the direction of the church, interrupting me among my duties weeding my father's cabbage patch; even if they were visions of angels in blinding light urging me to war, still it is hard to imagine finding the resolve to go, under the triple oppression of class, gender and education, and present myself to the local commander as someone who could reverse the nation's fortunes in war. The smirking looks of the men who show you in; the small room with its makeshift-headquarters feel, smelling of metal and sweat, and the impatient man who looks at you coldly as you enter. 'This is the Maid, Sir.'

'Go home and may your father give you a good slapping. Hussy.'

She doesn't. She stays and she comes to him again, with her stubborn ordinary face and her strong body. She has been sent by God to chase the English out of France. He finds her exasperating. Women are for something else, not fighting.

'I'll chase you and I'll give you something you won't forget. Take her away. Or give her to my men to indulge their desires.'

It would be hard now, let alone in the patriarchal fifteenth century, not to be afraid, not to go home and ask the angels for some easier mission. She comes back a third time and this time something changes: he listens. They give her men's clothing. They have a sword, a suit of plate armour made up for her, 'ung harnois blanc', so called because of the way light flashes off its polished surface. They give her a horse to ride.

It is such a strange story: the girl-boy who cuts her black hair (we know its colour from a single hair caught in the seal of one of her letters) into the bowl-shaped style of the time. The party of men who take her, riding often by night to avoid the English, to Chinon to see the Dauphin. The inquisition by the various clerics and scholars to check her veracity, her devotion. They make her wait six weeks while they watch her and test her faith. Then all

these men, these educated nobles and knights and captains-at-arms and tried soldiers, simply get up one morning and follow her.

France is abuzz with rumour. 'What is she like?' Everyone wants to know. Everyone is asking. And her appearance is gratifyingly iconic. 'I saw her mount her horse,' is the admiring account of one, 'armed all in white armour, except the head, a little axe in her hand, on a great black courser.' She bears the white satin standard of her own design, so terrifying to the English that they hallucinated a cloud of white butterflies fluttering from it when it first unfurled.

More chaotic is the account of her page, harangued by Joan for leaving her to rest when battle had once been started. 'I thought she had gone to sleep,' he pleaded, when she came downstairs like a whirlwind and in fury sent him out to fetch her horse. And meanwhile, in his own words, 'she had herself placed in her armour by the matron of the house and her daughter and when I came from preparing her horse I found her already in her armour'.

'Go and get my banner.'

The useless boy clattering about smelling strongly of sweat, puffing with embarrassment because she can be angry. 'And I went to find her banner, which was upstairs, and this I handed to her through the window.' The butterfly banner which is the terror of the English unceremoniously bundled out into the street through a casement open above, while below the teenage girl in armour snorts in impatience like her horse. Head back, Joan whirls her horse round, snatches at the banner handed down and charges, without her page, towards the Burgundy Gate. 'Get after her, quick sharp,' they tell the boy, which he does.

But she won. She won at Orléans. She won at Jurgeau, Meung, Beaugency, Troyes, Patay, Montépilloy and Lagny. She was aggressive. She urged attack rather than defence and, according to many, to everyone's surprise she fought with strength and expertise. Like a man.

Later, in her trial, this was seen to be her main fault; it was returned to continually by the crowd of men who harangued and tormented her in the dock and in her prison. Why did she wear men's clothes? It was evil. Why had she utterly and shamelessly abandoned the modesty befitting her sex, and indecently put on the ill-fitting dress and state of men-at-arms. 'It was abominable to God and man, contrary to laws both divine and natural.' And what had she to say about her sword? She loved her sword, she said, since it had been found behind the altar in the church of St Catherine whom she also loved.

But for now, it is 1429 and Joan, who is bent on ridding France of the English, is at the height of her success. She has God and nationalism burning in her eyes, she is seventeen and she is escorting her Dauphin to Mass in this booming cathedral. They are on their way to Rheims where the newly signed Treaty of Troyes will be overturned and he will be proclaimed king. Another twenty-five years and the Hundred Years' War will be over. Slowly England and France will disentangle themselves into separate countries and England will push itself, anxious, off from the Continent like a little boat, into isolation.

If you were standing wind-buffeted on those iconic Dover cliffs, would the Channel then have looked any different?

Has it widened, or is it the same? England and France seem further apart, more distinct. In England, although most of the aristocracy still speak French in preference to English, it isn't universal. Underneath, the balance has been tipping for some time. Take a walk a century earlier with the Benedictine monk Ranulph Higden as he goes about his travels up and down the country at the beginning of the fourteenth century, and you'll see.

Higden, born in 1280, wrote an account of England called the *Polychronicon*. It covers everything from history to topography to the ethnicity of the people. He wrote it in Latin, and less than fifty years later there was enough demand for texts in English for it to be translated by a Cornishman, John of Trevisa. At this stage the Anglo-Saxon thorn – þ – was still used instead of the digraph 'th' and the wynn – ƿ – was still used for 'w', so the text is rougher going than normal and must be scrambled through like the landscape it comes out of, all wind-blown tussocky grass and thistle.

As Higden saw it, there were seven tribes that went into the making of his country, including settled invaders. They were, in order of their coming, Britons, Picts, Scots, Angles, Danes, Normans and Flandrians. The Romans he splendidly ignores, despite the fact that he is writing in their language. By the middle of the twelfth century, he says, the Danes had gone without leaving a trace, although in English we would be picking their gorse and their thorns out of our words for another century or so. The Britons, Picts and Scots had been rammed into the island's extremities where they spoke their own languages. The Flandrians had been settled by Henry I at Melrose, in Roxburghshire, and then moved in a bunch to Haverford West, in Wales, where according to the book's Victorian editor they remained clearly distinct from the Welsh 'both by language and manners'. That left only the Angles and the Normans, who were 'mixed in the whole island' and the language that they spoke, up and down the country, varied.

'Al the language of the Northumbres, and specially at York, is so scharp, slitting, and frotynge and unschape, that we sotherne men may that language unnethe understonde.' Higden, who was born in the west, took orders at Chester. In his black habit, resolutely puzzling his way through the country, he came to the conclusion that 'burthe of the tunge' had been both unusual and difficult. In the thorny thicket of his own words: 'By comyxtioun and mellynge firste with Danes and afterward with Normans in many things the contray longage is apayred, and som useth straunge wlafferynge, chytterynge, harrynge and garrynge.' All of which hybridization, in his opinion, is due to the fact that English children at school 'against the usage and manere of alle other naciouns beeth compelled for to leve their owne langage and for to construe hir lessouns and here thynges in Frensche and so they haveth seth the Normans came first into Engelonde'.

Higden was writing in the 1320s or '30s. By the time that John of Trevisa was translating, around fifty or so years later, things had changed enough for him to make a note of his own in the text. 'Now, the yere of our Lorde a thowsand thre hundred and foure score and fyve, and of the secounde kyng Richard after the conquest… in alle the gramar scoles of Engelonde, children leaveth Frensche and construeth and lerneth in Englische.'

This, as he tartly observes, gives children the advantage of learning their lessons more quickly than before but with the disadvantage that, having done so, they find themselves knowing less French than their own 'left heele'. It is a given for both Trevisa and Higden that the English will want to leave their own shores, to 'passe the see and travaille in straunge landes and in many other places', either out of need or just out of curiosity. The English are adventurers already, in both senses. Higden, who has little good to say about his compatriots, finds them covetous, impetuous, deceitful, better able 'to wynne and gete newe than kepe her owne heritage', for which reason, with or without French-speaking left heels, the English (and this is only c.1340) are spread wide throughout the world in the strong belief that 'everich other londe is hir owne'.

Towards the end of the chapter Higden, lashing himself into a fury of disgust, reduces his account to a simple catalogue of national characteristics. The English are snobbish and discontented and self-aggrandizing. Those who prance about with minstrels and heralds as though they were great men are nothing. They boast and talk themselves up. They are gluttons. They are quarrelsome, murderous, dishonest. 'In gaderynge of catel, hoksters and taverners'. They are lecherous, argumentative, mercenary, envious and vain.

I turn off my computer as though surfacing from the bottom of the sea. I haven't looked yet to see whether medieval France had its own excoriating equivalent. Perhaps the French were more forgiving of themselves.

After Troyes and a sandwich we are more focused about our route. At Rupert's suggestion we will go on and backwards to our common ancestors the Celts – to Châtillon-sur-Seine and the Vix treasure.

'If you are interested in national identity you'd better have a look,' he says, 'and the Vix krater is an amazing thing. I've seen images of it but I really want to see it for real.'

'Good,' I say, 'I'm ready.' And I am. I'm still thinking about Joan of Arc and my own lack of faith. I am still wondering whether I've failed. 'Do you feel English?' I ask Rupert as we drive. 'I mean, do you feel like you love England, like you belong?'

'Well, I don't feel like anything else,' he says. 'And yes, I love England. I've never been very good at belonging, particularly.' He lifts one hand from the wheel, opens it so I can see the tendons in his hand pulled tight into the raised V of a Dupuytren's contracture. 'And I've got a Viking hand. Only Vikings get this, apparently.'

'That's disgusting. So what?'

'So I must have come over with the Normans.'

I look at him, at his Celtic colouring, with new eyes. 'Well, I haven't much liked the Normans I've met so far,' I tell him. He laughs. He doesn't care.

France seems to be relaxing into itself. Now, either side, there are many-windowed buildings in a softer landscape that rises and falls gently, with little woods in between, and the Seine in its adolescence, clear like a chalk-stream, its long green hair flowing. Houses more glass than stone, their shutters so close as to be almost overlapping, their red-tiled roofs rising steep, with finials at each end. We turn off the road at Vix and whip the van up a steep hill from which we can look out over the plain where the treasure was discovered. Little tumuli visible in the distance. Farm fields. And under our feet the Celtic citadel of the treasure's owner, from the fifth century BC.

The Celts are a phantom people. Geographically, at their height in about the third century BC, they ranged from the bottom of Spain across more or less everything in northern Europe, including the British Isles. They haven't left any literature behind so they appear only at second hand in the accounts of ancient authors. They are the Not-Greeks, and later the Not-Romans. Their tribes have names, the Latobrigi, the Volcae, the Tulingi, the Iceni, but opinion on whether the names were their own or whether they were given to them by others is divided. No one seems to know what they called themselves. No one seems to know whether they were one civilization with a common language, but with regionally different belief systems and burial traditions, or whether they simply look like one because their success in trading has left their artefacts spread throughout Europe. Their traditions, which persist in or have been claimed by Scotland, Ireland, Wales and Brittany, were oral. So here is a third option to add to that of Christ with no face or body and the Egyptian Mummy with no name or story: just a bundle of possessions – to leave only the things you owned behind, as proof of who you were. Because here is a long-lasting culture of great sophistication which has simply withdrawn in silence. It has put down its belongings, as if called elsewhere; left them lying about in lakes, or buried underground, for us to find and marvel at, turning them over in our hands and wondering.

Great, everyone says. More beautiful solid stuff. More facts and one conveniently decayed body. We can begin presuming.

The Vix body, found lying in a cart whose splendidly bossed wheels had been moved and ranged along the tomb walls, is in fact so decayed it is impossible to establish even its gender. The tomb has very few weapons, unlike other similar examples, and from the femur of the corpse it is possible to establish its age at death, thirty to thirty-five, and the height, five feet three inches. Very small and very peaceful for a man, or so it is assumed. Where its neck would have been is a huge golden torc, an ornament with a break in the middle and two great lion's-paw ends holding balls in their fine-haired, finely drawn claws. On the backs of the claws stand perfect little Greek-influenced winged horses. Around it, and still in the places where they had been worn or pinned to clothing, were bracelets, necklaces of amber, intricate golden pins. Jewellery. Definitely a woman. But to my eyes, the torc is expressive of great power, the balls at its ends decidedly male-looking.

The little notices that accompany the exhibits are cautious and concise, but on a wall to one side is a large illustration of a blonde-haired, blue-eyed lady who looks like she has just won a 1950s Good Housewife award. She is wearing the torc as if it were an Alice band, over back-brushed hair. A *New York Times* article in 1985 agrees: the owner of the tomb had been a princess, a sophisticated 'barbarian woman', who, apparently, kept her hair in place with a rigid lump of gold, ornamented at each end with lion's feet and testicles.

But the archaeologists with their little brushes and their eyes fixed in concentration are not influenced by newspapers. They are taking their time and assuming nothing. They say 'possibly' and 'perhaps' and 'in this case'. They divide the tribes stylistically and chronologically. The Hallstatt culture for instance, or the La Tène (which covers Vix), or the much later Insular Celts of the British Isles. Analysing the skeletal remains of the tomb's owner, they find that 'substantial problems with her hip joints and an asymmetric skull shape suggest that she would have had a waddling gait, and her head would have been held tilted to the right and her face somewhat twisted. These traits may be a consequence of either congenital conditions or childhood stress due to disease or malnutrition, or both.' So whoever she was, she had a highly unusual appearance, and with it cocked to one side it seems to me she could hardly have balanced the torc on her head as the woman in the picture is doing.

The famous statue of the Dying Gaul, who is a man with a handsome moustache, is wearing his round his neck. Trawling the internet in the campsite in my customary fashion, I find this is how it is more usually pictured, like a collar, the break at the front. Cassius Dio, the Roman historian, writing about Celts in England half a millennium later, describes Boudicca, like a proto-Joan of Arc, driving the Roman occupiers out of England, in a bright coloured tunic and a chariot with scythes on its wheels. By his account Boudicca had long tawny hair hanging below her waist, a man's harsh voice and a piercing glare. As at Vix both her tunic and her thick cloak were fastened with brooches, and round her neck she wore always a large golden necklace. But she also had a lot of weapons and, what's more, she was very good at using them.

I'm thinking of my see-through boxes, full of cheap clothing, as I stare at the untarnished, good-as-new torc in its case. It is perfectly possible that the torc's wry-necked owner was not a princess but a priestess or a seer. I've read all the information panels. That would be a rational conclusion.

'It's perfectly possible,' something else inside me says, thinking of all the clothes in my boxes that had been bought with the style of a new persona in mind, the long skirts ready for old age, or the designer charity-shop suits for improved efficiency, 'that it wasn't a woman at all but a small, weaponless, man who liked jewellery.' We come, and we go, and we leave our belongings behind us. How can we have any certainty about the people of the past when we don't even have any about ourselves.

Whoever the Vix people were, they were rich and they were traders. Along with the torc are objects from all corners of the ancient world: an Etruscan wine jug, Baltic amber and lignite beads, a gold necklace possibly from Syria, silver-ware and Greek black-figure pottery. The hoard's signature piece is a spectacular bronze krater, the largest vessel of its kind in the world, so big that the body it was buried with, at five foot three, could have climbed inside and stood up with inches to spare. It had come, in pieces, from the Greek mainland, possibly Sparta, via Marseille, which had been established by the Greeks as a colony (Massalia) in the sixth century BC. Even at the time the krater would have been an exceptional object. Herodotus has an account of something similar, given to Croesus, King of Lydia, by the Spartans in the middle of the fifth century. It was big enough to hold hundreds of gallons of wine and it was clearly unusual enough to be worthy of mention. In fact, it was so big, so unusual, that, until the Vix krater was found, historians dismissed its existence as an impossibility. Herodotus, we were told, must have been exaggerating.

How can we understand ourselves or judge our progress when our past is so long lost? Like a person with amnesia, we go groping back down the pathway to our beginnings, with our arms stretched ahead of us in the dark. When we throw a little light on things with our imaginations, we look at the lengthened shadows we have made and take them for the real thing. When we stop and try rationalizing instead, we go wrong.

I give up trying to work it out. 'Poor sweetheart,' Rupert says, looking at my troubled face. 'Let's just travel.'

OK, I think, why not? I can do that. I can travel as if everything were cut free from its moorings, mixing and flowing like a body of water. Maybe I can just float on its surface, let myself be carried for a bit.

I flick through the guide books in the shop while Rupert buys postcards. Have I heard of Beaune before? I'm not sure. The pictures look nice. 'Let's go there.'

In the van again, head resting against the doorframe, I watch the country of the Celts passing. How was it that they got quite so rich – rich and important enough to own something as stupendous as the krater? Well off is how this part of France still looks, as we drive on down through wine country, although when I look it up, scrolling through charts on my phone, it isn't, or perhaps isn't comparatively, coming sixteenth out of twenty-two regions. Presumably these fertile-looking fields produced their food, but the Celts also took tolls from any vessel going up or down the Seine, and they traded: copper, tin, iron, silver. And we, their descendants, are still trading. The few thin rappelling lines that the Celts cast out have multiplied and criss-crossed and interlaced, two and a half millennia later, to become a net wide enough to catch the whole world.

No one gets rich by staying at home, farming their own fields. The copper and silver mines along the Rio Tinto which have been in use on and off since the third millennium BC have given their name to a modern Anglo-Australian mining company with operations on six continents. Total, which I discover is French, deals in oil and gas at every level from extraction to refining, including trading, transporting and power generating (with a side interest in chemical manufacturing) and it has extraction operations in Indonesia, Qatar, the UAE, Oman, Nigeria, Norway, Russia, Yemen, Angola and Australia. We know all this. Countries, however emphatic they might be about their borders, operate outside them and it seems have always done so. There is hardly an inch of the world, once you start to look, that isn't prospected, staked out, claimed and trussed up in complex financial agreements; including areas under the sea, parts of the moon, and regions that are still under ice. Even in the teeth of apocalypse there will still presumably be money to be made. Some fortune hunter, some Count Eustace or other, frenzied with necessity, will be drilling the exposed polar caps, until his moustaches freeze solid or the rising waters cover his head.

'I'm not thinking about art or nationality any more. I'm thinking about something even more destructive,' I tell Rupert.

'I thought we were just going to travel?'

'We are! But I've just got this thought about money.'

'Right,' Rupert says. He has his wry face on. 'And what do you know about money?'

'Well, I know I don't much like what it does to people.'

'Right,' Rupert says again. He glances at me quickly as if unsure.

Eustace, up from the bottom of time's sea again, bobs to the surface like plastic trash.

'And how do you propose to live,' Eustace asks me, sliding into the back of the van, 'if you don't make money?' He looks at his fingernails, rather than me, while he is talking. 'What about your education, your health, the roads we are driving on, the technology that has created this van, which you like so much? Your computer? How are any of these possible without money, without trade, without manufacturing?'

To my fury, Rupert nods.

'You what?' I hiss at him. 'I thought you were supposed to be on my side.'

Even if he is right, I can't like Eustace. I don't want to talk to him. 'Wealth generation' is the name that we give to this activity he practises so relentlessly, which implies that the money wasn't there before, that it is being brought into the world in places where before none existed. I know about this at least, or I think I do. Wealth generation is not just a good but a necessary thing and those of us who can't give birth to money are worth less, as Eustace is keen to point out, in every way. But I can't help noticing that however much money is born, at individual as well as at national level, we still need more. I think of my life as it was when I was fixed in place, its blizzard of bills. As soon as we open our wallets, the money vanishes, as if our wallets were only full of smoke. Now how can we manage? And the populace, which has been told to keep shopping because the money must stay in circulation, is aghast. How are we supposed to buy all the things we need? How can we buy the new things that will allow us to throw our old ones away? And without new things, what on earth will we throw away next year?

Steal, presumably. And if you don't want to steal, borrow. Or, simply imagine it. If we spin it round fast enough and imagine it hard enough, we can operate at a deficit. It is like a party game. Keep going. Keep going. At all costs don't stop. So again we send out our Eustaces wearing their multi-national banners, hoping that when they have lined their pockets in the world outside they will remember they belong to a single nation after all.

Meanwhile, we sit at home imagining money; arguing with parched mouths about how much to ask for and trusting in trickle-down or un-evaded tax. When the Eustaces return they are outraged. They have mortgages, wages to pay, Jacuzzis to heat and helicopters to run. They have much less than they thought. Their overheads have galloped away in their absence. Their money too has gone up in smoke. And they've done their bit. They bought several things at a charity auction only last week, a fishing weekend, a dinner with an author, a picnic hamper. Didn't we see the photos? Keep it, we tell the Eustaces. Don't worry. Sorry for asking. Just don't take it abroad.

Some of this I say out loud. Eustace is mostly lounging in the back with his eyes shut. Once he leans forward and says to Rupert, 'What's that you are eating?'

'Gum,' Rupert answers. 'You want some?' They exchange a look that might be conspiratorial. I can see they are waiting for me to finish, and in fairness there aren't many breaks in which they might interject with opinion or invective of their own. When at last I do stop for breath and ask Rupert, a little pointedly, what he thinks, 'Maybe you should be a little more nuanced,' is all he says, glancing at me sideways as he overtakes a tractor.

'You *what*?'

For the real Eustace, the rewards he was given for fighting at Hastings, which had seemed at the time so considerable, within a year had begun to look paltry. He needed more. So he encouraged the already rebellious Kentish men to attack Bishop Odo's castle at Dover. Odo was the Conqueror's half brother and another possible patron of the Bayeux Tapestry, so it was a brazen move. Eustace's attempted land-grab was thwarted and he was banished back to France, although not in the end for very long. Smirking and looking at his disgusting nails, he tells me again, as he has done before, 'You can't keep a good man down.'

'Not everyone can be a Eustace.' I say this in my own defence and because this really is how I see it. 'While a very few people go out and give birth to money, many others are needed to stay at home and make a country fit for the Eustaces to come back to. Many people are needed, to empty the dustbins full of consumer rubbish, to grow food or drive it from one end of the country to another, or to make the dustbins that contain it, or the trucks that drive it around. Many more are needed to cure the truck drivers or dustbin emptiers, should they fall ill, or to educate their children.'

Eustace swivels his head. 'Look, you are boring me.'

'But these are necessary jobs. I'm sorry if I'm boring. A society is a whole thing; we need all of it to work. Even if you don't care about the people as people, from a practical point of view you must want them to be happy, and healthy and motivated, if only so that they go on producing and consuming. Isn't that so?' I ask him. No answer.

'In a healthy system,' I say, 'I would like to think that the money circulated freely and that people too made their way freely from the bottom to somewhere higher, and sometimes in the nature of things from the top to the bottom again. I would like things to be aerated with movement, for there to be both hope and the possibility of change in people's lives. I am afraid of a society where hope and choice no longer exist.'

'They have reality TV,' Eustace says. 'They have the lottery. There is hope.'

I twist round, ram my head between the front seats to face him. 'Something has changed,' I tell him, 'something has crept up on us like Grandmother's Footsteps, so incrementally that we haven't noticed.' Help me, Eustace, I want to say. Help me to understand. But my voice is too high. It is hard not to be hysterical. What happens when you have a mass of people at the bottom of society who feel thwarted or preyed on, or ignored? Eustace looks like he's stopped listening. He is picking his teeth with one hooked fingernail.

How, Eustace, Rupert, anyone, should we live?

'Look,' Eustace drawls, suddenly impatient. 'This is old hat. Read the newspapers. These people at the bottom that you are so worried about – they're all redundant. We don't need them. They don't matter. In twenty years' time robots will be doing all their jobs. Great things are being done in science.'

Rupert nods. 'That is true.'

'We have genetic engineering and stem-cell research,' Eustace says. 'We are inventive. We will think of something.' He goes quiet. 'I wonder...' he says to himself with interest in his voice. He taps his teeth with one fingernail. 'I wonder... these redundant people, could they perhaps be farmed? That's not a bad idea. I will look into it.'

In the silence that follows, the faces of children I once knew suddenly float up from the imaginary seabed, opening before me like little sea anemones. One small girl in particular, in white socks and with a high-up ponytail, horribly bullied by her mother. Every day she came out of school at the run, skipping with pleasure. When she started to say what she'd done in the day, she was shouted at in her face. 'Shut up. I'm talking.' When she picked up a stick to wave like a wand, she was asked what was wrong with her. Why couldn't she, for one moment, think? The girl looked at me, baffled. Think what?

But she could think, in fact she couldn't stop thinking. I don't know whether she was clever or not. I never saw her at school. But she was herself and she was beautifully alive, full of quickness and intelligence. There was in her a great willingness to understand and an instinctive impulse to think. Only once, when we played 'running away from home', did she become upset. In the role of her mother and finding her crouched in the cupboard under the stairs, I expressed my relief. 'No, you are angry,' she told me. She wanted me to shout and punish her. 'But I lost you,' I said, 'I've been looking for you everywhere.' She was almost tearful. She couldn't understand something and she needed to think it out. Why is my mother this way? Is there a choice? Is my mother bad? Am I? And if so, why do I still love her? She insisted: I *must* be angry.

Once it was explained to me, should I ever need it, how to tenderize an octopus. You bring it to the surface as quick as you can and then you beat it thirty-two times to loosen its muscles. This makes it flaccid. Children are not born to fit Eustace's system; they are too naturally lively. So their acculturation requires a similar process. The main thing is to shut off all vital signs before the onset of adulthood: batter them catatonic with consumer desire, muddle them out of curiosity and self-knowledge. At this point the person is no longer any use. Exhausted from the moment they wake up, most of them will look for the easiest option. Their curiosity will have been suffocated. Their faces will have closed and become opaque. Their eyes will be glazed and they will sit still, as their mothers wanted, burping overflow softly to themselves, their pale and fattened bodies spreading across new couches, and their pale and fattened minds listless with passivity. We will have done it – good work, everyone. What were once live beings are now just machines for consumption. We can pat ourselves on the back while the parents of the children, if they have stopped shouting, sit with their own backs turned, tapping muddle and loneliness into computer screens among a litter of cheap possessions.

'Spiritual genocide, Eustace. Do you hear me? Whole generations, child after child after child, our best and most valuable resource, bludgeoned senseless, just twitching occasionally with animal response to the prompts of various appetites.'

Eustace has slid away but Rupert and I go on hammering it out between us, because these are some of my troubles. Where is Joan of Arc? I would like her to see. Look, this is my enemy – and where is the armour and what are the weapons to fight that? Would you have managed? Is this just my nation, my culture? She would fix me with her fanatic stare. She would shrug with her French shoulders and she would answer that she hates the English. Well, Joan, I'm inclined to agree, only I'm not sure that it's just the English who are at fault. It is deeper, wider, more intrinsic than that. Why are we so individually greedy, so careless of each other, or of society as a whole? What did he say, the Chancellor, glossed and slick with choice? 'We will have the Gevrey-Chambertin and the quail pâté'? 'We will have boar with truffles'? Something about benefits being 'a lifestyle choice', or was it, 'Cancel the quail. We will just have benefits'? Neither Rupert nor I can remember exactly, and privately I am not surprised. It is impossible to hear what the men running Eustace-land are saying, there is such a hard clatter of silver spoons in their mouths.

Rupert, who has a more shaded view of things, who sees subtlety in place of absolutes, modifies everything I say. He doesn't mind that things are mixed, that good comes out of bad and vice versa. Mixed is how the world is, so he expects it to be that way. He thinks I should weigh things a little more. He thinks things are not black and white. He thinks, as he has said before, that I am taking an un-nuanced and over-emotional position. Both of us hate to argue.

'Well, in this mixed and shaded world of yours, I suppose we can both be right,' I say, exhausted and conciliatory.

'I'm right,' Rupert says, insistent for once, 'because I am looking at how people are and always have been. You're a little bit right because you have a point – it isn't a very good system but there isn't a better one. You could be more right if you calmed down, but even if you calmed down your point would not apply. Man is an imperfect species.'

'I thought that was what the whole effort was about, all this writing and making and speaking and thinking. I thought we were supposed to try to improve, ourselves as well as our society.'

'Only in your religion. Not in mine. Mine is an accurate depiction of the world as it really is.'

'I don't have a religion,' I almost shout at Rupert.

'Neither do I,' he says, 'I was speaking figuratively.'

In the heat of the discussion we miss the source of the Seine where we had planned to stop and eat our sandwiches. In my mind it is a clear spring bubbling out over pebbles among green grass. A beginning, a fresh and important and un-mixed origin. We are momentarily at a loss. But it is a good half-hour behind us. We stare at the map. We are unreasonably disappointed as we drive on in silence. Ahead of me, with its nourishing dews and its moderate and fertile plains Nuance appears and vanishes, like a mirage, in the dips and rises of the road. I can't help noticing that it is a word we pronounce as if it were still French, that there isn't an English word for it. I'm not just making excuses.

We reach Beaune in darkness. It's a town as beautiful as a stage set. Quiet. Old. Elegantly ornate. Stone again; stone streets and churches, stone arches, peaceful stone squares with trees. Around a corner we come upon a medieval belfry with clock faces on each side, under dormer roofs, crowned with a pincushion of pinnacles. Outside the cathedral a great crowd of people is gathered – at their centre, a medieval duke, expensive in black from head to toe, like a pinnacle himself, pointed, and articulated like an ant. Only his face gives him away as human: pale, under a top-heavy scrumple of black velvet, carefully balanced and looped together under his chin. He is Philip the Good, son of John the Fearless, murdered on the bridge by Joan's Dauphin. He is Joan's arch enemy, a man of great power. His court in the Duchy of Burgundy is grander than that of either England or France. His extravagance is legendary. I would stop him but there are hundreds of people around him, among them, always at his right hand, another chancellor. And I don't know which question to ask. Why is the world this mixed? Why do things look so lovely when behind them is such suffering, such waste? I let him pass; the long points on his wooden pattens give him a hobbling walk.

His chancellor, waving the crowds aside to make a passage, has the alert, miss-nothing glance of a hedge-sparrow. Did he look at me as he swept by?

We turn away to find a campsite and in my head I rehearse my questions for another time. What use – and I mean it in the strictest sense – are my democratic rights when I can't make head or tail of anything? Capitalist economics has become an arcane practice with its own language, which the uninitiated don't generally speak. I admit, I don't understand its complexities. How do I play my part, as I should in a democracy, when I can't balance a nation's budget, or manage its debt, or finance its welfare system? Is it enough to trust my instincts, each time I feel that our domestic priorities, or our foreign policy, or our bail-out system is wrong? I don't know. I don't always have the evidence to hand and I feel naïve. There are so many conflicting interests to assess; there is so much double thinking to be done and everything is so inextricably intertwined. I leave it. Everything will look different in the morning.

And it does, or at least Beaune does. It looks less mysterious, more composed and tourist-ready than it did by moonlight. Plenty of tidy, well-off people are doing their shopping. Vans unloading boxes. Wine shops everywhere you look, though we don't need wine. I have questions to ask and Rupert seems happy to wander, squinting through his viewfinder any time I stop. I am looking for the Duke I saw last night, following the flutter of black out of

the corner of my eye, down the narrow streets behind the cathedral. It turns out to be nothing – just a crow lifting out of the gutter on a breeze. He must be here somewhere; he runs this place. I stop in bafflement, looking left and right. Then something else – the swish of a heavy fabric and we set off, this time with purpose – the fur-trimmed robe of Chancellor Rolin as it swings out of sight at street corners. A chancellor will answer. We hurry after.

Rolin, whose first name is Nicolas, is getting old. You can see that from the grey look of his face, its skin hanging in pouches below the jawline, the wet, full, bottom lip, and its meagre opposite puckered as if in anxiety. As if, even with the stupendous riches he has amassed for himself, still he daren't stop. His bright, hedge-sparrow eyes at constant alert. Will there be time? Will I be deposed before I've done, or will I manage?

Why so restless, Chancellor?

Just one more negotiation, one more letter for one more position, for another levy, one more estate. As I say, he can't stop. And now, with the onset of old age, he is making bargains with God, trading charity for torment, trying to buy bliss.

> Moi, Nicolas Rolin, chevalier, citoyen d'Autun, seigneur
> d'Authume et chancelier de Bourgogne, en ce jour de
> dimanche, le 4 du mois d'août, en l'an de Seigneur 1443…
> dans l'intérêt de mon salut, désireux d'échanger contre
> des biens célestes, les biens temporels… je fonde, et dote
> irrévocablement en la ville de Beaune, un hôpital pour les
> pauvres malades, avec une chapelle, en l'honneur de Dieu et
> de sa glorieuse mère…

Famine after the Hundred Years' War, followed by plague, has left a countryside ghosted with people whose eyes look sick, whose mired and tattered clothes hang off limbs that jut like poles. Are they alive, these ghosts, or dead, it's so hard to tell. They have been eating bread made of acorns and their mouths are ulcerated with untreated tannin. Their stomachs too. For some the tannin is causing kidney failure. They walk painfully past us, down muddy lanes on swollen ankles, and their hands, full of retained water, dangle, oddly fat, at their sides. This little pile, here by the hedge, didn't make it. They ate bread that they'd made from fine-ground clay.

So Chancellor Rolin builds a hospital for the poor, largely at his own expense. It is a beautiful place, steep roofs covered in jaunty tiles arranged in geometric patterns, a complicated lacework of finials, a courtyard. Inside there is to be an order of nuns sanctioned by the Pope, a huge hall with closed beds down its sides, fifteen per side, a vaulted roof with decorated beams, a chapel, an apothecary, where medicine is made in huge copper vats, with pipes and crushers and distillation chambers. Next door there is a room full of jars on shelves, from which the medicines can be dispensed. All will be welcome. All the ghosts, whether man, woman or child. But only thirty at a time. So the Chancellor has answered, in a way, and his answer is, benefits, or to be more precise, health benefits; for the soul as much as for the body. He will heal both. And his foundation has persisted; it still exists, only now in the form of a modern hospital. It has lasted over half a millennium.

'What did it cost you, Chancellor? Sorry, which of your comforts did you do without, what sacrifice did you make, other than time and coffer-overspill?' I lean forward. I didn't quite catch that. But Rolin doesn't answer. His mouth is full of quail and Gevrey-Chambertin. He is at a banquet for the Duke's projected crusade. It is being held in a hall of the ducal palace at Lille, tables groaning with gold service. In the middle of the room a live lion is chained to a pillar. Tumblers, musicians, acrobats and a whole hunt, pass each other in succession, to entertain the diners. There is a church, with stained glass, and an organ and bells; there is a wilderness whose rocks are rubies and sapphires; a ship with masts and sails and sailors; a naked child on a rock, pissing a stream of rose-water. And that is just the decoration for the Duke's table, at which Rolin is the only commoner present.

Now we are getting to it.

The Duke of Burgundy's wine is brought to him carried above head height, so that it can't be polluted by the cup-bearer's breath. Some lives count. Some don't. Rolin, an entirely self-made man who was born the son of a local burgher, is neatly poised between the two, in the tricksy no-man's land of self-invention. Hated by both sides, history has never a good word to say for him. 'Il est bien juste,' Louis XI said of his hospital, 'que Rolin, après avoir fait tant de pauvres pendant sa vie, leur laisse un asile après sa mort.' His greed for gold, for land, is legendary, so much so that the Duke is supposed to have told him on one occasion, 'Non, Rolin, c'est trop!'

I've seen Rolin before, kneeling dutifully, dressed in furred damask, in front of a modest Virgin with the naked Christ child on her lap, in a picture by Van Eyck. He is ten years into success, already a knight and the Duke of Burgundy's chancellor. He looks at first glance rich, hard, obdurate; as though religion, for him, were not a live concern. Behind his left shoulder the landscape, of which he now owns so much, opens out: fertile fields with little hedges, vineyards, woods. Just above his hands, folded convincingly in prayer, is the church of his hometown, Autun, restored and extended out of his own pocket. You can see the covered passage going from Rolin's house to one of its chapels, built so that he and his wife can listen to a matins specially sanctioned for them by the Pope. This is the grand and comfortable life he has made for himself. But he isn't looking at any of these things. His praying hands are in a plane with the Christ child, but his face is angled out of the picture. His eyes look somewhere else, out past the Madonna's inclined head, like someone in church distracted by a thought.

'What are you thinking?'

Because it is obvious that that is what he is doing. 'Is it business?' Rolin's contemporary, Georges Chastelain, accused him of always 'harvesting on earth as though earth was to be his abode forever'. But the hazel eyes looking up out of his picture are surprisingly soft and faraway. I feel that I am interrupting. The dark hair looks lightly dishevelled, particularly when compared with a slicked-down later portrait, on the back of Van der Weyden's Beaune altar-piece. I have the odd impression of a public presentation of a private, internal moment. There is no one else there, no interceding saint to present Rolin to his God, as is the convention. Just himself, as he is in life, outrageously, right at the throne of power.

'What are you saying with your picture, Chancellor?' Because although some have suggested the painting was commissioned by his son, most have assumed that Rolin himself ordered and paid for it. Here I am, whether you like it or not; try to stop me? Or, here I am not, and never will be, no matter how many taxes I levy, or lands I accrue, because even with all the gold in Burgundy I can't change the colour of my blood? A man trying to fix himself, to make himself visible, permanent. Look at me. Can you see me now? Am I safely and irreducibly there? A man so solidly un-eraseable, so real, with his veins, his shaven neck, his folds of skin and all the goadings of his anxiety on show. I get both messages. I'm here and there's no getting round me. And, I'm afraid I am still nothing. I can be swept away in a moment by the aristocrats (as indeed in the end he was), if I lose concentration or if, sleeping for one second, I relax my hated grip.

Whatever Rolin is doing or thinking, whatever his preoccupations or spiritual shortcomings might or might not have been, the gaze of the child in the Madonna's lap is direct and focused. It is a kind painting. His hand is raised in blessing. Maybe, unlike everyone else, Van Eyck liked Rolin. At least Rolin saw the ghosts that moved so painfully about his fields. And if he couldn't control his greed, at least he was too clever or too personally exposed to ignore completely its effect.

We make our way back to the van and head off, leaving the fat lands behind, following the great slow loops of the Saône into smaller country. The fields are tighter, drier, holding on to the sides of hills. Little tussocky plots and rough stone buildings that give way, by evening, to the drama of Cévennes. The Gorges du Tarn clothed in autumn. There are round stone tiles on the roofs, many-spanned bridges over water that sounds everywhere and that changes – translucent, so even from a height you can see its pebbled bed – from vivid green, to blue, to brown as tea and back again. Wilder country and sharply cold. Crag upon stony crag rising against the evening sky. The road is single track now, diving through tunnels and teetering above the river. Bend after bend after bend. One star rising and half an aspirin-moon.

We drive over a broken length of chain onto a deserted camping-plot in the valley bottom. Empty grass squares, with stands at intervals for electricity.

Wooden washing blocks with padlocks on their doors. Trees rustling and the pale cliffs of the gorge rising high above our heads. We walk the riverbank as far as a stone bridge at the outskirts of a village, where the only shop sells us milk, eggs and a powerful and, in the end, inedible saucisson. In the time it takes to cook an omelette the van is warm. I read the anchor. I've got as far as Chaucer, an extract from the Knight's Tale, the Temple of Mars, which, spelling aside, is as far as the human race has ever got, and no further. Pictures of bombed-out cities float through my mind.

> Ther saugh I first the derke ymaginyng…
> The nayle ydriven in the head anyght;
> The colde deeth, with mouth gapyng upright…
> Armed Compleint, Outhees, and fiers Outrage;
> The carrion in the bosk, with throte ycorve;
> A thousand slayn, and nat of qualm ystorve;
> The tyrant with the prey by force draft;
> The toun destroyed, ther was no thyng laft.

'Come with me, Chancellor. You think religion is a commodity but I will show you something. There is no pretence at praying here, no holding your hands in devotion, while the sermon runs and your mind is totting up taxes.' Above the van, up the narrow stone ways that go over these mountains, the black shadows of people are passing, trying to be quiet. A long line of them, mostly women dressed up as men. They are following a guide, trying not to stumble in the dark. Refugees trying to reach Protestant Geneva because here, unlike in your picture, religion is life or death. Quickly, quickly, clutching their bundles to their chests. Up above the sleeping village of Pont-de-Montvert. But the guide is moving fast and it's tough going and at the back the young girl, who has never left the village before and is feeling dizzy, misses her foothold. Down the steep sides go her cry and the rock her foot dislodged, clattering and bouncing together. The column freezes.

It doesn't matter. They were going to be found anyway. The Abbé of Chayla, who was taught about torture by the Buddhists in Siam, has men posted at all the passes out of the village. There are always people who will tell you what you want to know if you make it worth their while. The column is rounded up and driven back down to the village, faster than they came up and as if they were sheep. In terror, stumbling, the poor girl who dislodged the rock is crying now. She barely has control of herself, whimpering like a dog. What will happen to me? What will happen now? Either side the villagers bear her up. Come now. Pray. Stand fast.

But she is right to be afraid. They are shut in the Abbé's own house, which has become a prison. Sitting waiting in the dark with the river talking outside. One by one they are taken out and questioned about their faith. When they don't recant and turn Catholic, they have wool soaked in oil bound round their hands and set alight until their fingers disintegrate.

You can hear their screams as far as the next village. Good. A warning.

All night, through our sleep, the river handles its stones. In the morning the village is out buying bread, their modern hands miraculously intact. Cars stop in the street for conversations held half in, half out. It is cold. Up the sides of the ravine, against a pale sky, the chestnut trees blaze with a fire of their own. The place seems immune, wrapped up in its own astounding beauty.

We walk above the Jonte. Air and water are running in parallel currents, above and below, and the months are visibly turning towards winter. We keep stopping for breath along the zigzag stone tracks. Through breaks in the trees the water is clear, full of shadows and reflections and its own mineral green. What can you do with water, except get in it? The two people in my head wake up and start arguing. I want to swim.

'Don't be ridiculous. All that ground we've won… it's miles down. It's probably dangerously cold.'

'It's probably magnetic. I can't help it.'

'I hope you die.' Etc., and etc., down the chestnut-leaf skid to the water's edge.

Mistake to put your hand in first. 'I told you so.'

At the top of the sky, as we undress, vultures slide slowly, crag to crag, on wings like hearth-rugs, keeping an eye. We put our heated bodies full of blood and edible flesh into one of the river's pools while they watch. Three seconds – maybe five. The water so cold it is like a clamp round your neck. You can't even breathe.

Out again and we walk on, our hair drying in the air. Up on the heights, we come across the ruins of a little chapel, with a window, up a rock-face ladder. It is the Hermitage of St Michel, built in the ruins of an older fortress. And then above it, as if that wasn't remote enough, round and up between a squeeze of house-sized boulders, underneath a flat-topped limestone plug, the remains of a ruined dwelling. So someone lived here – I can't imagine how – alone with the vultures and the wind.

Come with me, Chancellor Rolin. I've got someone I'd like you to meet. I haul him up this narrow scrabble: the man in the fur-lined damask, with the black silk belt, weighted and buckled and studded with fine gold, all of which the Duke of Burgundy gave him. He walks briskly. He's a strong man. The huge green velvet purse, the sign of his office, swinging and tapping at his leg as he goes, a little impatient because, well? What now? His fashionably padded shoulders crush between the boulders as he ascends to meet – who is it who lives here? I've no idea. Or when. But someone for whom society was distasteful enough to need to get as far from it as possible. A man with dirty hair and coarse clothing and something burning in his eyes that is beyond human, living in this little stone dwelling, half shack, half chapel, built into the cliff-face. Behind it an iron ladder let into the rock leads upwards. Rolin has a bad smell under his nose but I take no notice. We make the final ascent up the narrow ladder, as if we were climbing into the sky. When we reach the top, pulling ourselves on to the rock shelf, there is nothing. We are on top of the world, at incredible height, the vultures wheeling below us now. The hermit, who lives here, looks out as he often does. God's works spread out in majesty, the river a toy, the trees, the steep ravine, its strange people-shaped erosions, standing like sentries all along the gorge. Up from the bottom the river still sounds and in the distance the hills lay themselves out, layer upon layer, hazing into blue.

'And tell me,' Rolin says, his faraway eyes narrowing into focus, the full force of his restless mind tipping into mine. 'Which is more use, making money and building hospitals, or turning your back and curating your own soul, alone in this wilderness?'

'Rolin, I don't honestly know.'

I can't help liking him. He is so clever and so fallible. He doesn't necessarily return the compliment. And now, the country below us is burning. And I mean really this time. With the sanction of Louis XIV, 466 villages in the Cévennes have been set alight. Because the taking prisoner of a column of refugees has had a consequence. Like a line of dominoes falling, bitter and violent reprisals are in train.

Abraham Mazel, a wool comber by trade, having seen a vision, led his fellow villagers to the Abbé's house. They arrived at ten at night, singing psalms, to request the release of the prisoners. No joy. So they broke the doors and when the maimed and shocked column filed out again with their hands burned to stumps, the villagers set light to the house in revenge. The Abbé, trying to escape by shinning down knotted sheets into the garden, fell, broke his thigh and crawled into a hedge to hide, from where he was hauled out, dragged to the market place and stabbed fifty-two times; a thrust for every family member sent to the galleys, or tortured, or killed, or burned for their Protestantism.

The war of the Camisards. These were the self-styled 'Children of God', mostly agricultural workers, or workers in the wool trade, combers, carders and weavers, all of whom were Occitan-speaking peasants. None of them, including their charismatic twenty-one-year-old leader Jean Cavalier, an apprentice baker, had any military experience or training. Nevertheless, they managed for two years to fight a successful guerrilla war, holding off Louis XIV's army and even taking the seven-hundred-strong garrison town of Alès with only seventy Camisards. Throughout the Cévennes, goaded into fanaticism by almost two decades of Catholic oppression and with their religion outlawed, they massacred whole congregations, locking the doors during Mass and firing the churches. Then they melted back into the landscape down the paths that they knew like their own bodies. That man, against the skyline, leaning on his staff, lost in thought over his flock – was he there a minute ago? Has he been burning Catholics? Or that one, kneading the bread in the stifling bakery before dawn, or that one at his loom? No one knew. So it was easier to punish all of them. Burn their dwellings and turn them out into the fields like the damned animals they are. The soldiers corralled them into small spaces, cut off their ears and stacked them on their bayonets like kebabs.

'That,' Rolin says, 'is religion for you.'

'So is that why you were looking out of the Van Eyck picture, because you're watching for insurrection?' He doesn't answer. I look at the hermit. He only talks to God, so he doesn't answer either. He just walks away, back to his solitary life, tipping a bucket of cold water over his face to wash, eating his meagre meals, intoning his prayers, hands upraised, with only the vultures as congregation. He has turned his back on people. It is people who are the problem. Maybe he has a point.

We leave the campsite just as the weather changes. Drizzle on the coals of sweet chestnut and on the mountains creased into folds like the wimples of the sisters in Rolin's hospital. Little dry-grass fields opening out every now and then, as though all the water had sunk to the country's core. Rivers like veins. Cataracts booming into brown pools. Rowan berries, and the grey road winding southwards.

We drive into Nîmes briefly with its Roman amphitheatre like a plughole at its centre. In function and design amphitheatres strike me as ugly, however old. This one is almost complete and they still hold bull-fights here two or three times a year. It sits in its square, holed with entry tunnels all the way round, like a colander through which to drain away all that is worst in us. The subjects of Empire walking home afterwards through the wide streets, quietened inside by the spectacle of a lion shredding a gladiator to bloody ribbons; vicariously exorcized of violence. That way, a man might go back to his work contented. The pines, with the falling of evening, release their scent and someone's washing is strung still across a backstreet, so that living in a Roman colony doesn't look so bad after all, because life is sweet and, unlike the gladiator, his isn't over yet.

Free entertainment of the most spectacular sort is one way of keeping a people happy and united. Another, less obvious tactic for social cohesion is, as emperor, to claim divine descent; have your father posthumously deified and put up temples, so that the people don't question your authority.

Behind the arena is the little white temple to Augustus' grandsons and designated heirs. Gaius and Lucius, murdered despite their divine status when they were barely into manhood, probably by their stepmother. I would like to bring my hermit here. Walk him up the steps to the elegantly fluted columns, show him the coffered ceiling and the pediment where the boys' names are decipherable in pinpricks. What do you think of this, hermit? But he wouldn't come, or if he did he would rail and spit – because this is the devil's work – his hair and his eyes wild. They are polar opposites, I see that, your God and the Roman Empire. But your God too was a man, isn't that the point? At the time, his claim to divinity must have looked no less outrageous.

We don't stay long, just enough for Rupert to take some photographs. By evening we reach the Mediterranean in high wind. It is apocalyptic. Sand flying and the air grainy as if out of focus, waves like beaten metal chasing each other up the beach. On every side, dirty white Camargue horses graze behind pampas grass in mud-trodden corrals. It is Sunday so most of the shops are closed and somehow we have no food. We buy tinned beans in a miraculously open corner store. There isn't much else, just some flaccid celery and some ancient tomatoes. A girl, with long hair and purple leggings, on new roller-skates, moves her legs cautiously like scissors over the uneven road with a lollipop sticking out of her mouth; otherwise the people in the street have the rocking gait of riders. We walk, bent double, towards the pale block of the church, sucking to itself the last of the light, but the wind is too strong and the air too oddly thick for much more than a brief excursion.

The campsite is closed so we park under a breakwater in a lay-by already full of big vans. At the roadside is a shelter with a corrugated roof that has one tap and a toilet sign on the outside. The toilet, which has no door, just a part-screening wall, is a ceramic runnel in the ground. It is daylight and there are cars and people constantly passing. I stand in the absence of door, looking at the runnel, briefly at a loss.

We have driven a thousand miles since leaving Great Portland Street and it feels like it. I look at the sea that goes on towards Africa, and think of all the ground behind us. The waves of people that washed back and forth, building and destroying and building again, either escaping or looking for more, for the perfect place, the perfect city or just for rest, for refuge.

Ahead of me, in countries further south and east, people are once more on the move, heading desperately west and up the globe. To the London we left perhaps, drawn by the magnet of consumer capitalism. To the city paved with gold. Only it isn't. A city whose gold is in people's minds, and whose streets are paved with speckles of chewing gum. But still the people keep on coming. Shadowy columns of economic migrants and shattered refugees flowing, now the channels have been opened, like a river. Have you any idea, I would ask them, do you know how London can be? The London I left; littered with rough sleepers breathing a chemical air, begging a passing public who have baffled and exhausted themselves of pity. A city where people go to seek their fortunes and never come out. Where the buildings are tall as trees and taller, and the light is shut out and life is probably elsewhere, only here is where you stay because of magic, because you might, you just might, down this pathway or that, lay your hands finally on the golden egg. That's what I think as the sun sinks exhausted into its beaten-metal bed and the wind goes on into the dark.

2

The night in the lay-by is terrible. The wind never lets up, streaming and battering over the breakwater. The van rocks wildly and I think it will tip, or that the sea will rear in a tidal wave which, maybe even now, hangs teetering above us. Either way, the world is poised to end in a whirl of wind and water. Darkness of every kind.

When I do sleep, I dream. I dream that the door of the van behind my head is wrenched open and something old and cold and mineral comes roaring in. Original Evil with its horrible stretched face held in violent stillness. Everything, skin, hair, mouth, blowing back as if the wind's force was inside rather than out. I've heard this sound before. A silent roaring, present in the delirium of childhood fevers. I wake with my own mouth stretched, birthing a silent cry. It is pitch-dark and the wind is still raging. I can feel the weight of Rupert next to me, but I know absolutely no hope. My instinct is to pray, swiftly followed by the realization that for me now, there is nothing there. 'What are you doing?' my one self says. 'I told you.'

Oh help me, God who I don't believe in.

By breakfast the wind has dropped and against all the odds we and the world and the van are all still here. I feel jittery, as always after a nightmare, but slowly, while I eat my porridge, rationality reasserts itself. It's a slow day altogether; sunny and washed out. As if the great sheet of the sky had been torn into patches and strewn across the ground, the puddles in the lay-by are full of reflected blue. My feet are wet. The site is busy. High up in a converted military truck a man lounges in his cab on a purple cushion, his feet extended on the dashboard, reading. Everyone else is cleaning or otherwise managing their vans. Awnings are wound in or out. Brushes, cloths and miniature hoovers are put to work. Salt marks are rinsed off windscreens and bodywork. Water tanks are being filled at the standpipe. Rupert finds someone who shows us at last how to unlock ours and we queue to fill up. Meanwhile, I fall into conversation with the water-tank expert's wife. She looks yielding and delicately rumpled, as though she hadn't slept well either, or as though I'd caught her before she'd fully prepared for the day. There is an odd intimacy to being unwashed and under-slept. We talk not as if we know each other but as if we are, though still strangers, somewhere deeper than the polite surface. She is from the Loire.

'Where are you from?'

'England.'

'Aaah.' Pause. Her daughter had a pen-pal once, from England. The woman hesitates, looks anxious. Might we know her? 'A long time ago. They were pen-pals for years, for a long, long time. A girl from Nottingham. A very nice child.' She doesn't offer any details, just her own evident distress. 'Something went wrong.' She waits for a response but I don't quite know what to say. It is obvious that she doesn't really expect me to know. She can't remember the girl's name.

'I lived near Nottingham as a child myself,' I tell her. We stand in the close cloud of our stranger intimacy. Behind the van Rupert splashes through sky-filled puddles managing hoses and locks. Someone bravely or desperately goes into the toilet, to squat in the absence of door or lock.

'Then one day the child wrote saying things were not good. She was unhappy. We never heard from her again. We couldn't find her. Even now, with the internet. She is gone.' The woman looks at me, appealing through gathered tears, as though being English I might know an unhappy child in Nottingham. Between us almost as solid as a body, we pass each other a child's despair.

We talk about other things. She has never been to England. 'How does it feel to be English now?' she wants to know. I shrug.

'France is the same,' she offers, consoling. 'People can't afford to live on their wages. There is too great a differential. The young have been blocked from the property market, blocked from borrowing. They don't have zero hours here but they have so many short-term contracts and the banks won't lend unless you have a guaranteed indefinite contract, a CDI. Then,' she says, 'there are the refugees. This is very sad. People are suffering and there is war, but there are French people,' she repeats it, her hand clenched to her soft chest, 'French people, who are sleeping in their cars, who have to go to the soup kitchens to beg food.' She looks at me. I don't answer because I still haven't answered the question that precedes hers: who are French people? Are they Normans from Denmark, or Romans, or Celts? Who are the English? Or are French and English people simply the ones who got to those respective places earliest? When was the cut-off time? I had it first, as we used to say, tugging a toy angrily back and forth until it broke. I. Had. It. First. Again, I shrug apologetically at my stranger-friend.

I could tell her what I've found so far. I could tell her that, as Chancellor Rolin knows, there are people whose lives matter and people whose lives don't. Nothing changes, I could tell her. All animals are still equal. Some animals are still more equal than others. We all practise this; my children, for instance, are much more equal than anyone else's. But I don't say anything, so instead we stand companionably in our puzzlement, in silence.

The water tank is full. It is time to go. We part kissing each other on the cheeks. If ever I go to the Loire I must wave.

'Nice lady?' Rupert asks as he starts up the engine.

'Nice lady,' I say. 'Same problems – or some of them.' Rupert's phone rings and he sets it against his ear. Why do I think the little voice that comes out of it sounds like Eustace? Is it Eustace?

'Sounds interesting,' Rupert says and the voice goes on. 'OK… OK.' He is nodding, coaxing the steering wheel around with his knees. 'Count me in.' I stare at Rupert. Is he doing something with Eustace? 'I'll look into it,' he says, ringing off. He flicks the indicator and we turn out of the lay-by northwards.

'Was that Eustace?' I ask him, and then without waiting for an answer, 'Are you taking him on a trip?' Then, before he can answer, I say, 'Do you actually like Eustace?'

Rupert glances at me. He sounds almost surprised. 'Why, what's wrong with him? He's alright, isn't he?' He pauses, then he says, 'He's quite interesting. And he's got a lot of energy.'

'He's terrible, Rupert. He's a murderer for a start, and a liar.'

'Oh, lots of people are those things. And anyway, that's just how you've written him. That's just the Eustace you've made. He has other sides and other ways of being you don't know about.'

'Well, I've made him out of what there is, what I've read,' I say. 'I've made him out of what I know.'

'Which is very little – a couple of lines in the Anglo-Saxon Chronicle,' and then he says, turning to me, one eyebrow comically raised, 'Do you actually like Rolin?'

I don't say anything. I just smile back. I shrug my shoulders and I let it all go. I use his own line: 'Let's just travel.'

The Camargue, a huge river delta at the bottom of France, is an edge-place in every sense. Its identity is distinct and flamboyant, as though in defiance. Its language is different. Its traditions, which include bull-fighting games, court danger. Its swagger church here in the town of Saintes-Maries, visible for miles, was built, ready to fight, with a garrison housed above its apse. Its rare African-born saint is Sara, the patron saint of the Roma, who come in their thousands every May in pilgrimage.

We stop at the tourist office for information. The girl at the desk, disdainful and glamorously thin in scuffed jeans and cowboy boots, tells us Nîmes and Marseille are bourgeois. We can go if we want, she shrugs. She hates both. I don't tell her we've already been to Nîmes. She recommends instead the Gypsy Festival, the Provençal poetry of Frederick Mistral and the medieval fortress town of Aigues-Mortes. Provençal, an Occitan dialect, is the language of the Troubadours, ancient and literary, although still in use.

Will we understand it, if it's in Provençal?

Another shrug. 'I am Hungarian.'

So that is how, cowed by our provinciality, we find ourselves now out on the road to Aigues-Mortes and planning a circuit away from Saintes-Maries before looping back for the bull branding, which happens in two days' time and is a spectacle, she tells us, we don't want to miss.

Ahead of the van, the road unrolls itself as straight as a carpet. Are we driving on land or water? The light is hazy. Everything looks shifting, insubstantial. It is as flat as a lake for miles. On the map it looks hardly like land at all; a fretwork of threads, as though someone had dropped a mantilla over the sea just at the land's edge. On either side in the shimmer, flamingoes balance their pink pillow bodies on reedy legs, or lift in a mass and settle again, necks extended as if for a finishing tape. The road thinning into the distance, the rice paddies, the flat fields, everything looks as if it were ready at any moment to return to water, dissolve, like the salt that has been produced here since the Stone Age, as if the land's solidity were only borrowed from the sea, a temporary thing.

Aigues-Mortes. Dead water. What did I tell you? But if I were building a town on water I wouldn't do it out of great blocks of stone, with towers and turrets and high battlements, which is how this one is. It is fortified all the way round, with medieval walls, and gridded out like a garrison. Inside, it doesn't seem particularly bourgeois-free. Cobbled streets, tidy houses, cappuccinos on sale at tables with rattan or bentwood chairs, the choice is ours. WiFi. Gift shops. It is an odd mixture, both vaguely threatening and twee. At one corner of the square of surrounding walls is a tower, bigger than all the others and blind, except for a couple of long, hair-thin slits. It is stumpy and crude, the shape of a child's bucket-built sandcastle. It was built by Louis IX, in the thirteenth century, partly for defensive reasons, partly as a departure point for crusades. The seventh crusade and the eighth, on which Louis died of dysentery, both set off from Aigues-Mortes. The tower's name, like something out of Bunyan, is the Tower of Constance, and when not used by the garrison, it was used as a prison. Abraham Mazel, the psalm-singing Camisard who led the assassination of the Abbé of Chayla, was imprisoned here. For seven months he and sixteen of his fellow inmates worked away with makeshift tools until they had turned one of the massive stones in the outer wall, after which they twisted their bedsheets into a rope ladder, down to the ground and across the moat and away from Aigues-Mortes, fleeing by night across the salt-marshes. It was the only escape in the tower's history.

Looking at its brute upturned-bucket shape rising sheer out of the flats, it's hard to tell: is its brutality cause or effect? Is it the only answer possible to the landscape's extreme nature, the mosquito-breeding, marshes, the blistering saltpans, and the wind; or did its brutality shape its people? Or both, a chain of echo and response, that passed from the unbuilt through the builder, to the building and beyond? Because horrors happened here too. The summer of 1839, for instance, when workers needed for salt threshing were recruited from three different quarters: French peasants, whose own work in the fields was for the moment done, known as 'Ardèches'; itinerants known as 'Tramps'; and northern Italians known as 'Piedmontese'. The arrival of the Italians caused unrest. Some locals were without employment and Europe-wide economic crisis meant jobs were harder to come by than usual. With the heat of summer things simmered into riot. A squabble between some Ardèches and Piedmontese, who had been forced to work alongside one another, turned sour. The Tramps joined the quarrel on the French side, together with a crowd of unemployed locals. In the evening, returning from work, a group of Italians were falsely accused of killing local co-workers. They were attacked and chased into a bakery, which the rioters then tried to fire. At four in the morning help was called for but failed to arrive. Then, when the working day began, the rioters moved out to the Peccais fields where most of the Italians were employed and, while local marshals failed to calm or contain the crowd, the immigrant workers were massacred.

Horrible as it is, none of this seems relevant now in this polite town, with its little bags of expensive salt, gift-wrapped in ribbon. I try to imagine, to de-bourgeois these too-quaint streets, but I'm still wind-worn from last night, and I have had enough of men massacring each other. Give me some women for a change.

As if it had heard me, the sea holds something out on the flat of its palm. Along the coast at Saintes-Maries a boat has appeared on the horizon. No one has noticed yet. There is some disagreement about who is aboard. Some say there are men – including Joseph of Arimathea, clutching the Holy Grail to his chest – but I'm discounting them. I'm only interested in the women. There are three of them, or possibly four; the three Marys, I don't mind which ones exactly – say, Magdalen, Salome and Clopas. Some say Sara their Egyptian servant was on board. Some say Sara wasn't a servant at all but a gypsy queen, camped with her tribe under the pines at Aigues-Mortes, worshipping Ishtar whose effigy they carried ritually into the sea.

This is Sara the Black, Sara-le-Kali, as she is known to the Roma. There are many different variations of the story, all with different details, but as I am at Aigues-Mortes I choose the last of these, putting her down on the sandy ground, in the partial shade of the pines.

All agree that the boat and its occupants set out hurriedly, driven from Palestine after the death of Christ. It was fleeing persecution, its disputed passengers all religious refugees. No one can see yet, but what sets the boat apart, other than its mainly female cargo, is that it has no obvious means of locomotion. No one is steering. No one is managing the wind or plotting its course. It makes its way from Palestine with neither oars nor sails, as if one insistent hand were carrying it all the way, never touching land until it arrives on the horizon off the coast of the Camargue.

Long before it is seen, coming steadily on under its own miraculous power, Sara, sleeping in her tent under the pine trees, dreams its arrival. The weather is worsening. Three women, present at the crucifixion of a god not hers, are coming and they will be shipwrecked if she doesn't help them to land. She wakes up and runs through the dawn to the shore where the sea, which by now has whipped up as violently as last night, is throwing the little boat from crest to trough. Now it's there. Now it's gone. Wait, sickening seconds and – thank goodness, there it is. There! Gone again. And by now many people have noticed and are gathered at the shoreline arguing about what to do. There are women aboard, two – no, three, can you see? – being thrown against the bulwarks. The boat tips crazily, and the women disappear in a sluice of spray. On shore the people catch their breath and wait. Have they washed overboard? And now faint above the wind – or is it a seagull? – a wail. Then nothing. Then a definite cry. Arriving at the shore, Sara unwinds her robe and throws it out into the wind and, as she does so, it unfurls to many times its length and lays itself like a coloured road across the waters. The sea subsides and as the onlookers stare in amazement Sara walks out, naked, across the cloth to the boat and climbs aboard. And so the boat is brought safely in, under Sara's protection. On board, the women lay their hands on Sara's pagan head, blessing her and praying for her conversion. Sara becomes a Christian saint.

It's just a story. Even so, I would have some questions. If I were in terror of my life and a strange woman calmed the storm by throwing her dress on the water and then walked across it to save me, I might be tempted to ask about her religion rather than try to convert her to mine. But then I never knew Jesus when he was a person.

By evening we are out walking in the little white mountains known as les Alpilles. For several years, in my late teens, when Rupert and I were students at the same university, my family used to come here on holiday and he was once a guest. He had an earring, I remember, and an inability to stand still. To my surprise I bump into us as we were then, when we used to walk up to Les Baux in the evening, in procession, or out to climb over the fence to explore the Roman remains at Saint-Rémy, or to walk along the top of the Pont du Gard. 'It's a very long time since we met,' I say to my glossy teenage self. So different now. But my teenage self doesn't answer. It is worrying about its clothes, hauling its seal body up the incline, wishing, for aesthetic reasons only, that it were lighter. You should get some jump-leads, I think sourly as it passes, its head, by contrast, lightly floating with air. Between your head and your body you could even things out. Always gallant, Rupert's younger self has better manners. For a few seconds, as is his way with everyone, he gives me his full attention. I watch him fondly into the distance, gone already, as he fools about, springing over the rocks, an old-fashioned camera swinging at his side, the little wings at his heels fluttering.

Another campsite. They are all more or less the same, no matter where you are. Little privet hedges for privacy, with the hook-up points, like periscopes, in one corner. Trails of wires across starved grass. As I round the gravelled corner in the morning, with my toothbrush in my hand and my blotting-paper travel-towel round my neck, there is singing coming from the shower block. Quite loud. I'm not sure if I should go in. I don't want it to stop. It is a black girl, in wellington boots and leggings, vigorously cleaning and singing. She seems to be doing a whole church service. When she gets to the end of a hymn, she talks the prayers in between, mostly in Latin because this is a Catholic country. Saecula saeculorum and a great gush of water is chased towards the drain with a wide squeegee. I say good morning. She gives me a dismissive glance, but she doesn't reply. She can't stop.

She might be Sara, in the version of the story I didn't choose, servant to the three Marys, still serving all these centuries later. I'm sorry. It was wishful thinking to make you a princess. I don't know if being a saint is much consolation for lifetime after lifetime spent cleaning out shower blocks. Something about her is robustly authoritative. I am impressed – by her memory, for a start, her vigour, her conviction. Peeled and pale inside my cubicle I am afraid of being chased, along with the dirty water, down the drain. Probably, lifetime after lifetime, I deserve it.

After breakfast, which we eat outside in the hedged privacy of our plot, we head for Marseille. It is made of pale pink stone, scored and cross-hatched with the countless spars of boats bobbing in its harbour. I'm sorry, Hungarian tourist officer, but it is truly lovely. Where to start, that is the problem.

We start, as Rupert likes to do, as early as possible, with the city's foundation by the Greeks in the sixth century BC. Some rubble, some walls and, in the museum, the skeletons of ribbed boats that once came and went. They are remarkable. Giant fish bones picked clean by time. And I suppose it was in one of these, or something like, that Pytheas, the ancient astronomer and explorer, set off to find where amber came from and by accident bumped into England. He left the first written account of our country; as though the cold mists of our beginnings had thinned enough for a brief glimpse, before closing in again for centuries. He found a place subject to frost, its people tattooed despite the cold, living in thatched houses and hiding their grain underground like squirrels. He found plain food and plainer manners.

Pytheas disembarked, possibly at Kent, and travelled on foot as far as possible. And there, in the spaces between wilderness and thick forest, he came across what looked like a rudimentary society: men living uncomfortable but mainly peaceful lives. When occasionally they did fight they drove against each other in chariots. Otherwise they threshed their grain in barns because of the rain, and mined little knuckle-stones of tin for export. Pytheas returned to his boat and sailed on. He got as far as the Arctic Circle, saw the ice floes whose untethered, in-between state he compared to jellyfish, recognized the moon's influence on the English tides, and eventually came home to Marseille where he wrote it all down.

His account hasn't survived, except as quotation in the works of later geographers. Many of them discredited him on the grounds that he'd travelled further than it was thought possible; it was too improbable that a country like England could exist that far north, beyond known civilization. Strabo in particular was vindictively dismissive. Pytheas, he said, was a liar. He was a commoner so wouldn't have been able to fund such a journey. Besides, the Carthaginians had closed the Straits of Gibraltar so how could he ever have got out by sea as he claimed? He must have gone overland. Caught out in a lie, by Strabo's reckoning, before he'd even started.

There are several centuries between them. Pytheas, wherever he went, made his journey in about 325 BC. Strabo was writing in the first century AD, by which time Pytheas had long been an established source, although his works, the *Periplus* and the *Treatise on the Sea*, had both been lost.

I would like to believe him. I recognize his descriptions. They sound true. 'We are still tattooed, Pytheas, still being phlegmatic about the rain. Fighting is still something we do, mostly for fun, among ourselves at least. I think you found us, just as you said.'

I have never heard of Sir Clements Markham before – President of the Royal Geographical Society, and supporter of Scott's fated polar expedition – but it seems he believes Pytheas, too. An explorer himself, he has been to the Arctic twice. He has brought quinine back from Peru. In his many written works people have accused him of a tendency to romanticize and of a lack of scholarship but he is independent-minded and he is dedicated to his subject. Well fed and tightly buttoned into layers of felty-looking clothes, he has long cotton-wool side-whiskers and school-master looks. In the picture I have seen of him, he is busy reading at a heavy desk, but he half turns towards me, keeping his place in the little leather-bound book in front of him with one finger. Strabo's criticisms, he says tartly, 'are satisfactorily disposed of by the fact that wherever Strabo specifies a falsehood or a blunder of Pytheas, the explorer is approximately right, and the theoretical geographer is wrong. If Strabo had treated the statements of Pytheas with the respect they deserved, instead of calling him a liar, his own ideas would have been more correct. He would not have placed Ireland to the north of Britain. He would not have expunged the peninsula of Brittany from his map. He would not have placed the north coast of France in the latitude of Bordeaux.'

That is a Victorian dressing-down for you. If I were Strabo I would be keeping a low profile.

Marseille is a distinct place. Whenever unification was pressed upon it (by Provence, and later by France as a whole), it resisted, and when it was coerced, it bided its time and rebelled, again and again. At one point Louis XIV had to come in person, at the head of an army, to enforce its submission. It is no accident that when France needed a national anthem, something that expressed indomitable spirit and freedom from tyranny, it took the 'Marseillaise'. No matter if it was originally composed in Strasbourg for troops fighting the Austro-Hungarian Empire, it was taken up, and made their own, by the bands of fédérés going north to support the Revolution. They sang it as a marching song, to keep themselves fired up on the long road to Paris, and I sing it to myself, bloody banners and sacrificial generations and all, as I pass down these elegant avenues. Long lines of four-storey houses that might be sheet music. Each storey has a wrought-iron balcony that runs the whole length of the street, layer upon layer as if they were staves, with the windows as notes and their pediments, and occasional washing lines, as accented phrases. All of it unfurling, rhythmic, as I pass, in blues and pinks and greys, written in stone and iron, but as light as their opposites, the whole place a song.

And everyone, it seems, is here. Turks, Algerians, Armenians, Koreans, Poles, Greeks, Tunisians, Romanians, Comorians, Moroccans and Italians. Even, when we arrive in a little square where we have lunch, the English – I can't help noticing that's what the quiet couple at the next-door table are speaking, although they order fluently in French. They have the same flotsam look as us: cast up, storm-worn, our ears ringing with bombast, escaping. Soup followed by moules frites for €9.50, so like everyone else, that is what we have. As if by mutual agreement we keep our voices down. We would all, I think, like to be the only English here. For a long time there is just the chinking of spoons and the burr of quiet conversation. Then a red-trousered man, a cartoon rosbif, scarlet with wine, blooms like a peony at the back of the terrace. He is talking to a table of young men and his voice is empire loud. 'Brexit ay oon day sastre.' We catch the eye of the quiet couple next to us and laugh.

From the separate islands of our lunch tables, in contravention of our national character, we strike up a conversation. They have a flat in Montpellier, though they live in Manchester. They look alert and thin and interested.

'Everything changed when Bowie died. The world went crap,' the woman says, with just the trace of a northern accent. She's funny and quick, sitting up straight like a little girl. She is applying for an Irish passport. She doesn't want to be English any more. As if you could shrug nationality off, like a coat – choose another one – which of course on paper you can. So why should it matter at all? Our exile, if that's what it is, is voluntary, and we are moving against the flow, south and east, instead of north and west. What kind of migrants are we? It doesn't occur to any of us that we might not be welcome in the countries we have chosen. Entitlement is our birthright. We are from England.

As we talk, in the shorthand of shared culture, I wonder whether we ever in fact left. Or are we still and always there, crouching in our cloud-hung tattooed selves, looking out at France through England's eyes? Perhaps this is what Mariette's legacy meant. Perhaps it was an admission that, through a lifetime spent in Egypt, he never really left France.

There are so many divisions between us and the world, so many filters: education, temperament, age, nationality, colour, culture, class. We see only what we are conditioned to see.

In Marseille, there are many things I do see, but with my filters in place there is also much that I miss. Jacky le Mat, Parrain, assassin, world champion trotter, stunt-driver and opera buff, who has survived one assassination attempt, sits drinking in his regular bar, with his back to the door because who would try to kill a man back from the dead? I don't see him. Nor do I see the cellar where, newly released from prison, he tortured his informer having kidnapped him from Algeria by night, in the Cessna aircraft he flew himself. I don't see the narrow streets where the gang members of the French Connection, running prostitutes and heroin, wait for each other in black leather coats under lines of washing. I don't see the judge who convicted them, lying in his own blood in the street, shot dead in broad daylight. Or Tany Zampa, le Mat's friend and rival, dead in his prison cell with a noose around his neck. However hard I look. I can imagine the gutter glamour, but I can't see the reality of it: the sound of the trap shutting, as it does in places where the local employment options are mainly criminal. Imagine, as a teenager, turning, so early in life but already too late, to find the exit barred behind you. Imagine making the mistake of doing the small errand for the big boss before you've had time to think about the choice you were either too young or too lazy to make, or didn't, in the first place, know that you had. I can't. Or I can imagine, but I can't see. You have to be poor, and probably callow, and possibly immigrant; you have to be hungry, or desperate, or reckless, or brutal, to see all of that.

So we go, unseeing, through the streets of the Panier district, 'Suburre obscène', as a municipal report described it in 1942 – this sewer, this filthy excrescence – 'un des cloaques les plus impurs, où s'amasse l'écume de la Méditerranée… C'est l'empire du péché et de la mort. Ces quartiers… abandonnés à la canaille, la misère et la honte, quel moyen de les vider de leur pus et les régénérer?'

Much of the district was dynamited by the occupying Germans in 1943, which was their solution to its hopeless and long-established corruption. And whether their solution was effective, or whether I just can't see it, there is no pus or scum visible today; no obvious prostitutes, or gangsters from Corsica, or the Maghreb, as we walk the streets, jaunty with painted houses, towards the museum. Only the odd tourist. Instead we find Pierre Puget with his strained and sensitive looks, in an old-gold dressing robe with pale green facings, sitting on a bench and working at his designs.

'What are they for, Puget?'

He has the fevered expression of someone who has dreamed a dream too far. He is a sculptor and an architect and he has been asked to design a statue of Louis XIV for Marseille, but he has forgotten his commission it seems. He has let himself get carried away. Looking over his shoulder at the plans I can't help noticing that this isn't just a statue – this is a whole royal square, a tiny plinth in a sun-shaped plot, radiating out into a great sweep of buildings, an oval, centred at one end on the main boulevard and open, through a grand triumphal arch at the other, to the sea at the old port. Columns, pediments, balconies, colonnades; it is an architectural fantasy. Coffered ceilings, statues, balustrades. And if it isn't just a statue then it isn't just a square either. Puget is dreaming a whole city. It will be as elegant, as theatrically extravagant as anything at Rome or Venice or Versailles. This, his grandest design to date, is to be the town's face. It will be the first thing you see when you step ashore at the dock.

Because Marseille is his city. He was born here, in 1620, in the despised Panier district, the son of a stonemason who died in a fall from scaffolding when Pierre was only two. All the more extraordinary that by the end of his life he should find himself redesigning the place of his birth.

At fourteen he was employed in the Marseille shipyards, carving ornaments for the galleys. By sixteen he could manage the design, construction and decoration of an entire ship himself. It was early in life to master a trade, so he took off for Italy where he trained as a sculptor and painter. He worked on the Palazzo Barberini in Rome and the Palazzo Pitti in Florence. Travelling and working, back and forth between France and Italy, he didn't come home for forty years. Not until 1685 did he finally arrive back in Marseille, with his head full of ideas and half a lifetime's experience to put them into practice. Elsewhere, as he draws up his design for Marseille's waterfront face, other plans of his are already in execution. He has drawn a fish market and a town hall, some of the sheet-music streets and a house on one end for himself, ornamented with a sculpture of his own making, and now, in the Panier district where he was born, a hospital for the poor. For several years, it is as if the city that he dreams raises itself, block by block, off the paper in front of him.

Puget takes his designs to Versailles, where he shows them to the King, in person. But something goes wrong. Suddenly he finds himself treading air. He is mocked. The King had only asked for a sculpture, not this great folly. He didn't ask for a wedding cake. The court laughs. Puget's vision is presumptuous. There isn't enough money to spare, what with the war against the Dutch. Or perhaps troublesome Marseille, with its ideas of independence, doesn't need encouraging to be any grander than it is. Whatever the reason, the designs are rejected. In the portrait painted of him by his son Francis, in 1690, Puget looks worn and sad. It is just after his rejection and his eyes are fixed dreamily beyond the viewer, as though he were still looking at what might have been. 'Marseille, my city,' because the ghost of his imagined towers and crescents haunts the streets where he walks, 'you could have been so splendid.' Four years later Puget dies.

'I tried,' Puget could have told Rolin, had he come visiting from the fourteenth century. 'I too built a hospital for the poor.' Rolin in his costly clothes, with his heavy tread, making his way through Puget's improved streets. 'But I didn't have much money. Mine didn't have a foundation behind it, so it didn't last as long as yours.' Because Puget's hospital for the poor, the Vieille Charité, lost its philanthropic function long ago. The answer to the Panier district's persistent scum problem, devised by its own son, is now the archaeological museum.

What do you do with the beggars, the immigrants, the vagrants of a city? This is my question and I am thinking of my own city as I ask. Rolin cocks his head, listening. The answer is often, as it was here – sweep them all into one place and shut them up before they can become criminals. There you can sort them out. The migrants can be sent home, the natives kept in gender-divided dormitories, and the children put to work – though neither man says so outright.

'Here,' Puget says instead, waving a fevered hand, the old-gold cuff on his coat flapping against his wrist, 'my vision for civic improvement.' If the truth be told, he isn't concerned with getting vagrants off the streets – he just sees a chance for a building. If he thinks anything, it is that in these cool, stacked, stone colonnades the vagrant population might better themselves. He is an architect. He understands the echo that sounded so clearly at Aigues-Mortes; how a place can influence its population and vice versa. He has taken care to design something that is beautifully balanced and harmonious and disciplined.

Whoever's idea it was to clear the streets of undesirables, the plan was put into effect and energetically prosecuted by bands of officers called chasse-gueux, beggar hunters, out day and night looking for people they could subject to charity. Often the chasse-gueux were brutal enough about their duties for the townspeople to find themselves taking sides with the beggars. After all, in this contrary and underdog-loving place, this city whose anthem celebrates freedom, why shouldn't people live in the street if they want to?

Puget's institution, flourishing at first, was always more a prison than a hospital. By the time of the French Revolution it had fallen into neglect. Over the years it served various purposes, including acting as garrison for the French Foreign Legion until, by the early twentieth century, it had effectively become a slum. People who had nowhere else gravitated here: those who needed rehousing after eviction of one sort or another, and the little band of Sisters of Mercy who tried to provide them with relief. Seasonal workers connected with the port, assorted packers of anchovies and bananas, set up under its cool colonnades. Rats and flies followed. Then the people made homeless by the German clearance of the Panier district in the Second World War came looking for shelter: roughly a hundred and fifty families crammed together in a building that was ruining around them. These colonnades, the flowing curves and ellipses of its church, all sprouting weeds and crawled over by indigents. It was an outrage, people said, clicking their tongues and pinching their noses as they passed. Now it was the building they felt sorry for, not its inhabitants. It was time for the town to step in once more. The occupants were evicted, the building repaired to its former graceful beauty and a new use for it was found.

The new occupants of the rooms, when we buy our tickets and stroll through the galleries, are docile and they too are all immigrants. Masks and skulls collected from Africa and South America stare out of wild, inlaid eyes, and Haida carvings put out their tongues. In the rooms on the floor below, Tanagra ladies balance under complicated ancient hats, bending their slender necks, while, in the case next door, whole crowds of terracotta heads gather and wait in silence. And at the entrance, among the Egyptian finds that it seems no French town is complete without, an ibis, elegantly mummified in Issey Miyake pleats, rests its black beak on its chest and puts its feet up like a human. Everything is grouped according to its origins, little ghettos all apparently equal in importance, silently side by side, in perfect society.

It is evening by the time we leave the museum and we have to get back to Saintes-Maries for the manades, the branding of bulls from the half-wild Camargue herds, taking place in the morning. We climb into the van, balancing baguettes and coffee on a little cardboard tray, and head out through the long streets that still seem to be defiantly singing. On the other side of the road, a car passes. I turn my head. My parents driving through the night to Italy. And in the back, my small self, with my sleeping sisters and my baby brother, sitting up in a nest of bedding. I am about seven, leaning into the space between the front seats. My parents are so glamorous. They radiate a mysterious energy, talking to each other in quiet voices as we speed through the dark city. My father drives fast, with his elbows lightly bent out sideways. And I remember the foreign street unrolling itself as we passed. I remember registering its spirit, how thrillingly different. The balconies, the shutters with louvred surfaces. And I remember a man in a beret and a striped shirt passing on the pavement the other side, pushing a bicycle. I think he had strings of onions round his neck, or round his bicycle, or both. My father telling me, in a joke accent, 'He is a Francheman.' Exactly like in the books.

Did it happen? Who knows. Probably not. Possibly I imagined it. It is one of my most vivid and defining memories. My parents, the dark, the speed, and France.

It is an early start. I am still fumbling around in the van, crawling around the bed trying to retrieve socks. Rupert is up and outside, shrugged into all his usual rumpled gear, with his hands in his pockets and the light behind him. His hair and beard are haloed at the edges.

I have been reading Bunin. And this is a day like a Bunin short story, made out of pale colours, its elements arranged and rearranged in different compositions as if it were not a day at all but a painting. At 7.30 in the morning the Camargue cowboys, the Gardians, assemble in a scruffy car park. Slowly they unload their white horses. They have long poles with little blunt prongs at the end and they wear black velvet or corduroy jackets, jaunty little homburg hats, coloured print shirts and patterned ties. There seems to be no particular hurry, no obvious programme. We keep asking, are we in the right place – this car park with its broken concrete buffers and its giant puddles looks unlikely. When are they going to start? Is there somewhere else where proper things are happening? The Gardians look down at us from their positions in the saddle while their horses wheel and stamp. Who knows? They have no idea, they say, when it will start or what will happen.

Really?

We don't ask again. They look as though they would like to prong us aside with their poles. Meanwhile, the townspeople are gathering on foot and on bicycles. Some little boys, dressed like their fathers, are hoicked up into man-size saddles on horses of their own. A lone woman arrives in a tight-buttoned, full-length, black riding-habit, wearing a cloth cap and seated side-saddle. With that the troop moves off, at the trot, towards the beach. At last. Four men, middle-aged and made out of pâté and butter and wine, ride abreast at the front of the column. They have coloured standards attached to their poles and stirrups that are like silver cages for their feet. They sit up easily, reins held in one hand. They are cowboys. We run alongside to keep up.

Down the backstreets of the town the procession goes, clip-clopping on tarmac, and out to the edge-land, half sand, half earth and marram grass where the sea lies beaten flat under the metallic light that I now so associate with the Camargue. The Plage Est, a great expanse of white sand and water, stretches ahead of us under the morning and behind it, equally flat, are the marshes, the étangs and salt sansouires that the country here is made of. They are easily flooded, quickly drained and dried, and quickly baked to a cracked plain. Poor-looking land. Thin dry grasses. Tamarisk trees. Dry little flowers. Undifferentiated from water, the distances are crowded with flamingos, dotted with free-ranging white horses and black bulls, the Camargue's characteristic and only flamboyance.

Once, while still at Cambridge, Nabokov, who admired Bunin's colour-filled short stories, praised him, 'in this blasphemous and tongue-tied age', for calmly 'sensing the beautiful in all things – in manifestations of the human spirit and in the pattern of lilac shadow on moist sand'. He could just as well have been describing the Camargue. That is what it is like this morning, in its Bunin-borrowed colours – impossibly, even ridiculously aesthetic. And underneath, where both danger and brutality glimmer, it is spirited, and in all senses cavalier.

Ahead of us the Gardians ride out onto the sand, under a grey-blue, grey-pink sky, against a gleaming sea. Black jackets, white horses and the criss-cross of poles and standards at angles. Sometimes they ride through water, still at the trot, so that sheets of spray rise glittering either side. Sometimes they ride between pools on thin bars of sand, so that horses and riders are doubled by the water's reflection, as if two worlds met at a fold. Then, when they reach the open strand, they ride free, wheeling wide and coalescing and wheeling out again, like the figures of a dance, or like birds flexing and gathering in a murmuration. The side-saddle woman gallops through the shallows, the sun behind her, her tight black habit flying, revealing a scarlet lining. At the back of the beach, by the dunes, there is a fire and a party of women are cooking bacon.

Some of the Gardians have dismounted already, their horses tethered in a circle, heads facing in, shifting their weight from hoof to hoof, tails swishing. There is breakfast for all of us: bacon baguettes, cheese, pâté and red wine in plastic cups. Where the dunes start, against a stationary tractor, a forest of poles has been planted. Young boys gallop up and down and a handsome man in wellington boots with spurs makes announcements through a microphone. The Gardians draw lots. There is to be a competition.

After breakfast the Gardians mount, poles in hand, and array themselves, backs to the sea, poles against the sky, in one long line. They might be an army of crusaders. One by one, in the order in which they will compete, the names of the teams from each manade are called, four to a team. To the accompaniment of wheezing from the local brass band they ride forward, bowing and showing their standard. Then they wheel and spur away, still in their teams, to the far end of the beach where a lorry full of bulls is parked. In front of the tractor, in a small metal cage, the very old, the very young, and the very nervous, huddle for protection. Everyone else mills around. When the bull is released a team of Gardians ride at the gallop either side, keeping it between them the whole length of the shore. At about level with the tractor they try to rope it, flipping it over with their tridents under its belly, as it runs. Once on its back it is branded and tagged, cheered and slapped, no hard feelings friend, loaded into another lorry to be released out onto the sansouires again.

It went wrong as many times as it went right.

Often the bull ducked or doubled back to break free, careering towards the scattering crowd, or made off sideways fast across the marshes. Each time, the Gardians who weren't yet involved spurred their horses, thundering from all angles across the sand to head the bull off as it plunged into dykes and étangs. Horses that had sunk at the gallop came rearing out again in great sheets of spray, their riders, backs arched, trident in hand, intent. Suddenly there was urgency and bravery and brutality. Hard not to feel your heart swell and your blood pounding in your ears. Hard not to hate the men and the horses for the terror of the little black bull, straining and plunging for freedom. Impossible not to thrill at the men and their horses, in all the drama of their danger and speed and spray. And in the end, who loves the bull more, the outsiders like myself, anthropomorphizing and intellectualizing, or the men on the horses, who know it, and raise it, and risk its horns and respect its temper?

Who will explain it to me, this nacreous place, with its pale sea and its opalescent sky; with its men on horseback, tridents angled like crusader lances; its fortified church in outline like a cutout against the landward horizon?

'Marquis Folco de Baroncelli-Javon,' Rupert says, his mouth full of bacon baguette. A man in a black velvet coat and a coloured shirt stoops over my hand with nineteenth-century chivalry. 'He should be able to tell you all you need to know.' He is the person who 'invented' the Camargue after all, with his broad face, his moustaches bigger and more jauntily curled than Eustace's, and his unconventional Italian origins. And his family, although they arrived in the fifteenth century, still in the late nineteenth century see themselves as different – as outsiders. For a start, although they live in Avignon, they speak not French but Provençal, which might have started as the language of troubadours but which now is only spoken by peasants. They are artistic, bohemian. His brother Jacques makes silent movies. Folco is a poet. He and his sister Marguerite belong to the Provençal literary movement, the Félibriges, whose leading light is the poet Frederick Mistral.

Most independent-minded of all is Baroncelli's grandmother, Madame de Chazel, at whose mas near Bouillargues, Baroncelli spent his childhood. In the long summers she sent him to Saintes-Maries, to the seaside, and it was at her instruction that little Baroncelli was taken at the age of nine to witness the annual May pilgrimage. In the heat and the thousands-strong crowd that pressed to get into the church, somehow his hand slipped free of whoever was put in charge of him. Somehow the bodies shuffling forward carried them with him and somehow, instead of entering the church the normal way to venerate the three Marys, Baroncelli got swept to the side door, the gypsy entrance.

There in the dark interior of the crypt, his hair slicked back tidy and dressed like the little gentleman he was, he looked so wrong the Roma couldn't help but notice. Who is the little Milor? The pale boy in the huge white collar and the coat with velvet facings? An old gypsy woman picked him up and carried him right to the altar, where the statue of Sara the Black stood, with its polished face and its white inlaid eyes gleaming in the half-light. 'Si tu es venu jusqu'ici, c'est que toute ta vie tu protègeras notre peuple.'

Popular myth spins itself like a pearl round the speck of human grit at its centre. I like its particular reality, its showy type of truth. The world is your oyster, Baroncelli.

He doesn't want the world. He only wants the Camargue, which his well-bred, wine-estate wife can't bear. He likes its extreme nature, its land which is water, its blazing heat and extreme cold, its sand-laden winds and mosquito-infested marshes. In particular he likes its people, its cowboys, who own nothing – not the houses they live in, not the horses they ride – and who manage the herds of semi-wild bulls, careless of the only thing they do own, their lives. They are hired hands, at the bottom of the social order.

Baroncelli is twenty-six when he moves, at his mentor Mistral's instruction, to his own mas near Saintes-Maries. He is a man in a romantic dream, a sort of Orlando, whose love is a place. It doesn't matter that at that time the Camargue bulls are scruffy half breeds, or the bull-fighting games of the region a disorganized type of brutal and bloody inter-species scrapping. He is solemn and ardent about his vision. He writes solemn and ardent poetry, and he edits a magazine called *L'Aeoli* in which the traditions of Provence are enumerated, expounded on and upheld. In his eyes the bulls are a noble breed worthy of comparison with the Spanish fighting bull. The reckless men who run them, dressed anyhow, in assorted rags and sabots, are not impoverished peasants, but rural knights. What he likes best is that man and beast have become degraded, almost to obliteration. No one cares about them now, and besides, the Eustaces have plans for the Camargue: it will be drained and turned into a money-generating seaside resort. It is flat so it is an excellent place for aeroplanes. There are endless possibilities. Sweep it clean of bulls and flamingos. Get rid of the scum and we can get started.

So Baroncelli finds his quest. Whether it was the gypsy woman, or Sara the Black herself who whispered to him in the crypt, his blood fires at the sight of oppression and he is spurred to action. Like Puget, he dreams a

place. Alone, he will kick the Eustaces to kingdom come. He will raise the Camargue to its dreamed self. He will save and enshrine its traditions. He will raise the dignity of its people and he will breed a race of fighting bulls, as fierce and as noble as the bulls in Spain. And he does.

'J'ai voué ma vie,' he says solemnly, 'à un idéal: la Provence, et je n'ai embrassé mon métier que pour mieux servir cet idéal, pour me trouver plus près du peuple provençal, pour mieux arriver jusqu'à son coeur et pour mieux l'aider à sauver son passé de gloire, sa langue et ses coutumes.'

It isn't all romance. Some of this involves reasonably hard-nosed publicity – when Buffalo Bill's Wild West Show rides into Nîmes, for instance, Baroncelli cannily offers a band of Gardians to help out. In the exotic context of Cowboys and Indians the despised local cowhands can't help but look glamorous. Besides, by now Baroncelli has formalized their dress. They wear the black corded jackets, the bold shirts and the moleskin trousers of today. They look picturesque and they ride with daring and conscious swagger.

To protect the changes he has already made for the generations to come, Baroncelli sets up a foundation called the Nacioun Gardiano. It is designed to standardize and enshrine Provençal dress and tradition. He has an emblem for the Camargue designed and cast in bronze; a cross incorporating an anchor, a heart and the three-pronged tridents of the Gardians. Slowly the Camargue identity is realized and the myth begins to disseminate, representation becoming real. And although to some it might look like aristocratic fantasy, Baroncelli's vision is politically hard-edged. His support, which is always public, is backed up by financial contributions of his own, so freely given that he is soon bankrupt. Over big and small issues, whenever necessary, he campaigns. When the bull games come under threat, he marches to preserve them. Horrified by the carnage of the First World War, he demonstrates, this time as a pacifist, and is imprisoned in the Fort de Peccais at Aigues-Mortes. In the Spanish Civil War he declares in favour of the Republicans and later, when the time comes, in favour of the Communist mayor at Saintes-Maries.

Baroncelli never gives up, even in the face of penury. He runs himself out of funds and both the fifteenth-century family hôtel particulier in Avignon and his beloved mas de l'Amarée have to be sold. Never mind. The locals give him a piece of land and he starts again. He builds something solid and practical and he goes on. There is always another cause and, whether it is Buffalo Bill's example, fighting for the rights of the Native American Indians, or Sara the Black still whispering at his shoulder, in 1935 Baroncelli manages finally to have the Roma pilgrimage at Saintes-Maries recognized and given the Pope's sanction.

'I've done it,' leaning back in his chair, in the modest mas that he built for himself. 'I've done as you asked.' And now he is old and ill. His wife dies and, in 1939, another hated war breaks out. In 1942 the Germans requisition his newly built mas. Disoriented and almost out of energy he is moved to Saintes-Maries and then to Avignon, but his fight is gone. In 1943 Baroncelli dies. He is laid to rest, with all the dignity he had fought to give them, by a troop of Gardians, on foot, leading their horses by the bridle and with their tridents pointing at the ground.

In the afternoon, before we leave, we go to watch the bull games that Baroncelli formalized and campaigned to maintain. They are held in the little arena facing the sea, with the church in outline watching over the top of the stands. From inside I can see that there are people who perhaps can't afford the tickets, up there, on the roof, looking down. Outside, a young 'raseteur' as they are called, limbering up like a footballer, stretches against a lamp-post on the promenade. And inside, on the sandy floor of the arena, women and men parade in Provençal dress, to the same abysmal brass band as this morning. It looks different from how I expected. It looks a little made up; all the tat, all the sham of spectacle. Women in the audience, their hair frizzed like scouring pads, their faces drink-blown, sway to the band. We all look brutal, all of us, our lowest selves. At the back, where we are, in the standing room only, a quiet man with a great beak of a nose watches with sad eyes, while his friends fat or scrawny, some with gaps in their teeth, listen to a devil, a George Clooney with green eyes, in black corduroy and a black velvet cap, telling them at length how it is done.

'When I was young…'

Because when he was young the bull was a giant. When he was young he was the fastest. People died when he was young. But the bulls now… The bulls now are pussy cats. He is so handsome, so full of himself, I can't take my eyes off him.

The doors at the back open and to music from *Carmen*, wheezed and honked out at varying speeds, the raseteurs enter, dressed head to toe in white. It's difficult to tell; like this morning, sometimes it's a game, sometimes it's serious, and the line between the two is impossibly fine. What they do is so dangerous. The bull is full grown, its horns in the shape of a lyre, long and curving upwards. And they run in front of it, trying as they go to snatch little prize tickets attached with string around its horns. They have nothing but a kind of metal comb strapped to their right hand.

The air is thick. The crowd repeatedly gasping at the danger of the bull which charges the stands full tilt and tosses the planking of the barrier up into the air. The boys call the bull, sometimes by its own name, as if it were one of them, sometimes just, 'Hé! Taureau. Hé!' Raising the arm with the claw-strapped hand. Leaping at the barricades, one foot on the top, one foot on the lowest level of the stands, grabbing at the top rail and swinging out and back. They are so light, they are flying.

The bull is black and they are white, graceful, courting danger, full of life. Bright white clothes, blood-spattered in some cases where they'd caught a hand, or grazed themselves, as they leapt. Because blood is the point of the game. Blood is the missing colour that fills up the heads of the crowd. Black and white waiting for red, the secret we all share; holding your breath in a frenzy of dread, which might in fact be longing. When will it come out? Now? Is it now? And when you see it, your own stomach flips because it's your blood too.

The best of them win repeatedly, wheeling back against the stands, arm raised to show the prize ticket as their name and their prize is boomed out across the arena.

He has a sharp face. See him, that one, set his intention, a certain look. Concentration in all his features, leaning forward, running. The click of his decision like closing a gun barrel. And I can see the danger. But as he approaches, calculating, he has more time than the others, not just saving his skin as they do, but turning to face the bull head-on as he passes, the leisure to make one perfect upwards snatch, the little ticket on its string swept skywards before he flies up to the stands, chin up, arm up, to applause.

I am the one! Look at me! And the crowd's answering roar.

After three courses we left. We needed to get to the border by supper time. I waited in the town, looking at Baroncelli's giant anchor while Rupert fetched the van. No one around except a family of tourists looking for a supermarket. The van wouldn't start so it took a long time. As I waited, the pompiers passed, sirens going, lights flashing, heeling round the corner like a boat, in the direction of the arena. So it had happened. Which one had it been? I thought of the constant winner; it couldn't have been him. He was too good. He seemed so intent, so easy. But that was the point. He was the one who knew what the risk was, and took it deliberately all the same. He was the one who faced the bull, chest open to the charge, challenging as though they were equals, as though it wasn't horribly weighted in the bull's favour. 'Hé, taureau! Hé. Hé!'

What slip was it, what split second of inattention, his foot unluckily skidding on the sand, to be gored, flung as he leapt, too late, for the stands?

Later, heading out on the straight road away from the town, the air ambulance lands on some hard-standing, at the edge of the marsh, and I see the pompiers again, lights flashing, careering out to meet it with the boy in white inside. Instinctively I fold my arms across my stomach. I can see red.

We leave it all behind. We drive past other places, towns and memories flashing past – Saint-Maximin with its surprising church. The long wild stretches where my brother and I holidayed in the eighties, our little sloughed skins still bicycling now, along roads that run the ridge of the mountains, wondering if we are lost. The helter-skelter down again, which he free-wheeled much too fast, round the hairpin bends whooping, risk-taking, with both legs out straight to the side. Cars passing us fast both ways, and at the corners, on a bicycle, it is hard to stay on your own side. 'Please be careful!' And my voice lost because he's long out of sight. But all the way to Nice there is something I am trying to understand – some inbuilt compulsion to risk, or to combat, even to war – some meaning I snatch at, as if it were a prize ticket. For a long time the white bird-boys go on flying in my mind and the black bull charges.

We wake up in that make-your-mind-up place, Menton, with its fluid, ever-changing border. At first, as part of the independent county of Nice, broadly French, then Genoese, so broadly Italian, then Monégasque, then French, then Monégasque again, though this time under the protection of Sardinia. Then a 'free city'. Then Sardinia again, then given back to France, then taken by Italy and finally French again, for the moment. And at some point, meanwhile, the Americans, and the English freezing in fog-bound shires, discovered it as a place to winter. They came out in their thousands, opening like pale butterflies under the sun, and began building uncharacteristically fanciful villas and making gardens. Queen Victoria herself came, swagged and buttoned, and sweated it out under huge parasols held by other people. There is a fountain in her honour on the seafront. Lawrence Johnstone, the creator of Hidcote, bought a farmhouse here and made a sub-tropical garden that is still open to the public. Even Nabokov, who had been on my mind in the Camargue, as if in premonition, came and sat here in the Hotel Astoria, in the February of 1960, waiting for Kubrick's decision on the screen-play for *Lolita*.

Bright, bright light and heat, as if we'd arrived by accident at the equator. Palms and lemon trees when I open the shutters. And the Mediterranean only inches further round the coast from the Camargue, not beaten metal at all, but its bluest, holiday-advert, self. What are you hiding, Menton? All this glamour, this whirl of cars and elegance, everything money can buy. What is it you are trying not to look at?

The little medieval town clinging to its rock stares into the water, where its pastel, patchwork, reflection stares back and says nothing. Only the villas with their hospital-cool rooms and the grand and shuttered hotels know the answer.

Don't mention death, anyone. Don't mention decay. On the beaches, in bikinis, all along the Riviera, Lolitas look over their dark glasses. Lose yourself while there's still time. Try sex. Try gambling or driving at speed, or narcotics. Try drink or Catholicism, or both. Just don't mention sickness. Don't mention blood.

Because blood means something different here. It isn't risk and heroism. It isn't health gaily confronting the thunder of its own mortality. It is something else that rampages here. The people in white move efficiently up and down long corridors, while their patients, an anxious crowd of all ages, sit in marble stillness and just hope that it will pass them by.

If you wanted to make a collection of invalids from the last two centuries, Menton would be a good place to start. They are all here, drained and emaciated, hoping for a cure, Katherine Mansfield, Swinburne, Prince Leopold, Yeats. And in the Cosmopolitan Hotel, Aubrey Beardsley, hooped over his drawings, as thin as a question mark, sits writing letters to his friends and family.

'Menton is a truly sociable little place,' his tone is as bright as the light outside, 'and the strong English contingent here furnishes me with quite a number of people to talk to.' He is twenty-five, the same age more or less, as the bull-running boys. He can't run and he wouldn't want to; he has had aggressive tuberculosis since childhood. Something else is roaring towards him bigger, blacker than a bull. He can hear its hooves all the time, coming at him through the heat-struck days, and he can feel them, especially at night, shivering the ground with their approach, up through the legs of the hotel bed, and into his own bones. By day he works at his own blood-shadowed black and white art, developed and mastered in defiance. But he is still frightened.

'There is a famous Egyptologist here,' he says brightly, 'one Tyler, who looks like a corpse, has looked like one for fourteen years, who is much worse that I am, and yet lives on and does things. My spirits have gone up immensely since I've known him.' Under the desk his legs, no thicker than the candlesticks on his newly Catholic mantelpiece, are painful to look at. He is worried about the sinfulness of his drawings for *The Yellow Book*, for Wilde's *Salomé*. Could they be burned? Could someone see to it they are destroyed? Just in case.

In England, someone makes non-committal noises and puts the drawings carefully into a portfolio. These must be kept for posterity.

In the heat-thickened stillness the hooves are drumming. In the last photographs of him before he dies, the voile protecting Beardsley's bed from mosquitoes shines with whiteness. He sits, like Jacky le Mat returned

from the dead in Marseille, with his back to the door. When will it come? Now? Is it now? He looks at his books and he faces his crucifix among the upholstery furious with conflicting patterns. He tries not to listen. He carries on with his commissions when he has the strength and he turns repeatedly towards the window. He trusts in the light. Light is life. And it's so strong here, surely it must be catching.

It isn't, and in two months and five days' time something voluminous in black, straight out of one of his own drawings, enters the room more quietly than he'd expected, and blots itself across Beardsley's life; across the shining white of the curtains, across the patterned bed, the patterned carpet. A flood of soaking red.

We are staying with friends in one of the nineteenth-century villas above the sea. Tall cool rooms and, below the window, when I open the shutters, French police in dark glasses are lounging in a little hut next to the railway line. They are there to catch the economic migrants looking for work, or the refugees who walk the line from Italy into France, hoping to find asylum, or both. It happens all the time, according to my friend. You see people pulled in, arrested. 'How do they know?' Stupid question. Despite Beardsley the picture here is mainly white. The policemen tip their chairs in boredom and go on waiting.

Later, driving into the Italian hills the other side of the border, to find some waterfall pools to swim in, we are stopped by the road being closed for repair. Traffic cones and orange plastic tape and not a great deal happening. The workmen saunter around in hard hats, their trousers cinched underneath cannonball bellies. We will have to walk it. There isn't a way round. So we step over the barricades and set off and as we do we are overtaken by three thin boys, in their early twenties at most, very dark, in jackets and hoodies to protect them against cold – in this heat. Anxiety is coming off them in waves. They are looking for a way over the mountains. 'Because people aren't monsters,' my friend says, 'they help. "I should try that way if I were you." They don't say exactly, but they indicate. "Over there, I don't know, it might be worth a shot." And a wink and a jerk of the head in the direction of some pass or other that might get you up and over into

France without a policeman in shades interrupting. I don't say anything as they outpace us. I don't know where they are going.

'I can smell war now,' my friend says as we walk, 'the extremity of the times.' I look at her in surprise. So that's it – she's right, that's what it was – I felt it too: the lurch of the London streets that I left, so sunny, so unnoticing, while the world we know, eyes glazed, fatted with distraction, sleepwalks into catastrophe.

'I make stories for each of them,' she says, as if apologizing. But watching them pass us, it is hard not to. The boys so distinctive, so noticeable. The fine-cut melancholy of their features, their physical thinness, their liquid and wary eyes. I am also human, even if I seem other, each side says silently to the other, although to them most likely we aren't. There is no difference, if you are desperate, between unable and unwilling.

Maybe we should stop and listen. Maybe we should call them back. Because, although their societies are broken, although they look as if they are behind, perhaps they are really ahead. Perhaps what they know is where we are going.

We bolster ourselves with tea, sitting outside, on a scruffy veranda above the river. An Italian mountain-town recently restored by Dutch incomers, picturesque, rough, a million miles in feel from Menton. There is washing hanging in courtyards glimpsed through archways, and children with tangled hair pop out of alleyways to stare, or to pound footballs against the ancient walls. In the hostel, which is run by the Dutch as an organic farm, students on working holidays play cards at the next-door table. The town is quiet. Among wooded hills, old stone towers sprouting weeds point at the sky and, in the bottom of the valley, as we drink, the river sounds. We have crossed our first border since coming into France without even noticing it; the magic line on the ground which switches language on and off, like you might switch a light, and which some may cross naturally, as if they were leaving one room and going into another, while others may not.

Higher up, somewhere in the trees, the boys we passed file in silence up the mountain paths. The line on the ground which we crossed without noticing is raised against them like a wall of glass. We sip at our tea and they go on walking, sliding, looking for purchase. They think France, if they can reach it, will be better. But now, at the top of France, at Calais, the Jungle is burning and the people who had managed to cross all the borders it took to get there are moving on again, shouldering their worn-out bags, dressed in their assortments of donated clothes. Trying to disappear. It seems that some change has happened. It seems that they aren't really people any more. They are just overspill. Their camp is built on a former landfill site and they, as a result, are now a new kind of litter to be swept away. They are a problem for which we can't find a solution, from which I for one am just running away with my hands clamped over my ears. Don't tell me, tell the governments. That's what governments are for. I can't do anything. I can't hear you. La La La La La La La. I am not listening.

'What *are* you doing?' Rupert asks, turning round on the path.

'I'm singing.'

In the ice-cold river, later, we let the water shoot us, delighted, from pool to pool, the fragile vigour of our bodies our only certainty.

Borders only really make sense where land meets water. All other barriers are invented and therefore arbitrary. At the top of Italy, as in all the European countries to its north and east, borders have been, until very recently, fluid and changing, breathing in and out as if in imitation of the sea. It is only with the rise of nationalism, in the nineteenth century, that borders have become enshrined as something not just fixed, but sacred. France was ahead in this, in part thanks to Joan of Arc who had a definite vision of her put-upon country as a nation, separate from others, governed by a king who took his right to do so directly from God and whose authority was therefore absolute. But long after Rolin's Burgundy had capitulated, rolling itself, along with all the other dukedoms, into the greater whole of France, Italy was still a region of separate and changing autonomous, or semi-autonomous, states. Lord Acton, writing in 1862, a year after its initial unification, saw the spread of nationalism as a Europe-wide phenomenon which he watched with anxiety and mistrust, and which grew, as he saw it, largely out of the overspill of ideas after the French Revolution.

Acton was a historian and a polymath but first of all he was a Catholic. As such, his thinking is characterized by a subtle and complex infusion of tradition with liberty. Liberty, which he defined not as the 'power of doing what we like, but the right of being able to do what we ought', and tradition were for him twin sacred lights. And nationalism and socialism were his demons.

In the early nineteenth century Catholicism was still, in England, effectively an outlawed minority. The Relief Act of 1829 gave Catholics the vote and almost equal rights, but Oxford and Cambridge continued to debar them from entry until 1871, so Acton studied instead in Munich, from where he watched his demons wake and stretch out of sleep, first in Greece and the Balkans in the 1820s and '30s, and then stalking north and west, on into Italy and Germany, to use his simile, like dissatisfied souls in search of bodies.

Part of his objection was practical and part of it was moral. In terms of practicality, he saw the ideal of nationalism in particular as reactive, rather than intrinsic. Put simply, it rose wherever the ills of society were the product of foreign oppression or intervention. It offered an intoxicatingly simple solution to complex and often long-established evils. Kick out the foreign oppressor and we will be free and self-governing. To Acton, solving a practical problem with an ideal was like eating medicine at meal times instead of food. Theories of an ideal state were useful and even necessary. They were a response to real evil and an impetus towards its removal. They just weren't practical.

This was Acton's worry, that nationalism looked only forward to the descendants and inheritors of its newly won freedom. It drew a temporal line, kicking out, overnight, the hated past, the old identity, evolved over centuries and established by history, in favour of something new, something that was decided only by invisible lines on the ground. Who were the French or the Italians? They were all the people inside the lines, in this place or that, at this particular time. I think of my troubled friend in the Camargue campsite worrying about refugees and foodbanks. Once the lines are drawn the people inside are cut free of history. Or rather their history starts afresh. From this moment on, whatever they have been historically, they become first and foremost an ethnological unit. This was the moral ground for Acton's mistrust. Nationalism, once in place, trumped everything else – anyone coming in from outside had to bow to this in terms of identity. The system was airless and rigid and monomaniac. To Acton, watching these ideas grip the countries of Europe by turn, nationalism was not just a fiction; it was both absurd in concept and criminal in effect. He was worrying, ahead of time, about the ability of European nations to remain open and flexible, because only through change, and adaptation, as he saw it, would they ever flower into progress.

'The co-existence of several nations under the same state,' he writes in his 1862 essay on nationalism, 'is a test, as well as the best security of its freedom. It is also one of the chief instruments of civilization… A state which is incompetent to satisfy different races condemns itself; a state which labours to neutralize to absorb, or to expel them, destroys its own vitality.'

Driving through tunnels, rocked by passing Italian cars speeding in the opposite direction, his words are ringing in my ears.

'I think it's interesting,' I say to Rupert, 'the idea that history is something that *can* happen as much as something that *has* happened.'

'History means the study of past events.'

'I know, but he seems to be implying that history is a live thing.'

'What are you talking about? Who is "he"?'

'Lord Acton, who wrote this essay I've been reading about nationalism. He identifies it as a problem when countries kick out history, as a way of self-identifying, and decide to use geographical limitation instead. He seems to be implying that history is not just about the past but about some kind of philosophical possibility of future past – that history is something important to manage, or curate, as a nation – that you could make decisions based on how you want it to look in time to come. I've often thought that history was regrettable or inconvenient but I've never thought of it as a live concern, let alone potentially dangerous. He seems to suggest that you could limit it or close it down somehow. I've never thought of it like that before.'

'Is he planning on the end of civilization?'

'What do you mean?'

'Well, without exterminating the human race I don't see how you can envisage limiting history.'

'I'm not envisaging anything. I'm just interested in Lord Acton.'

'Right.' It's dark and we haven't yet had any supper. Rupert has been driving for hours. 'I'd love to continue this conversation but do you think you could get interested in the map?'

We are trying to reach Lake Garda. It is like being caught in a bad dream. Endless suburbs, all of which look the same, advertising in neon lights things we don't want. Roundabout after roundabout, little suburban houses with fences, as if mountains had suddenly pushed up under Milton Keynes. More neon. More roundabouts and, at every one, 'Sexy Shop' flashing in pink and blue, alongside pizza and some kind of chicken. Then more houses. And at no warning, in one of the housing estates and without my advice, Rupert swings the van right, up a little rise to a grassy spot where the road just comes to a halt at what looks like a wood. It is a wood. I am too tired to wonder what it is doing in suburbia. A track leads in among sweet chestnuts, and to one side a steep cliff drops away, over which I spit my toothpaste, picturing it landing on someone's lounger or lawn mower. It's not polite but it's not as bad as bird shit.

In the morning, we wake to find ourselves parked among scrub – brambles and scarlet smoke-bushes, burning with autumn. Around the van, a drift of condom wrappers and little pinches of used toilet paper. 'Welcome to Italy,' Rupert says.

I have forgotten about Lord Acton because someone new is waiting for us at our collapsible breakfast table. All night, in and out of the rocking tunnels, in the dark, we were driving without knowing it into a Beardsley drawing; the overwrought sensitivity dressed in simplicity, the lightless-ness, the flowing eroticized death. Where else could he be from, this horrible little man with heavy-lidded eyes? He looks barely human. He looks like something that Beardsley thought up to goad the Victorians with, holding the paper casually in one etiolated hand right under the noses of the thundering patriarchs, as if to say, 'I beg your pardon, I believe this is yours. I found it on the floor. It must have dropped out of your mind.'

'Is he a friend of yours?' I ask Rupert. 'Do I have to meet him?'

'I think you'll find him pretty attractive,' Rupert says, because he's read the book, 'if he pays you attention. Most women do.' He seems to be in a bad mood.

'Attractive?' I ignore the proviso. That is simply never going to happen; this little polished grotesque who lisps his greeting at us this morning. His face is unpleasant so I make the mistake of looking at his feet. They are clad in shiny handmade shoes that fit tight as fish, ornamented with pink-stitched phalluses.

And he isn't a drawing. He is real. He has a soft, high-pitched voice, and behind the contrived and languorous delivery, there is a note of hysteria, something overdone. He barely acknowledges me as I say hello and sit down, just a limp flick of his wrist. He tells us swaggering stories as we drink our coffee and he calls for war. He spouts nationalism and the purity of heroism and the scent of pines. He wants us to go to his house above the lake. He wants to show Rupert his antiquities. Rupert doesn't even ask

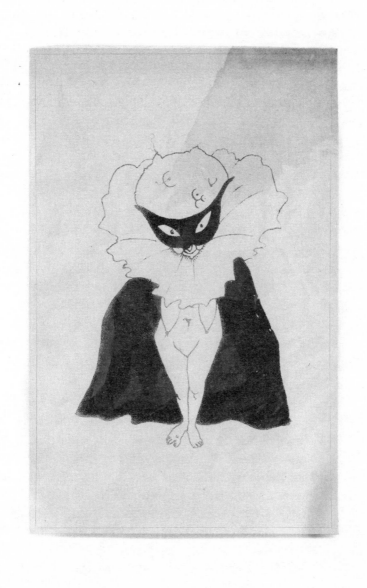

if I want to. He just says yes, jumping up with enthusiasm. 'Great,' he says with energy, 'I'm on.'

I don't get it. 'Why are we even talking to him?' I ask, half trotting to keep up, they are moving so fast. 'He's repulsive.'

'We will go first to my little museum,' d'Annunzio says, turning back to us as he hurries ahead.

'It'll be worth seeing. You can ask him about Lord Acton,' Rupert whispers at me. 'Ask him your questions about history. He seems to have collected a lot of remnants for someone who wants to kick it out.'

'I didn't say he did want to kick it out. I just said that's what Acton said,' I whisper back, cross because I'm still trying to keep up. 'You ask him.' Are we arguing even at the run?

So in his nonchalant way, when we come to a stop, Rupert does. The little grotesque doesn't answer the question. 'We live in an infamous age under the rule of the multitude and the tyranny of the plebeians,' he tells us, his chest swelling outwards like a pouter pigeon's. War, he is keen to make us understand, is the only hope, a great national war, to reinstate glory and nobility and sacrifice.

'Who said anything about war?' Rupert asks, aside.

'My friend did, remember? When we passed those boys on our way to go swimming.' Rupert looks genuinely puzzled but the little grotesque isn't listening to either of us.

'This next war that you seem to fear,' he says, letting us in through a side door to a small museum. 'This next war, I summon with all the strength of my soul!' He has cabinets full of uniforms, weaponry, a whole aeroplane, and he waves a small hand as he shows us, gabbling about bravery, about rose petals and about the thrill of voluptuous desire. It is in his books, he says. Have we read them? It is all in his poetry and his novels. Only after a while, somewhere between his fevered brain and his lips it all gets tangled and turned inside out, so that what comes out of his mouth in the end is what he meant to keep hidden, his private horror.

'Flesh, flesh,' he gibbers in front of a white linen night-gown, a round hole, ornamented with gold thread at groin height, 'this brutish thing, full of veins, tendons, ligaments, glands, bones, full of instincts and needs; flesh, sweating and stinking; flesh becoming deformed, sick, covered in sores, callouses, wrinkles, pimples, warts, hairs.' He thinks he is just writing fiction. But I am not stupid.

We emerge into a courtyard – surprisingly pretty, flights of stairs leading up to gardens and a view of the sea. 'Come! Let me show you my house, my bosom's nest, the place of my creative soul.'

No thank you, Gabriele d'Annunzio. He is the first monster we have met, which is surprising. Usually, on such a quest, there are monsters everywhere. I try to step round him. But like all monsters, it isn't that easy. Hesitating, one foot on the threshold of his house which is bright like a daffodil, above the lake. Narcissus.

'Come in, come in.' I intend to sit this one out, here, in this courtyard, looking out at the sea, but as he addresses me it is not so simple. It is his eyes that are the problem. Looking up, against my better judgement and because his shoes are repellent, I find them light. I can't help it. Oh my goodness. His eyes are beautiful. 'His 'clever, often witty, often cruelly indifferent eyes', runs one man's description. I reach a hand back in the direction of Rupert.

'Sarah Bernhardt compared them to little blobs of shit,' Rupert murmurs, reading my thoughts. I am reassured. You have to arm yourself against monsters. They are designed to be compelling.

'Sarah Bernhardt,' he says, without changing his tone, 'was his mistress.' I try to look at something else. D'Annunzio's head is bald save for a sprinkling of smoothed and scented red hairs. He has a permanent erection. He holds out a hand, in gallantry, to help me in. I step into the house, as if magnetized.

We are gathered in the little antechamber, me and Rupert and a French family made up of two women, one in thigh boots and curled peroxide hair, a plump and knowing child and a tall man in an overcoat with swept-back grey and flowing hair. So we are definitely still in a Beardsley drawing. The guide is apologetic; she can do the tour in Italian or in English. If we want French then it has to come out of a little Dictaphone she is holding. What language would we prefer? The Beardsley man is sneering. 'We speak

French, Italian, German and English.' For some reason he says this preening his hair and looking at me.

'French is fine,' I offer in a small voice.

He stoops towards me. 'It is better in French or Italian. In English it would be barbaric.' He says it twice. He stinks of wine. I flush as if I had been slapped.

Why is English barbaric? But I don't ask it out loud.

Briefly, in this horrible crepuscular hallway, heavy and hideous with pretension, Shakespeare and lovely Wyatt, and Langland and Chaucer and Donne, and Hopkins and Hughes, and Beckett and Dickens step lightly past me in procession. I love them. I love their air and earth and windy sun, their mist and cloud and rain; the gathering of so many weathers into one, the gathering of so many languages. I think there are tears in my eyes. This glittering, rough, surprising whole is *my* whole, my language, where I live. I clench my fists as I think it. And it is famous for its beauty. Isn't it? Craven, I smile. French it is.

D'Annunzio was a photophobe, I think in every sense, although ostensibly as a result of temporary blindness after an aeroplane crash. The rooms we go in and out of are all the same, dark, upholstered in gilded suede or damask, the ceilings corded with ropes, lit with rock-crystal lamps. Every surface is crowded with knick-knacks, sculptures, animal fur, velvet, bronze, gold. In this room, on a dais, in a bed the size and shape of a coffin, d'Annunzio likes to lie alone with his arms by his sides, his eyes popping, wallowing in his mortality. This is his personal aesthetic, his temperament, but it is in happy coincidence with the times through which he is living. It grows out of them like mistletoe grows on a tree: the nationalist obsession of newly unified Italy; the end of Romanticism, and the sterility of the urban, industrialized, present; the bourgeois hypocrisies of domesticity, its small morality, its denied sexuality. All of these are gifts to d'Annunzio, whose works, opposing them in fevered language, give expression to the central ideal of a new movement called Decadence. D'Annunzio is the champion of what Symons calls the 'disembodied voice', reached either through sensual oblivion or through blood-letting and violence.

'Look at all this junk,' I say to Rupert. Rupert is scornful of possessions. I am hoping to impress him and I'm hoping that he won't notice that for a split second, as I met d'Annunzio's gaze, Rupert's prediction was proved right. 'All this talk of beauty and it's so ugly.' I say it loudly so d'Annunzio and the Beardsley man can hear. I want to call d'Annunzio on his luxury, on his sensual overload and his disembodied posturing. 'I will buy you some see-through boxes, d'Annunzio. Then we will see – when all your possessions are stored, when you are nothing but your tiny body, your bald head and your heavy-lidded intelligent eyes; without all your paraphernalia, your jewelled junk, what kind of man will you be?'

D'Annunzio turns aside. He is more interested in the French woman in thigh boots. And besides, without his possessions, his tiny body is still strangely attractive to women and his bald head goes on apparently producing some of Italy's finest writing. Added to which, as he leans now to tell the French woman, he is a military hero. That aeroplane in the museum, did she see it? He himself flew it, has flown it many times, as a fighter pilot all through the First World War. He flew it over Vienna, and he took part in the famous raid on the Austrian harbour of Bakar.

'And you?' he whips back around, to ask me in return. 'What do you have to offer in this time of crisis? Your boxes are no different from my words. They are a response to the same conditions and they won't last as long.' He is rightly dismissive. Like me, he wishes for a god but can't find one that fits his requirements. So he makes one, in his own image. He creates something that is almost a cult, a fit-all for fanatics of every kind. 'It is too late,' he tells me as he turns, heading to the exit. 'Science, in case you hadn't noticed, is incapable of repopulating the deserted heavens, of restoring happiness to those souls whose ingenuous peace has been destroyed… we no longer want truth, give us the dream.'

'Is he right?' I ask Rupert later, when we are alone at our campsite again. 'Is that where we are? Because this is my worst fear. This is what I am looking for answers to. Is it too late? Is distraction the only thing art now has to offer?' As I bend over my computer in the van, d'Annunzio suddenly seems horribly prescient. His words, still horribly effective, refuse to die.

On whacko sites, weird, proto-Fascist, militarist groups quote and re-quote them next to pictures that show masked gunmen kneeling before crucifixes. The writing that goes with the pictures is a garbled mix of spirituality and perversion. It talks of purification through bloodshed.

'Don't look, sweetheart,' Rupert says, suddenly kind. 'It's just some little man. You have to remember that. Come and look at the moon.' He holds out his hand, which seems something solid, something warm and human. I put away my computer and do as he says. He is right. Once all the men in it have gone to sleep the world looks comforting and like it might endure.

'Sometimes I'm frightened of the internet,' I say later, in the dark, but Rupert is not listening because he has fallen asleep. I lie on my back, listening to him breathing, and try to take his advice. Don't look. But little men can be so dangerous. They get listened to and now, ever since the invention of film, they won't go away. You can find d'Annunzio anytime – if you want to – on YouTube, forever perfect in uniform, on a podium with the veins in his temples bulging and his eyes ablaze.

'We are waging our war,' he shouts at me, fist raised, as I lie trying to sleep myself. 'Blood is spurting from the veins of Italy! We are the last to join this struggle and already the first are meeting with glory... The slaughter begins, the destruction begins... All these people, who yesterday thronged in the streets and squares, loudly demanding war, are full of veins, full of blood; and that blood begins to flow... We have no other value but that of our blood to be shed.'

I feel I've heard this before, more recently from the mouths of other fanatics, scarved or suited, this talk of blood and glory. 'Can't you see where this leads? Don't you care?' Again, 'No thank you, d'Annunzio.'

Breakfast is Rupert's favourite meal. It is always porridge and coffee and he likes to be the one to make it. We sit either side of the narrow table adding things to our bowls in a ritualistic way – bananas, walnuts, honey. If Rupert's food looks especially attractive he photographs it before he eats it.

'What's the plan?' I ask him. I haven't slept. I hope it isn't more war.

'A walk above the lake. I want to photograph the sheep we saw,' he says with his mouth full. He especially likes sheep for the way they give back light, most of all when the light is slanting.

'Well, that's fine by me. I want to get away from blood and nationalism and death. I couldn't sleep much because of war.'

'That may be difficult,' he says, 'war is what we humans do.'

Is it? Is there no progress? Won't we change now we can see at close quarters what war is; now that it is no longer possible to avoid the knowledge that we are mostly waging war on people who are just like us? I think of the strangeness of our times, in which we can hear the voices of the ordinary people who sit under the bombs we have sent. You can read their matter-of-fact preparations and their liberal puzzlement. Because in 2003 I sat in the green cool of England reading the blog of a young architect in Baghdad.

Today my mother and I bought masking tape and packing tape. Today we bought tins of beans and stocked up on rice and matches. Today we made blackout blinds and taped up the windows so that the glass wouldn't shatter inwards and fly in our faces. It is x o'clock. Today we are waiting for the bombers to arrive.

Or words to that effect.

Every day, inconveniently articulate, unmistakably educated, amusing, the blogger recorded the details of his life under bombardment, while around him the buildings, some of which must have inspired him to his training, were ruined. Every day, I read his words. It is I who am doing this, I thought, whether I like it or not. I am part of England and this is what democracy means. The rule of the people. I am waging this war on architects and their mothers. I am their enemy.

Surely, at some point, we will sicken ourselves.

But we don't. It seems instead that we are inured. There is just so much of it about. Today, as we walk looking for flocks to photograph, someone has thought up the notion of a united Italy, free from Austro-Hungarian control, and now at every step there is another battlefield. Behind these sheep, for instance, whose raised heads seem only to be considering their side-to-side mouthfuls of morning grass, young men from several countries hurl themselves after empty ideals into the epilepsy of war. The French and the Piedmontese and various allies, all possessed by Acton's demon of nationalism, have come to grips with the monster of the Austrian Empire. We have got stuck at the bottom of the barrel.

'What is happening?' I shout at a heavy-set man standing on the sidelines, as all around me maddened men attack each other with sabre, bayonet and rifle-butt. When they run out of weapons they seize their enemies by the throat and tear them with their teeth, while I reel, gasping for breath. 'Here come the artillery,' the heavy-set man shouts at me suddenly, pointing into a thundering cloud of dust. Meanwhile, Rupert goes on photographing the light. He is amid the flock now, shoulders hunched, entranced, the sheep around him luminescent.

It is the Battle of Solferino, June 1859, and the bystander, who is kindly and practical and has sideburns like shrubberies, is Henry Dunant. He is really here on business, he tells me over the battle's noise – he has a corn-trading enterprise in Tunisia and he needs Napoleon III to establish land and water rights. The colonial authorities are slow and slippery. He couldn't get anything done from afar, and success in business is often a matter of timing, so instead he came to the battle. When it is over he will ask. He hasn't thought about how that will work. He hasn't thought about what battles are, or how this one might affect him. He was thinking only about business when he set out.

But here, at first hand, things are different. He is a steady and peaceable person. He won't ever recover from this sight. He won't ever forget, by his account, how in battle like this, 'the guns crash over the dead and wounded, strewn pell-mell on the ground. Brains spurt under the wheels, limbs are broken and torn, bodies mutilated past recognition – the soil is literally puddled with blood and the plain littered with human remains.'

The fighting, which started at four in the morning, continues into evening and in the intervening time a gale springs up. The soldiers have had nothing to eat or drink since battle began and a cold rain is now falling. There is fighting everywhere you look, in the streets, in the fields, in the lanes and in the little local woods. Foot soldiers whose advance is hampered by orchards and vineyards fall under a hail of grape-shot, tangled in these carefully tended vines.

Night falls and it is impossible to find anyone among the carnage, by torchlight. The horror is too great. The helpers who went out to look for friends or family stumble home dazed. So the wounded are left, in ditches and gullies and under piles of enemy dead, starving, exhausted, their blood flow unchecked. Many, who might have been saved, die during the night. Dunant walks away to his lodgings, unaware that for him monumental internal changes are taking place.

When he gets up again, and for days afterwards, he sees ragged files of casualties pass on the roads, hands on each other's shoulders, in tens of thousands, or heaped groaning into carts with little scraps of canvas laid over them to protect them from the sun. Come here, d'Annunzio, I would like to say. Come here, with your nationalist calls to arms. Are you really telling me that nationhood is worth this? But d'Annunzio has a glazed look in his eye and his goatee beard is pointing skyward. He grew up listening to accounts of Solferino, its martyrs and heroes, its twenty-year-olds who sacrificed themselves for the glory of Italy. He thinks it is a triumph. I will find someone else to talk to.

Dunant for instance, who is clutching his head at the sight of the battle's aftermath, muttering under his breath. 'But good God, what is this?' Because it is chaos. 'And is no one doing anything for these poor brutes? Is there no provision?' Dunant, who came to further his business, is stopped in his tracks. The men who can't walk, still lying on the battlefield, heaped like trash, the dead and the dying undifferentiated. The pitiful cries, the extended hands.

'Help me. Please help me.'

Dunant is in some ways a practical man and now he thinks of marshalling the local women. The whole of the surrounding area has become a makeshift hospital, private houses, tents, rigged-up shelters, even the church, but there are very few doctors and nothing like enough nurses. The wounded and dying are everywhere. He sets to helping. But several times he stops, staring with his mouth open into the middle distance in despair. There is no real structure here; it is all so amateur. The doctors are almost asleep on their feet, one surgeon so exhausted he needs people either side to support his arms as he cuts. Dunant snaps back to attention and the present again. If no one else will take responsibility then I must. And suddenly Dunant is everywhere. Beds. Bandages. He bangs on the doors of the village. 'Get the French to release the Austrian doctors they've taken prisoner. It doesn't matter whose side anyone is on now. These are all human beings in the end.'

Out of the houses the mothers and daughters come, holding up their skirts at first because of the mud, or the blood, or both. Then dropping them again because there's no point.

'Tutti fratelli,' the shocked women say, stripping off the various uniforms to get at the wounds and bathing the bodies that are all the same underneath. 'Tutti fratelli,' and the phrase goes round like Chinese Whispers.

Meanwhile, Dunant, all thoughts of corn trading gone from his head, organizes and pays for the buying of supplies. He buys tents and camp beds and medicine and bandages. Day and night he makes his rounds, trying to alleviate suffering, unqualified to offer anything much more than comfort. It is shocking, what he sees. He doesn't know it yet but it changes the course of his life completely. When he has time, he writes it down, partly in exorcism but partly because there must be an account of this. People must understand the seizure of war, what it is like when it happens and what it is like when it is over, when the seizure has passed and men come to themselves again.

'With faces black with the flies that swarmed about their wounds, men gazed around them, wild-eyed and helpless,' he writes, wading in memory through the jumble of the wounded packed into the aisles of the local church. 'There was one poor man, completely disfigured, with a broken jaw and his swollen tongue hanging out of his mouth. He was tossing and trying to get up. I moistened his drying lips and hardened tongue, took a handful of lint and dipped it in the bucket they were carrying behind me, and squeezed the water from this improvised sponge into the deformed opening that had been his mouth.'

I am squeamish. I look around the quiet hilltop for Rupert. He is nowhere in sight. I put my hands over my ears. 'Please stop, Dunant. I don't need telling that war is bad. I am practically a pacifist. I don't want to know.' But Dunant can't stop.

'Another wretched man had had a part of his face – nose, lips and chin – taken off by a sabre cut. He could not speak, and lay, half blind, making heart-rending signs with his hands and uttering guttural sounds to attract attention. I gave him a drink and poured a little fresh water on his bleeding face. A third, with his skull gaping wide open, was dying, spitting out his brains on the stone floor. His companions in suffering kicked him out of their way, as he blocked the passage. I was able to shelter him for the last moments of his life, and I laid a handkerchief over his poor head, which still just moved.'

Dunant doesn't forget what he's seen; how could you? He spends the rest of his life, even through personal bankruptcy and penury, trying to realize his philanthropic ideas. This must never happen again, these men in agony, untended by anyone except untrained civilians. There must be an organization of professionals to care for the casualties of battle. He is too realistic to hope that there will be no more war. 'That will never be,' he tells me. 'Not only will that never be, but there are already,' he says, 'new and frightful weapons of destruction, which are now at the disposal of the nations.'

'I know, Dunant, I know. I live in your future.' Dunant ignores me.

'War in the future,' he says with emphasis, setting off down a track to the village, 'will only become more and more murderous.'

Well, he was right, and although it took his whole life's energy to do it, the makeshift hospitals that sprang up at Solferino in essence never quite went away because here, thanks to Dunant's vision and persistence, were the beginnings of the International Red Cross.

Ants are apparently the only other species to make war. I'm sitting by a bend in the track taken by Dunant, waiting for Rupert, watching a line of ants march past my boots. 'How trapped you and I are, despite our clever heads, in the stupidity of our natures.' The ants are manoeuvring something huge and dead towards their ant heap. They have no interest in my opinion. But the sun is shining now, and Rupert appears with his floating step and his camera, so he and I head off to walk the heights, above the lake, in shirt-sleeves. If I can't solve the puzzle that is mankind, still,

I can rest. The country around looks peaceful and bucolic. The red of the smoke-bushes flares against the sky above and the water so blue between. The ground at our feet is starred with tiny dianthus and colchicums, their faces opened flat to the sun. It's hot so we climb down the long way from the heights to the lake shore and strip off, swimming out in water that is soft and very still.

Stationary on the lake's surface, there are little bits of reed. It feels almost thick, nutrient rich, although the water is clear and it goes on and on, stretching away as far as you can see into the distance. At the end, instead of horizon, just the blue blurring of water into sky, as though if you kept going, you could swim without noticing it up into the air.

One swan keeps us company. Nothing else. Or nothing else I can see, because in fact far below, on the mountainsides of the world underwater, a carpione, one of the salmon family which, the whole world over, is found only in Lake Garda, noses through crevices where the cold springs come jetting out of the rock. He's as beautiful as if Beardsley had been down here with his pen, his silver back blotted with startling black spots, his eyes white with stored light, the eye-shine that allows him to see on the lake bottom.

He is a fish. He has a completely different experience of the world, not just because he lives in one lake, but because he lives in it (and therefore in the world) in a different, non-human way. He has less power to act and none to influence, but still, he sees a different order.

And like a man might live his whole life between hunger and sleep he goes on, down there, working the bone levers of his jaws through the blue glooms. Maybe he sees a shadow passing fathoms above. Maybe he feels it, like something on his own skin, because he doesn't know for sure where he stops and the water starts. Fairly sure, he might think to himself, if it was in his nature to think, there is at least strong evidence to suggest that there is a world above, under different conditions in which, translated, he might live a different life. A world that sometimes penetrates his own. 'But now I am hungry,' he thinks. 'Now I am sleeping. Now I am hungry again.' He has good peripheral vision. Maybe he noses up a little to see. The inept scissoring, jerking along the skin of his sky. He knows a human when he sees one. I don't know how a fish would talk but I know, if I were one myself, what questions I would ask of my race; the race that wars, that constantly meddles and spoils in one-species-oriented improvement. A race that visits its tantrums, and its indiscriminate and inept curiosity, on the rest of the world, picking everything up, putting everything in its mouth, like a giant toddler.

Up from the bottom something swooshing and booming like sonar, and then the voice from somewhere I can't see, the words capsuled like bubbles, bringing something old and fish-cold to the surface.

'I want to know, can I ask—' I swivel my head in surprise. The fish appears, just below the water's surface as if hung on an invisible string. I can see him swaying slightly, opening and shutting his mouth, as if he were talking or chewing, the gills at the side of his head rhythmically flaring. The time-lapse between the release of the bubbles and their arrival, the bursting of the words into air. I swivel again to see if there is anyone else. Rupert is further out, snorting water. He has swapped himself for something more animal. He isn't talking.

'Can I ask you?' again. A faint pop, pop and the smell of fish. 'There aren't many people around and I'm fast running out of time...' I look down into the water at the carpione, levering away with his jaw bones. 'When you move about in the world above mine, do you move like this, or do you move better?' He pauses. Does he mean to insult? I have no idea. He goes on, 'I mean, do you fit, or does it seem that you are in the wrong place, that you've landed in this world by accident, that you belong somewhere else, somewhere better?'

Now it's my turn to look like a fish. I open and shut my mouth. 'I don't understand your questions.'

But he has lost interest. Fish have short attention spans. 'Forget it,' the popping bubbles say. He sounds despondent. 'It really doesn't matter.' He flips away, and then as if changing his mind, turns. 'Just one more thing, these people of yours, do they show any signs of running out, or are they still in good supply?'

'Which people?'

'I'm just curious. I heard you mention casualties. I wondered... the death from which you are – correct me if I'm wrong – currently running. Is it just individual or is it a whole species?'

'I'm not running from anything, fish,' scissoring my arms and legs, head up like a tortoise. 'I don't know what you are talking about.' The swan eases away as if on rollers.

'Sorry. I must have made a mistake...' He is too polite or too tired perhaps to go on. It doesn't make any difference to him. He is only killing time, waiting for extinction, which for him is imminent. There are none of his type anywhere else. None of the attempts at transfer to other lakes have been successful. He lets my shadow pass over him as he hangs, stationary, in the water below. He would shrug if he could, but he has no shoulders. What is it he is thinking as he swims away? Just maybe that it is odd that something so vulnerably naked and inept could see itself so otherwise. The fear of death he can understand. That's only natural, although in him it is reactive, an instinct for self-preservation, not something that drives him to change.

For him, it is a matter of scale: how big, how significant do you see yourself compared to everything else, he might ask. Because, he might say, I see you as very small in this lake, which by the way is my place, my identity; very small and very bad at swimming. And yet...

Just for a start, I suppose he must think, we have done a lot of fishing. 'You will be a lucky devil, finding this delicious fish in a restaurant,' the guide books tell us. 'Carpione are excellent when flavoured with fennel and baked in a salt crust.' Then, I suppose he must think, there are our nets and our lines, our out-flows and emissions, our sprays, our habits of cultivation, our motor boats, our plastics that lie on his world's bottom and don't rot down. But what he doesn't realize is that God put us in charge of creation. He has no understanding of that: that all of this, himself included, is designed expressly for our use. He just wonders how it is that something so comparatively small could be so successfully, so comprehensively destructive.

'I just thought,' the carpione says quietly, flicking his tail as he dives. The little bubbles of his words bursting on the surface have a cold smell. 'I just wondered, since it's your world too…' Then nothing. I can't hear him any more. He must have gone down to his deeps.

Fool.

You stupid, stupid fool. In the stories, it is always the animals that have the answers. The snake tells us, or the mouse, or the horse, or the fish or the bird. Have you forgotten? Humans aren't a parallel. They are just more of the same. Get him back. Say sorry. Ask him again, and truly this time, what he recommends. If it isn't too late, in every sense.

Forlorn and dripping on the shore, I look along the line of water to where Rupert has beached himself further down. He is flat out, sunning himself dry on a rock. No help from that quarter. I think about calling the fish – how would one begin to do that? – but the surface of the lake looks impenetrable; blue glass. I don't think he can hear me. I don't think he will come back, or not just for me. Not now.

So I dress and instead I call them all here, to the shores of Lake Garda; I call all the larger than lifetime, significant people, Dunant and d'Annunzio. All the people who have left a print, whether for good or bad. Not Beardsley because he is too ill but Jacky le Mat, Puget, Baroncelli. I call Joan of Arc, who comes followed by a little black cat. I call Rolin. I call Eustace, who can't make it. He has got his hands full already, he says. He is trying to be in two places at once. He is busy. He is building an expensive concrete wall. It is to guard the puddles and the smoking ruins of the Jungle, empty now apart from a small child, cowering in a ditch like a rat. And he is busy in Dakota, where he is getting impatient, waiting with his drill and his pipeline, his moustaches full of the rich smell of oil. He can't come. He really can't spare the time. 'OK, Eustace, don't worry. We can do without you.'

Mariette and the Mummy, with its stretched leather face and its piano-key teeth, arrive together. He is leading it by the bony hand because its eyes don't work any more. Dickens comes, in dandy style, with a notebook, hoping for a story. He has made friends with the couple from Manchester. The three of them sit on a rock, already deep in conversation. I hear 'politicians' and 'tailcoats' and 'You were only supposed to blow the bloody doors off'. Dickens nods and scribbles. He seems excited.

Everyone appreciates the lake. How could you not? Singly or in drifts they approach the water, such a swathe of shining colour at a distance, so translucent closer to. There is no evidence to us that anything is spoiling or already dead. On a day like this it is a miracle. 'What heaven. Aren't we lucky? What are we here for?'

'You are here to make sense of things, as you tried in life. You are here to see if some key to life can be forged out of all the things you have said, or been, or done.' I don't tell them anything about meeting a fish. I just hope. I have nothing to offer the carpione, or nothing he would recognize, but he had his own questions which I failed to answer and I sensed that they were somehow urgent. So perhaps, seeing all these people gathered on the shore, he might be tempted to come back and try again. If he does I will not be so stupid a second time; I will ask him mine in return. Then maybe I will get my answers. And if he doesn't answer directly, then at least I hope he will provide another, outsider's perspective, something bigger than human, something broader, something more lasting.

It is Joan of Arc who sees the fish first, listing to one side in the shallows. Maybe it's because she is the simplest, her just-above-peasant origins putting her at ease in the natural world. Maybe it's because in her armour she looks most like a fish herself. Either way she kneels down, ignoring her greaves in the water.

'Are you ill?'

'I am dying,' the carpione whispers. Close to, the Beardsley black spots are filmed, the yellow eye already cloudy.

She stretches out her hand. 'Then let me give you comfort. Let me bless you, brother.' She raises her eyes briefly to the sky as if asking something and then bows her head, her lovely lips moving in Latin. She is concentrating, the black bobbed hair falling sharp, in line with her nose. 'Confiteor Deo omnipotenti et vobis, fratres, quia peccavi nimis cogitatione, verbo, opere et omissione: mea culpa, mea culpa, mea maxima culpa.'

'Well,' the carpione says, the cold and bubbled voice a little ragged, 'I don't know what you left undone. It was mostly the things you did that did for me, but don't blame yourself. You weren't the only one. It's been going on a long time, but it's nearly over now.' He sounds very tired. 'It is nearly over.'

Joan stops in surprise, mid-sentence, sits back on her haunches. She frowns. The fish has reacted improperly to the word of its maker. Has she failed to recognize a demon? She looks up at the sky again. Around her a vigorous discussion breaks out.

'He isn't a Christian,' someone says. 'He's a fish.'

'I thought fish were the symbol of Christ. Am I wrong? It seems a bit inconsistent, at least.'

'You can't blame him. He doesn't know any better.'

'Whatever he is, he is rude.'

'He's not rude. He is dying. Didn't you hear what he said?'

'It's not my fault he's dying. I don't even live in Italy.'

'It's just, if you're asking' – the watery voice of the carpione is faint. The people stop talking and lean in to listen. 'We creatures all live in the world,' he says. 'We are part of it.' He is working his mouth with obvious difficulty now. 'But you men, as if separate, live only on top of it. It seems you have something else in mind. You are always looking at something else, something more, or bigger, that would make a better fit. Forgive me, I just don't understand at what, or where.'

Only Rolin seems to answer directly, his head cocked, looking at the fish, one eyebrow raised. He nods. 'On it or off it,' he says with a wry smile. 'That's about right.' No one else seems to understand the question.

Or perhaps they are just not interested. D'Annunzio, for instance, chest out, is trying to attract Joan's attention. She has finished praying and stands at the shore, brisk and practical, taking off her greaves and gauntlets. 'Often have I stood by,' d'Annunzio tells her, 'and watched within myself the continual genesis of a finer life, wherein all appearances were transfigured as in a magic mirror.'

'My point exactly,' says the watery voice, but d'Annunzio doesn't hear. He is in full flow, facing Joan now, his little pointed beard lifted. He believes in nobility, he is telling her, 'in the man as in the woman, in their equality, the hunger, the desire of our twin souls to burn, to purge in some celestial fire'. Joan stands up, her legs slightly apart in a boyish stance, her hands on her hips. 'You and I have, do we not,' d'Annunzio says, 'an aspiration to rich and ardent life? To nationhood, for instance.' He raises one hand, convulsed like a claw. 'Blessed be the youths who hunger and thirst for glory, for they will be sated. Blessed be the merciful ones, for they will cleanse a luminous blood and bind a shining grief.' Spit is gathering at the edges of his mouth. Joan watches, looking slightly surprised. She is no fool and, besides, he is blaspheming.

Baroncelli and Jacky le Mat have slid away. They don't think much of words. 'I'm obsessed by opera,' Jacky says. 'That is the art for me. Opera and horses.'

'Now you're talking.' They walk out along the shore, exchanging views about risk and honour, and the cult of manhood. They talk about horses they have known and ridden, about speed and skill and killing bulls and the elevated life of danger survived.

Puget is hovering at the edge of the circle. He would like to discuss the divine right of kings with Joan. They share an absolute belief in monarchy. He would like to show her the grandeur of his designs for Marseille, celebrating his king, for making of his hometown a heaven on earth. He is sure she would understand what a fine opportunity had been missed.

Only Rolin is left looking down at the fish. 'Self-aggrandizement,' he says, scuffing at the pebbles with one pointed foot. 'We are an anxious species. We can't imagine a world without us individually at its centre. We cannot believe that we are nothing.' But the fish is yawing in the shallows. It looks suddenly unstable, as if it were difficult now to keep equilibrium.

'Since I do it by God's command, and in His service, I do not think I do wrong,' Joan says, answering for herself with the insistent clarity of her prime, before she was broken or made ill with interrogation; before the fire.

Rolin bends his head to her. Whatever it takes, he might have said, but he doesn't.

I can't help looking at him. 'You sold her,' I hiss at him, aside. 'The papers were passed to you, weren't they? You were there with the Duke of Burgundy, at Compiègne, when she was taken.' He turns, his arms crossed, snug inside the damask sleeve of their opposite. He must be sweltering in all that garb.

'She was taken in war.'

'But you sold her. You were the one, were you not, who negotiated her price? Did you really need it, that extra ten thousand livres that went to fatten the already groaning coffers of Burgundy? That was blood money.'

Rolin's eyes narrow, hard as metal tacks. 'It was ransom. It was not usual to have prisoners murdered.' He clears his throat. 'Remind me,' he says softly, looking away across the lake, 'whose compatriots they were who burned her at the stake – yours, or mine?'

'Blessed be those,' d'Annunzio, almost shouting now, has lost himself in his own rhetoric, 'who, waiting and trusting, have not wasted their strength, but preserved it by means of a warrior's discipline. Blessed be those who shunned sterile loves to keep their virginity for this first and last love of their life.' He breaks off, panting. He can't help himself. He is looking at Joan, his eyes and his trousers bulging. 'Those clothes you are wearing my dear, my Saint...'

Joan looks down at her controversial male attire. According to the catalogue of her tormentors: shirt, breeches, doublet with hose, joined together and fastened to the said doublet by twenty points, long leggings laced on the outside, a short mantle reaching to the knees, or thereabouts, a close-cut cap, tight-fitting boots and buskins, long spurs, sword, dagger, breastplate, lance.

She is wearing them for her own safety among men.

'Oh come,' d'Annunzio says. 'It's not so simple. You are well dressed. You thrill as I do to the finer things. Everyone knows you were wearing a loose cloak of gold cloth when you were taken.' He swallows. 'And I can't help noticing,' he says, 'all these laces and ties. So many cords, so many bows.' His eyes run over her body, up and down. He seems out of breath. 'You have laced your boots to your doublet.'

'It is against rape.'

Has he heard, or is he too far gone? D'Annunzio reaches a hand to the laces, pinching them between finger and thumb, stroking and slyly untying.

He is in something of a hurry. To my surprise, with deftness and great speed, Joan fetches him a slap across the side of his bald head so vigorous as to send him sprawling. It is done with no apparent ill-feeling. Rolin throws back his head and roars with laughter. Joan turns to look at him, her eyes wide. She smiles. She doesn't know he is the man who sold her to her enemy.

The fish leaves. He can't help finding people ridiculous. 'I still think,' he says as he swims unsteadily away, 'I still think that it all comes down to scale; to scale or perhaps to borders; to where you think you stop and elsewhere starts.' Acton, if he were here, might agree but nobody else is listening now. The Mummy lets go of Mariette's hand and moves to the lake shore, its black stick arms raised to the sky like bull's horns. Its head is back, its little chin raised and a humming sound is coming out of its ancient, tented ribs. It is praying to Hatmehyt, the ancient Egyptian fish goddess. 'What is she goddess of, Mummy?' The Mummy's voice is like sticks scraping against each other in a small wind.

'Life. And protection.'

Along the shore, away from the crowd, as he always does, Rupert is taking photographs.

See-sawing now through the shallows, the carpione, unprotected and with his life ebbing, gasps out his communication bubbles. 'What is it you are doing?'

Nothing surprises Rupert. He looks up from the viewfinder, his eyes the same colour as the lake. 'I'm getting the fuck out of it for a while.'

'No, I mean what are you doing with that apparatus?'

'I'm documenting,' Rupert says, squinting again through the lens, pointing now at the carpione. Click. Click. 'I'm just photographing things as I find them; as they are. I live in a tricksy world and they say the camera never lies.' He lowers his camera. 'I take a picture every day. I can't tell whether things really are the way they seem. It's completely pointless but I like doing it.'

'Not at all,' the carpione says in exhaustion, 'not at all. It sounds sensible to me, to make a record. You never know…' His voice tails away. 'I find that too… that things are always looking different. When I was young, for instance, I could see the other side of violet.' Then he says with longing, 'For myself, I haven't yet got to the end of water.'

'I can quite understand that,' Rupert says, looking out across the lake.

The swan we saw in the morning disappears its neck, leaving just its body visible, as if someone had thrown an unwanted pillow onto the lake. The trees, bending forward, look for their roots and find instead their crowns reflected. Quietly the carpione dies. Just the whisper of water displaced as his body rolls over. At the sound of it Rupert, unsuspecting, looks down to see him belly uppermost, oddly stiff on the water's skin. 'Oh,' he says, out loud. Squatting down he rights the fish, taking it in both his hands. 'Oh, no.' He looks back along the shoreline, as if to call out, but the Mummy, who is the nearest, is still praying. Everyone else is busy. For a long time he stays like that, just looking at the dead eye, the sunken flesh on the now nothing body in the beloved lake's shallows. Then he checks his light meter and takes a photograph. 'I'm sorry,' he says, to no one.

3

Nothing has been learned. The carpione has died without offering a solution and I feel somehow at fault. We stand looking at the dead fish, bobbing at our feet. 'What do we do now?' I ask Rupert, my face stricken. Ashes to ashes, dust to dust. A fish doesn't seem to belong to either thing. 'You can't bury a fish. Earth would be a fish's hell.'

'No,' Rupert says, 'you can't bury a fish. Just leave it in the lake, I suppose. Something will probably eat it.' We look down again. It seems tattered already, some kind of scum clouding its scales. Can decay be so quick?

'Do you think we should tell the others?'

He glances up the shoreline. 'I'm not sure they're interested.'

'I'm going to tow it out to deeper water. That at least will be more dignified.' I start wading out to swim and Rupert, himself again, smiles.

'OK, sweetheart, you do that.'

I pinch the fish by the tail and, swimming a kind of one-armed sidestroke, pull it along with me back out into the lake. I am sorry I took offence at its questions. 'I should have seen you were as puzzled as I am,' I say to the corpse, yawing along beside me. I would prefer it not to touch my body, although I try not to think that. I try to concentrate on my apology. This is, after all, a funeral of sorts. 'I could have offered you companionship at least. I could have told you that I too don't understand. Because I don't. I have so many questions of my own. I could at least have told you that.' I don't take it out as far as I might. It has become a self-conscious exercise, carried out half in sympathy but half also in superstition, as if to placate the gods of fairy tale. And it's tiring swimming with one arm.

I leave him belly up on the face of the waters and turn back. Rupert is waiting for me, amused, in the shallows. 'All done?'

'All done.'

He rubs my back dry as I am trying to put on my shirt. 'You are really bad at drying yourself.'

'I know. I just don't really care. It's hot. I'll be dry in a minute and anyway we need to find someone else to ask – now that the fish is dead.'

I already have an idea who that might be. I have discovered, in my nightly searches, a fifteenth-century poet, Christine de Pizan, who wrote, among other things, *The Book of the City of Ladies*, in which she argued, against the grain of the times, for the value and necessity of women in society. In its pages, she built an imaginary city which she peopled with famous women from the past, mythical as well as real. She is forthright and insistent about women's quickness in learning, and talent for government, and she is sure that a just society is possible. It seems worth a try. We leave the little knot of significant people behind. D'Annunzio has found the couple from Manchester and is trying to muscle in between them. The Mummy and Mariette are hunting for shells.

At the van, I hold open the back door and settle Christine de Pizan on one of the benches. She sits bolt upright, clutching at the sides in alarm as Rupert lurches through a three-point turn. Her voice, anxious, with its precise French accent, floats forward. 'Is it quite safe?'

'One hundred per cent,' Rupert says emphatically, accelerating away.

A little further along the road we find Joan, striding out, in her armour, her face scarlet with heat. 'Get in!' I say as we slow up, level beside her. Christine's last poem was a paean to Joan of Arc, celebrating her victories, written just before her own death and Joan's capture by the English. Her face when Joan heaves in to sit beside her is that of a star-struck teen.

We are driving to Ferrara, to meet Ariosto, because he too is a poet and because, although I wouldn't say so to Christine, I think he understands better than anyone else how human life is designed as if it were a wood; both for good and for bad. He knows its paths which start open but lose their way in thickets. He knows its towering, light-shut stands in which you can go out of your mind, or round in circles. He knows its groves and streams and flowered glades, and he knows how, passing from one to the next, you can be so busy negotiating the trees that there is little hope ever of finding your way out, let alone seeing the wood as a whole.

'Why do you need to see a wood as a whole?' Rupert asks me, looking at his phone which is ringing again, and pressing 'ignore'.

'Well, because then I will know what it means and therefore how to be.' It seems so obvious. I can't believe he needs to ask.

598 _ MUSÉE DU LOUVRE
Le Sueur _ Clio, Euterpe et Thalie _

'Haven't we had this conversation before? Why do you keep thinking there is a meaning?'

'Because it keeps looking like there is one.'

Christine and Joan suck in their breath. It might be because they think there is God, or it might just be that Rupert is driving too fast. He *is* driving too fast. 'There isn't a meaning,' Rupert says, indicating left. 'There isn't a point and there isn't a solution. I've told you. Just be. Relax. Just enjoy it.'

'Well then, why bother with morality?'

'Who said I did?' Rupert likes to think he is amoral. If so, he is confusingly kind and ascetic and disciplined. I mentally list what I see as virtues. 'Everything I do, I do because I want to,' he says, guessing my thought. He believes only in temperament.

Joan is crossing herself as though she had fallen in with the devil. Christine leans forward and I hear her whisper, 'He is a pagan. He doesn't yet know.' She has confused him with an ancient Greek because of his profile. I hear her whisper, whisper, and then I hear 'looks like' and 'Hermes'. Well, he is a pagan but if he were Hermes he would also be a god, which would be a different problem. I think, disloyally, of Ariosto who was a man and who therefore had human worries. He will know what I mean. He has mapped it in his epic poem, *Orlando Furioso*: how people behave when they think they believe, how they try to be noble and try for society, how they look for meaning and go to war over it: their different gods and their fears and their muddled loves. Ariosto has been a diplomat and a courtier and a lover as well as a poet, and he knows wickedness and trickery and danger and temptation. He belongs to the world a hundred years later than Joan and Christine. He knows all the ins and outs. He will help.

The van feels very full. To begin with I keep anxiously turning round, thinking, as I did at the beginning of the trip, that the cupboard doors have come open, that everything has fallen out and is now clattering about in the back, but it is only the armour. Joan sits legs braced as if about to be thrown, frowning at the gear-stick. The little black cat who follows her has curled up in the space above the cab and Christine is lying flat on the bench opposite. I think she is praying.

Out on the road towards Mantua we slow down. There is an obstruction, a crowd of people dressed up in rainbow colours and mounted on horses. Rupert perks up – he thinks it may be a festival. At the head, a plump lady rides with her plain companion. We crane our heads forward to see. They are mounted on ambling horses, palfreys as they used to be called, their many and complicated clothes swathed and belted, their skirts wrapped round their feet and shoved into stirrups. Each of them must have on at least two dresses. The plain woman in black, with random gold rectangles like some anachronistic design from the Festival of Britain. The plump one in red, with ribbons holding up quantities of extra cloth: whole ruched-blinds-in-waiting at her shoulders, and festoons of white sheeting falling out of long, bell, oversleeves.

They are Elisabetta Gonzaga and Isabella d'Este, sisters-in-law and best friends. Self-educated intellectuals, they love each other's company and they often travel like this, out on a spree, while Isabella's Gonzaga husband Francesco is away. Lake Garda is the furthest they've ever been. It is so exciting. The scenery, the freedom, the conversations they have in the saddle. And while they talk, their horses step their smooth and outmoded gait. Left legs, right legs, left legs, right. The bells on the harness jingling, and the gold and embroidery flashing. Round them a hive of attendants buzz, all mounted, all also talking.

'They look fun,' Rupert says, slowing down. 'Let's see if they'd like to come along.'

'They are both notable,' I say to Christine. 'What do you think? They could easily be part of the City of Ladies.' Christine is leaning forward to see, something about her like an excited child. They would make a welcome addition. We will ask them.

Isabella, when we draw level, looks like the Mona Lisa. 'Is she the Mona Lisa?' No one in the back seems to know what I'm talking about. She has asked Leonardo to do her portrait, which he has so far only sketched out. I have seen it before, the velvet delicacy of Leonardo's red chalk drawing. He asked to draw her as he preferred, face on, but she refused. She wanted the portrait done in profile like an emperor on a classical medal. Still and sideways on like this, you can't really see how she is in life, her energy, her anxiety, her ability. Her one visible eye turned away from the viewer, as she wanted, as if purposely keeping her real self hidden. She looks powerful and placid, only half of which is true. Her heavy hair, which might be red or might be brown, is netted in a transparent veil. It looks like the kind of mat a swarm of bees makes draped from a tree. She appears matronly, when really she would so much like to be a match for that harpy, newly arrived in Mantua, the blonde Lucrezia Borgia who is everyone's fancy, including Isabella's husband Francesco. Horrible slender neck. Horrible mane of honey-coloured hair to tie men up in; horrible slender fingers for stroking and caressing, horrible eyes, horrible horrible biteable little red mouth.

'Why am I so short and so stout?' Isabella asks herself continually when she is alone, batting at her fat thighs with little furled-up fists. Three years after the Leonardo drawing and a year into her marriage to Isabella's brother, Lucrezia is already Francesco's mistress.

Isabella is stuck in a conversation with herself. 'No,' she thinks privately, 'the Leonardo drawing, however masterful, however like, won't do. It isn't quite right.' And out loud she says with a little, mock-modest laugh, 'I'm afraid I shall weary all Italy with my portraits.' Then after a while, and privately again, 'Who else? I want more. There isn't one pretty enough yet.' Lucrezia is so much the favourite. Isabella hates her. They will never be friends. She runs through her list of painters. She chooses another. Picking unconsciously at her palm with pudgy fingers while she waits for the result, while under her breath she says, 'Don't paint me old. Don't let him paint me old.' Lifting her chin like a bird on the look-out, to avoid the doubling.

So the kind, plain Elisabetta is a better friend to have, a good, kind friend and a loyal and faithful wife to her invalid, impotent husband, who is suffering from pellagra. She was offered the rare option of divorce because pellagra's symptoms are diarrhoea, dermatitis, dementia, photo-sensitivity and aggressiveness. She has refused. She will nurse him until his inevitable death. She has sad, slow-looking eyes and a fleshy face like a baker's wife. She is virtuous and clever. Lucrezia by comparison is a nothing, a trashy little harlot. She is just for bed.

Isabella and Elisabetta are at the centre of a vivid life of patronage, collecting and culture. Elisabetta is literary muse to Baldassare Castiglione, whose *Book of the Courtier*, published in 1528, is set in her company at the court of Urbino. It is a series of conversations about morality and nobility and it was one of the literary sensations of its time; published in six different languages and distributed throughout Europe. In England, in particular, it was instrumental in defining and developing that concept we think of as so peculiarly our own: the English gentleman.

'So to be an English gentleman you have to behave like a Renaissance Italian?' I am asking Rupert but it is Isabella who answers.

'But of course,' she says dismissively. 'Everyone knows; we are the pattern.'

'I should indeed like to read that,' Christine says, leaning her head out of the window.

'I believe it is widely available,' Isabella answers with a wave of her hand as though she really didn't have time.

'I have more than one copy,' Elisabetta's quiet voice offers, overlapping Isabella's. 'I would gladly give you one if you were to pass by Urbino on your travels—'

'Of course,' Isabella cuts in quickly, her voice a little too loud, 'borrow one of mine. I too have many. Have it. It will be my gift, should you pass by Mantua.'

Isabella, who is also present in the book, is perhaps less focused on virtue than her friend. Her interests are politics and literature and art. She is very aware of her public image and position, and she is busy buying and commissioning on a grand scale. Some have called her the first lady of the Renaissance. Mantegna, Titian, Perugino, Costa and Correggio all work to her commission and she is not afraid to dictate. 'The picture must be like this, exactly,' and she sends a little sketch, minutely detailed. 'The owl must be in the olive tree just so, and Cupid here and Venus there.' An army of fauns and satyrs must be coming out of the woods or over the hills. I would like Polyphemus and Mercury and Uncle Tom Cobley and all. 'You are free to reduce the figures, but do not add anything to them. Please be content with this arrangement.' While to another, she simply says, 'We are glad to hear that you are doing your utmost to finish our studiolo, so as not to be sent to prison. You can paint whatever you like inside the cupboards, as long as it is not anything ugly, because if it is, you will have to paint it all over again at your own expense.' She is, as I said, a kind of royalty.

'Oh, very,' she tells me, when I ask whether she knows Ariosto well, the van keeping pace with the horses. 'Since childhood more or less.' They are contemporaries, if you can be contemporary with royalty. She is his patron, as were two of her brothers, but she counts him as a friend. Have I read the *Furioso*? He said such flattering things. She directs me to Canto 29 in case I missed the reference – God's decree, after the death of the heroine Isabel, that in future every woman of that name 'shall be sublime of spirit, beautiful, noble, kind and wise; she shall achieve the mark of true virtue, and afford writers cause to celebrate the praiseworthy, illustrious name, so that Parnassus, Pindus and Helicon shall ever ring with the name of Isabel'.

Isabella, arm raised like an ancient bard, to sing her own praises, lets it fall. If we are going to Ariosto then they would love to join us. Indeed she will guide us. There is something commanding about her that, even had we wanted to, makes it impossible to refuse. I look at Rupert. Well, we were going to invite them anyway. Rupert shrugs.

We brake and they dismount, waiting at the little back door for someone to hand them into the van. Rupert with his cool courtesy comes round the side. Elisabetta steps up first, and then Isabella heaves herself on board. She is animated, full of information. 'Ariosto, let me tell you – he lives in a house he designed himself, a modest cottage with a big garden at the back giving onto a little elm wood beyond. We can all go together. How delightful.' We introduce Joan of Arc and Christine. 'A professional lady poet, well, what an oddity. How did you come to write verses for a living?'

Isabella is not quite comfortable. The van dips appreciably as she bundles herself and her quantity of fabric a little further up on the bench. Christine, who has made room for Isabella in the back, clutches again at the sides in anxiety. We should trim the ship, I think, but how to say so without offending anyone. Joan and Elisabetta tactfully change sides.

'My husband died, my captain, my true love, when I was only twenty-five,' Christine answers in her high, precise voice. Because it is true, her husband died suddenly, abroad, in an epidemic, and the news struck Christine to her knees. She has a pale and pinched face. She looks lost.

How a door can open, she is thinking, in a room where you are completely happy, and through its everyday aperture, at no notice, you are sucked out of childhood into something cold and adult. Although, even as it opened her sixth sense warned her; even before anything was said, something in her knew. Looking up, with a gripping at her heart, as the messenger came into the room.

'What?'

'In God's name what?'

Hurled into the howling horror of the world. Like being born a second time.

'The news, my lady... May God help us to understand his purpose.'

'What news? In God's name, what news?'

'I had to provide for my three children and for my ageing mother,' Christine says, hauling her mind back to the present, smoothing down her dress, missing out her free-fall into denial, the fevered hysteria of the days that followed. 'I often shivered under my fur-lined cloak and my fine surcoat that I couldn't refurbish but kept as nice as I could; and I spent many bad nights in my beautiful and well-arranged bed.' Which is the oddness of loss, when life takes the one thing that lit it and gave it meaning and tells you instead to busy yourself with money. Everything turned upside down.

The shame when the bailiffs came. The shame when men cheated her and her children of the money that was rightfully theirs, which they repeatedly did. The lies, the fraudulent claims. The double shame when she had to approach a friend for a loan. No, she couldn't go through that again. Isabella is watching her sharply. Joan and Elisabetta exchange glances.

'And did you never take another to husband?' Isabella asks.

'No, in truth. I loved him. I married scholarship after that.' She speaks simply, in staccato phrases. She has made a net of precision and restraint and economy of speech, behind which her agony, unseemly and all consuming, is held from view.

'That was a noble course to take.' Elisabetta, who passionately loves her sickly husband, looks at Christine through eyes that are heavy-lidded, pulled down at the corners as if not by gravity but by sorrow. Isabella, who is expansive, offers her hand in a gesture of surprising affection. It is a hard thing to survive in a world run by men and this she understands. 'At least,' she says, 'you didn't suffer the misery of infidelity.' Because of her whoring syphilitic husband. Because of the Borgia.

Friendship springs up like something quick between these three clever women: a little green thicket. 'I was always a stranger,' Christine says. 'I am Italian you know.'

'Well, of course.' Isabella claps her pudgy hands. There had to be something; she knew it all along. There was some hidden bond between them. 'That is it! From where?'

'From Venice. My father was a noble and renowned man, a philosopher, an alchemist, an astrologer.' Christine smiles. He had been called to the court of Charles V of France when she was a little girl of four. 'A great king,' Christine says, 'a good ruler who could have done much, only he died too soon.' And after him came the mad King, the one I saw lying on his bed, the one made of glass, under whose rule the whole of France, the body politic, splintered into shards. Civil war. 'I warned France in my writings.' Her voice rises. 'I begged it not to let its own blood, because what a waste, what a disgrace is a divided nation. And what in God's name,' Christine says with passion, 'are the consequences of civil war? Do you know?' She looks round at the assembled company. No one answers.

She had foreseen it all at the time, but of course you can stop war as little as you can stop weather. 'Famine is the consequence,' Christine says, her voice rising again. 'Famine, because of the inevitable plundering and destruction of all goods; non-cultivation of the fields which will cause rebellions by the people who are brutalized and robbed by the military, oppressed and pillaged from all sides; uprisings in the cities because of the outrageous taxes that will be levied on the citizens and inhabitants in order to raise money; and above all,' Christine says, 'the English who are waiting in the wings and will checkmate us if Fortune lets them.' She warned France, long before Joan of Arc. She warned it of the English King, the cruel and scarred Henry V biding his time, across the water. No one listened.

Sometimes the careful net of precision and restraint loosens and something of Christine's inner violence slips out. Her neck stretches like a bird's, its sinews humming with tension. 'Cry therefore, cry, ladies, maidens and women of France. Clap your hands with great cries, for the swords are already sharpened that will turn you into widows and rob you of your children.' She stops abruptly, bows her head in embarrassment, as if to say: I am forgetting myself.

'I fled Paris when it came,' she says, in a carefully neutral voice. 'I joined my daughter in a priory.'

Isabella is leaning forward. 'How interesting. I too have witnessed war but I couldn't retreat into a priory – I didn't. I like to govern, you see.' And she does. She had brilliantly brokered peace with Louis XII while her husband was for several years a prisoner of war. When he was released, bitter and outclassed in diplomacy, he left her. She paid a heavy price, but she doesn't mention his desertion. 'I couldn't do it every time,' she says instead. 'I was present at the sack of Rome when it happened. I turned over my house to two thousand refugees. My son was among the invading army.'

The women bend their heads in silence. War is always complicated.

But then there is Joan with her simplicity and her fanaticism and her vigorous practicality. She looks puzzled. She doesn't understand this sitting by, on the sidelines. She likes direct action not just manipulation. She likes fighting and she very much likes men, as companions, as equals. Fighting men, that is. She has been very brave in battle, wounded, steadfast, quick-witted. She clears her throat. 'Helping to raise a scaling ladder against a wall, I was hit by an arrow between neck and shoulder.' She puts her left hand up to indicate the place: 'Here.' It had gone in half a foot deep, so that the arrow came out of her back. She shows her scar, puckered into a purple pit, still livid. The ladies suck in their breath as if they were one body.

Even so, Joan tells them, she retired only as long as it took to stuff the wound with cotton wool soaked in olive oil and bacon fat, to stop the blood flow. Another time, she was knocked on the head by a rock thrown from the battlements. It ripped through the iconic white banner and dented her helmet, so that she reeled, her head full of stars, hanging at her horse's neck. And she was so talismanic that if she was hurt the army instantly lost heart, as it did then. The French line wavering in its advance, turning ragged, the men faltering. They were on the point of retreat, until she sat up again, wheeled her horse round to face the enemy. 'Amys, amys, sus! Sus! Notre Sire a condampné les Angloys.'

'Indeed,' Christine says, her back very straight, her legs braced against the corners, because she doesn't want to disappoint Joan. Joan is her heroine, France's long-awaited saviour. But she is an extreme person with an intense interior life, so she always goes a step further than expected. 'Indeed, we are all of us men, are we not?' She means it literally. She is so surprising. 'I was, in fact, transformed from a woman into a man, by Fortune who wanted it that way,' she says. No one seems to know how to answer. Is she serious? She is so oddly insistent. 'Fortune transformed me, my body and my face, completely into those of a natural man.' She says it several times in different ways, while we raise our eyebrows, try to understand. Is she a little mad? 'Then I became a man.' Her voice is precise, almost pedantic. 'I who was formerly a woman am now, in fact, a man.'

Looking at him sideways, I can see Rupert is in his element, a vanload of cracked women and one fashionably gender non-specific. Isabella, however, is clear. She is a ruler, a born negotiator. She neither needs nor wants to change her sex. 'Well,' she says after a while, 'Fortune it seems hasn't quite completed the job.' She is looking at Christine's thin body. 'Or are you hiding something?' Rupert's sudden laughter fills the van.

Christine doesn't answer. She looks out of the window, retreating to her in-between place, her place of neither one thing nor the other. If you are born to power you don't know how it is to fend for yourself, to turn the gender-order on its head, to try for your own money and keep your family; to face down all those wolfish men who take dominance for granted, and talk, and cheat, and assume you don't understand. Joan sits like a puzzled boy, her legs apart, her elbows on her knees, frowning, and Elisabetta Gonzaga has fallen asleep with her mouth a little open. 'Tell me,' Isabella says, changing the subject, because she also thinks of herself as a leader in fashion, 'this little pavilion you wear on your head?'

She means the great cloth horns that Christine wears, the white veil pinned up and falling in flags to either side. Christine de Pizan puts one hand up, recalled to herself. 'Oh this? It is a templar and veil. We think it modest not to show the hair.' So, still a woman after all.

'Yes indeed.' Isabella looks thoughtful. Now that would be part solution to the Borgia problem, those cascading tresses that her fingers can't stop twining.

Changing the subject in favour of my own obsessions, I twist round to the back. 'So, what is Ariosto like?' I ask Isabella.

'Un uomo simpatico, messer Ludovico: un po volubile, un po caparbio.' But he doesn't like being bound into service, not at all. 'He grumbles and mutters under duty. He wants to write, you see, but he must make diplomatic missions. He must keep his family, his brothers, including one who is deficient, and his sisters, his mother. He has been in the employ of my brother the Cardinal and my brother the Duke. Otherwise, about his two bastard boys, or his garden, he is sweetness itself. Now he has his cottage, built to his own design and his little wood of elm trees. He is happy there. Spesso sulle sue labbra guizza il sorriso. His smile is always flickering at his lips.'

Christine, who has been listening, looks up. The bondage of service. She knows about that. The lonely providing for dependents. Her face brightens. Perhaps she will enjoy meeting this man.

Ahead of us now Ferrara is rising out of the flat lands, a pink city, made of brick, with sometimes white stone facings. We pass between its grass-topped walls and to the right, there, its fantastic moated castle which belongs to Isabella's family, and out the other side into its wide cathedral square, where medieval-looking shops tuck in behind a spolia-ornamented arcade, while its population passes to and fro on bicycles. There are bicycles everywhere.

On one corner someone has even managed to turn one into a piano. He has extended the crossbar to fit a keyboard and he is sitting at it in a battered tail-coat, playing Mozart with concert style.

We weave, under Isabella's direction, through the narrow streets to where Ariosto lives. Rupert is gallant about her confusion of left with right, turning the wheel suddenly as she changes her mind, while she tinkles her annoying laugh for him and the traffic stalls, hooting with displeasure. This is the street. Here. At the end, or no, halfway up.

There is no little wood of elm trees now. Dutch elm disease gutted Europe of its elms in the twentieth century, and even if it hadn't the streets now stretch away behind, covering the place where the trees were rooted before. But the cottage is there, although it is not a cottage, more a small town house, with the wide-spaced proportions of the Renaissance.

'I have high expectations of this,' I say quietly to Rupert.

'You are nothing if not persistent.' He looks at me with his usual non-committal half smile. 'Try not to be too disappointed,' he says softly. But I've read the *Furioso*, he hasn't. So I know what it contains and this time I am sure we have come to the right place.

We pull up to the kerb and all pile out. And here he is, Ariosto, 'tall of person' by all accounts; 'of complexion melancholy, of colour like an olive, somewhat tawnie in the face'. The hair which was once so black and springing, now slipped like a hood to the back of his head and his bony crown bare.

The ladies go first, Isabella performing her introductions while I stand hesitating at the back. I have to gather myself to follow. I feel I have arrived at his door, the solid stone jambs, the worn step, as if cast up after shipwreck. If you are puzzled by the intractability of human nature, if you are bothered by the mess of life – your own, or anyone else's – then I can tell you, Ariosto is the person to turn to. Because he knows how the world is mixed, this man. He knows how the good, out of bodily need, often serves the bad. He knows how everyone has their quest and he knows how questing is at once both noble and absurd. He knows how you can journey for years only to end up where you started, how blind it is possible to be, how the thing you are looking for can change beyond recognition while staying the same. And he knows how a person can go mad in a wood.

Come in, come in; his eyebrows thin, his eye a little hollow but very full of life and very black. His teeth passing even and white, his cheeks but lean, his beard very thin, his shoulders square and well made but somewhat stooping from reading. 'The house is small,' Ariosto says, 'but suitable for me, clean, free of expenses and purchased solely with my own money.'

We follow through the door, Joan of Arc with her open-air stride, stepping over his threshold in her breastplate, followed closely by her little black cat. Ariosto blinks, his mouth for a moment open, and suddenly he holds his arms out to her in pleasure and surprise. 'My own, my Bradamant! How are you here?'

'No, no, you are mistaken, Messer Ludovico.' Isabella has her hand on Joan's shoulder. 'He thinks you are a character from his book. He thinks you are Bradamant, sister of Richardet, a female knight.'

'Is she French?' Joan asks Christine. Her mind is strictly nationalistic. Her face is pulled into a frown of honest concentration.

Christine scurries forward. 'This is Joan, the Maid of Orléans, who raised the siege, who freed France. Une fillette de seize ans. Is this not strange?' Christine has little sense of propriety. Any occasion will serve to extol her heroine so there is no stopping her. Ariosto listens with folded hands, his head cocked to one side. 'Joan, to whom weapons weigh nothing, as if she were bred to be a warrior, to carry arms and a standard, she is so strong and hardy. Never was there such strength, not in a hundred, not in a thousand men. And she's not finished yet!' Christine says in triumph. She has got her singing voice on, her head tilted back in its templar, her foot tapping her rhythms, one hand making a little sweep in the air as she ends.

I could tell her, because she doesn't know what happens. She died in her priory before Joan was captured. I could tell her about the stupidity of Joan's inquisitors day after day, standing round her in the cell. Did St Margaret speak to you in English? Joan's brisk response. Why should she speak in English when she is not on the English side? I could tell her about their insinuating questions, their prurience. The smut of their own minds rising as asphyxiating as the smoke that was to come. How did the angels look when they came to her? Did you touch them? How were they dressed? When what they mean is, was Michael naked? Because if he was naked, if you even thought his member, then you are damned for a witch. How the nonsense of it all, day after day, muddled her and wore her down.

I could tell Christine about the trickery of the English guards who took away the female dress she had been forced to adopt, emptied instead the banned doublet and hose on her bed so that in the morning there was no other option. 'Sirs, you know this is forbidden me: without fail, I will not accept it.' So she kept to her bed, because she'd been taken out and shown the scaffold in the square, the pyre waiting. I could tell Christine how in the end, when her need for the privy overwhelmed her, she got up and put on the banned clothes because there were no others – how the guards crowed in triumph that she had gone back on her word. And I could tell, poor country teenager, how they pounced on her, bound her, dragged her to the stake. The reality of death by burning. The ear-splitting screams. How loud she screamed, in horror, in pain; screamed continually, foaming, gagging, until the smoke choked her to death, after which she was burned twice more in quick succession to get rid of all remains. The black cat sunning itself on a step, cast in surprise onto the pyre, as was customary at the burning of a witch. Because all this really did happen.

Or I could tell Christine about Joan's fanaticism, her violence, her determination to crusade, her hatred of the unbeliever, all of which is also true. But I don't. I let her have her hero.

So we all go into the dark of Ariosto's stone house. Rupert slips away to photograph the entire contents of the town's archaeological museum. He will come and find us later. I nod at him when he tells me but I'm barely listening. 'You could be Bradamart,' Ariosto says to himself softly, in incredulity as Joan passes. He is still not sure whether he is in his head or out of it. I sympathize, thinking uneasily of BritAnnia on her stoop. Text and the world it represents are never as distinct as we think, just like Ariosto's twins, Bradamart and her brother Richardet, who are so identical that sometimes even their parents couldn't tell them apart.

'Perhaps it was a sister of mine you saw.' He is quoting his lines under his breath while looking at Joan's broad back passing into the dark of his hall, the bobbed hair swinging. 'One who wears armour and carries a sword at her side... one day she was wounded in the head and to heal her a servant of God cut her hair till it only half covered her ears.'

He notices that I'm watching him and he shakes his head as if to clear it. He smiles. 'It is sunny and hot. We will go into my garden. I will bring you refreshment and we can tell each other our stories.'

Christine, perched on a chair, begins. She describes her widowing and the threat of penury that followed hard on its heels. She describes how she found the strength to carry on. 'When I was left a widow at twenty-five, with three small children and my mother to provide for, my mourning was so intense and my eyes cried so much that Fortune took pity on my unhappiness. She came in my sleep and she touched me all over my body. She palpated and took in her hands each bodily part, I remember it well. Then the little ship of my family which had lost its captain struck a rock with great force. I awakened and felt myself completely transformed. I touched myself all over my body, like one completely bewildered. Then I felt myself much lighter than usual and I felt that my flesh was changed and strengthened and my voice much lowered, and my body harder and faster. Then I stood up easily. I found my heart strong and bold, which surprised me, but I felt that I had become a true man; and I was amazed at this strange adventure.'

Ariosto listens, sometimes head bowed, sometimes with his quick black eyes fixed on Christine. He doesn't look at all surprised. Christine's story could be something he'd written himself. 'So you made a living by your writings.' He sounds impressed. 'What did you write?'

'I wrote about chivalry and its effect on women. I wrote for women, you see, to make a place for them and so they might know what they are. In order to bolden them to their place in society. We are much needed, you see,' she says to Ariosto. He dips his head.

'Indeed.'

'I wrote *The Book of the City of Ladies*. You may have heard of it. I drew together all the ladies of note since time began and I created a city for them, defended against men, and I discussed female strengths and virtues, without the voices of men telling us what it is we are or should be.'

'I see,' Ariosto says. 'We have much in common.' He too had been bereaved, he tells us, at the same age as Christine. He was twenty-six, leading the life of his dreams, a poet and playwright at the court of the d'Estes, when his father's sudden death left him head of the family. He was one of ten children, so he had more dependents than she. He had been catapulted out of his carefree poet courtier's life into one of anxiety and responsibility. He had to take diplomatic work for the d'Estes that he didn't like. He had to travel and negotiate and administer often at risk of his health and sometimes at risk of his life. He only found happiness very late. 'You are our equals in everything,' he says softly to Christine. 'It is just that the world isn't built that way. I too have my City of Ladies – a little less virtuous than yours. Forgive me.' I can't tell if he is teasing. He offers to recite. It might entertain us. He loves to recite. He chooses carefully, so as not to offend Christine, his voice round and rhythmic in the autumn garden.

'The warriors made their way from the ship to the city, where they found haughty damsels, their dresses tucked up, riding through the streets and tilting at each other in the square like so many Amazons. Here no man was permitted to wear sword or spurs or any armour unless he went about in a band ten-strong. The remaining menfolk were all busy at their shuttles and spindles, their reels, combs and needles; they were dressed in feminine attire falling to their feet, which gave them a soft, languorous air. Some, though, were kept in chains to plough the land or watch the herds.'

I am looking at Christine's small mouth laughing.

Ariosto turning to me, with such courtesy, asks, 'And your story?' I had almost forgotten that I am here. Cough. Flush. My hair falling forward over my face so I have to hold it up as if it were a curtain, one hand to my head. It isn't a difficult question.

'I don't think I have a story. I mean, I haven't. I mean, not yet.' How many times is it possible to say what you mean when you mean nothing at all? I try a few more times. Nothing. 'I came to see you,' I tell him. 'I was hoping you would help. I was looking for something, for a way through life, you know? A direction, if not a meaning.' I look at him. 'I don't really know how to be.'

Isabella has sat too long and she has no difficulty being. 'Come,' she says to the others, 'let me show you the garden.'

Ariosto rises and bows. He gestures towards his garden with one long hand. 'Please, help yourselves. I must fetch something from the house.' Then he disappears into the cottage. When he returns, he hands me his book, his *Orlando Furioso*. It is dedicated to Isabella's pinch-faced brother the Cardinal. 'Don't take it too seriously,' he says, smiling. I don't know if he means his book, or my life.

'But how did you do it, Ariosto?' I can ask him straight now Isabella's gone. 'How did you work so long, in such a world, for someone you must have despised?' He doesn't answer. He just raises his long eyebrows, half smiles. He whispers something thoughtfully, half to himself, something I can't hear and I lean forward.

'Zerbin.'

'What did you say?'

'Zerbin; whose promise prevailed over his inclination.' A knight from the *Furioso*, whose adherence to the principles of chivalry and nobility was so literal that he ended up serving a murderess. 'Leaving his chosen path to accompany the wicked old woman with whom he was charged, and to whom he was as partial as to the pox or even to death itself.' Ariosto smiles at me. 'Zerbin,' he says again, as though that explained everything.

The lonely figure of Zerbin who is so shining an example of knightly honour but who, trapped in his promise to protect, is caught into protecting evil.

'So is it principle that is dangerous, or inflexibility, or both?'

Ariosto smiles and opens his hands. He is only showing things as they are. Talking to him I have the same feeling I have when I talk to Rupert, as if my thoughts were running on rails, while above and around me swallows flicker and cut arcs and switch direction in the sky.

Zerbin dies, untainted by the evil he serves, still a hero and a knight. I look at Ariosto. Was that his own hope? His midnight prayer? Don't let my service to these monstrous decadents count against me. Don't let their corruption spread and corrode my soul.

'There are many parallels, I'm sure,' Ariosto says, 'should you choose to look. Life is made like that. It can't help repeating its pattern.'

Even if you don't look, sometimes you can't help but hear, because the echoes are so loud they ring in your ears. Or so the pinch-faced Cardinal, for whom Ariosto wrote, was to find. He was no fool. He saw perfectly well the story at the centre of the *Furioso*, despite the apparent extravagant praise. When presented with the dedication, he thumbed the book through. 'Where did you find all this trash, Messer Ariosto?'

From you, my lord. From you, although he doesn't say so. He just bows his head in silence as he always does, a half smile on his lips. If the hat fits, my lord. He is remembering when the beauty, Isabella's nemesis, Lucrezia Borgia came to marry Alfonso d'Este, how she brought with her a cousin, Angela, whose little pursed mouth was so appealing. Who sat her horse just so, with the fat, gold-twined braid of her hair swinging lightly at her back, her blue eyes down. From you, Ariosto thinks to himself, in response to the Cardinal's question. That's perhaps where I got Orlando's madness from – from your lust for Angela. That great volcano of sexual rage that boiled and burned and branded; the damage you did in your disappointment. That's where I found my Orlando's love for Angelica the faithless, who chose instead of him a beautiful foreign boy.

It isn't true, of course. As he said to me, it's just an echo, just one of life's repeats, told to himself for private satisfaction, to redress the balance of a hated employment. Or it isn't wholly true. 'That's where I found his torment,' Ariosto says under his breath, 'his destruction, tearing up the forest, slaughtering men and animals, frenzied and debased.'

Because on later days, when Angela had been at the court for a while, the Cardinal, who was vowed to celibacy, was seen breathless in a passage, pressing up to her in a way she did not like. She had already made her choice, Giulio, the Cardinal's illegitimate brother. 'Giulio's eyes alone are worth the whole of you, Sr Cardinale,' Angela's answer to the lascivious request. He should know better. And the Cardinal, like Orlando in the inn, lying in his bed which stung him harder than a field of nettles. So he lay in wait, or had his men do so. And they sprung the pretty boy Giulio on his way back from hunting, beat him till his face was pulpy, slashed at his eyes with their knives and left him blind. Meanwhile, the Cardinal brought the court the news himself. 'Something terrible has happened to Giulio.' Watching Angela's face as he said it. 'He is alive.' He put his hands together as if in prayer, bowing his head, his eyes eating up Angela's shock. 'Praise God, he is alive, but his face… His eyes are worst affected… I just can't imagine how it happened.'

Handsome Giulio, who tried and failed to take revenge and whose death sentence was commuted only after Isabella intervened, was imprisoned in Ferrara castle for forty years and released only after the Cardinal's death. And here he comes now, an old man tapping along the streets of Ferrara in the outlandish clothes of forty years before, like someone in a fairy tale, woken out of time. He sees out of one eye these days, in blurs. He keeps stopping people in the street. He keeps asking courtierly about the beautiful women he knew before. 'There she is,' someone answers with a smirk, thumbing at someone across the street, that crone painted like a doll, limping on arthritic ankles. 'That's her.' Giulio doesn't hear or doesn't want to hear. He has been shut into his head so long, and he's too old now to get out.

Rupert returns, wandering into the garden. 'How was the museum?' I ask him.

'Same old same old.' He asks me if I am ready to leave, and I am.

'Anyone else coming?'

'Only me, I think.'

'Good,' he says, with emphasis.

So we leave everyone there, the poets of compromise, Christine de Pizan and Ariosto; Joan of Arc with her cat sunning itself on the lawn; Isabella d'Este and the shadowy, silent Elisabetta Gonzaga. Ariosto, pottering among his guests, telling them about his plants. He loves the idea of growing things, only he is so inquisitive; how is it exactly that they grow? What is happening down there in the dark? He stops mid-sentence – looks thoughtfully down at the tamped earth of his sowing lines. Are they doing it yet? He often spoils his seeds with impatience. Nature is too slow and he just can't wait. He keeps digging them up to see how they are getting on. Stooped now over a line of capers he had sown, that through some miracle speeded up their gestation enough to survive his probing. Watching them with such pleasure. 'I look at them every day. See how much they've grown?' he tells me when we go to say goodbye. I haven't the heart to tell him that from the look of the seedlings the capers have failed, that the green shoots are just common elder.

We go back into the bicycle-filled town. We make other ordinary stops: a museum, where there is an exhibition about the *Furioso*. 'I just want to glance at it,' I tell Rupert as I lead him in, 'we don't need to be long.' There's much more we want to see – we want to look at the d'Este castle, at the buildings old and new, the diamond palace, the post office which is Fascist in architecture. Listening to us talking, the lady behind the glass at the museum asks where we are from.

'England.'

She calls to her colleague. Her colleague wants to live in England. 'Some English people are here. Come and talk.' We laugh and shake our heads.

'Stay here,' we tell her. 'It's so nice. We are taking a break. You speak such good English already.'

She is pleased. She loves English but, she says, 'I can't speak French. Ma me mou mou ma mou. I can't speak a word of French.'

'French!' We roll our eyes, playing the nationality game, hiding our recent love. 'Who wants to speak French?'

We are quick, as I promised. We are soon out again, hurrying to the monumental post office, where we pay a parking fine and are told we may not photograph, as we have been, the fat columns, the green ceramic ornaments like palm trees, with the beautifully symmetrical clock-faces above them. Whatever the politics, the building is lovely. Ariostan sprezzatura; classicism with style and humour and none of the solemnity of neo-classicism. Before, I might have asked how this could be, that out of such brute stupidity could come such lightness, such loveliness, but now I have the *Furioso*, which is the book of the world as it is, where everything is so mixed and so constantly in flux as to be impossible to separate out into certainties. It suddenly hits me: is that it? Is the muddle in fact not the question at all but the answer? I have to know. 'Wait there,' I tell Rupert, running back the way we've come.

He turns round in surprise and then I hear him follow. 'What the… what are you doing?' he asks, catching me up. 'You can't just set off like that. Where are you going?'

I'm concentrating. I hope I can find it among these medieval streets, past the bicycle-piano, the afternoon light cleaving a path, as if prising these almost-touching buildings apart. 'I'm going back to Ariosto. Sorry. I have to ask something.'

'Well, you're going the wrong way,' he says. 'You should've turned left out of the square.' It's annoying, his sense of direction, my utter lack of one. I frown and we back-track. 'There,' he says, pointing down the street. 'I'll wait here.'

At the door again, ringing the old iron bell. Ariosto looks surprised to see me. 'I said I was leaving but I have just one more question. You see, this Fascist architecture, it is just like your seeds; the bad so often comes out of the good and vice versa. Does it matter, Ariosto?' I ask him, still clutching his book, still out of breath from running. 'Should I not like it then? Should I do something?'

He looks amused at my earnest breathlessness. Always threshing away, working my legs and arms, awkward, across the surface of my life. Always battering away at being. 'Spesso sulle sue labbra guizza il sorriso.' But he is kind. 'Keep going,' he says, so faithful to the world. 'Don't worry about the undertow. You will certainly fail, we all do, but it will only be for a while.' He opens out his bony hands, looks at his palms and turns them over. 'Beauty and absurdity both at once. That's how it is. What can I say? Ugliness and loveliness, whether inner or outer, intertwine and change places. Loveliness declines into ugliness. Bad blossoms into good. Keep trying.' He raises his eyes to me. 'Nothing lasts. Nothing at all.'

I miss him as we drive out from the city, my head resting against the passenger window. Ariosto's particular grace is acceptance. I think of his life of trials and sacrifices. I think of how he remained true to himself despite them, keeping his simple tastes even at the glittering court of the d'Estes. Because he was always frugal, avoiding strong wine, eating only plain food. Even now his favourite dish is a mess of turnips flavoured with vinegar and mustard, prepared not by a cook but by himself. He habitually gulps it down, standing up, as fast as he can manage, so he can get on with something else. He is happy. He has his love at last, Alessandra Benucci, and his two illegitimate boys. I will try not to bother him any more.

Heading for the border, we hit Trieste in darkness. We are staying just outside it, at a campsite up a steep hill, looking down over the Adriatic.

But there are so many hairpin bends in a long and impatient tail of traffic. There are no place signs. We go too far and have to turn. We hunch over a small geo position blue dot inching across a space that is neither road nor not road. Where are we? It seems to be moving even when we are standing still. Are we caught already in Ariosto's undertow? Is it traffic passing, or the sea that makes this swishing sound?

The Adriatic is silent. Lights winking on its surface.

When we finally arrive, having passed the turning several times, we walk out to look over the edge of the bluff. Standing anxious with this black expanse opening seemingly endless below. I have never been to the Balkans. I feel everything I know is behind me.

Luckily we are still ridiculous. In the morning, at a tiny crowded campsite, we eat our breakfast at our fold-out table, in front of the van. Porridge and bananas and coffee. It is still a ritual, passing each other the knife to slice it just so, a small tie to the life we left behind in England. The little metal coffee makers with their nipped-in waists stand like waiters at our sides, one each. Everyone who passes laughs. It is busy. People troop back and forth to the showers, carrying their towels and their toothbrushes. New families arrive, some Germans with a little girl back their caravan into their allotted plot. The woman unpacks quantities of Tupperware containers and a folding table like ours. The man unhitches. Looking up from her little boxes the wife screams – he has forgotten the brake and the caravan rolls with what looks like slow deliberation backwards, down the slope.

'Stop! Stop!' She looks suddenly wild, shouting at it as though it had a will of its own and could respond. It doesn't. It keeps going until it comes to a juddering halt against the barrier just over the lip of the hill. The barrier is bent but it holds. I imagine it making a different decision, the caravan hurtling on over the top, to drop like a meteorite onto the suburbs of Trieste.

We all go quietly back to our national breakfasts. Salami and cheese and gherkins. Little bread rolls and jam. Odd rusks. Hot chocolate. Porridge. 'Good appetite,' we say to each other formally, as though nothing had happened, while we read the news on mobile phones and tablets. Elsewhere, Italy is suffering earthquakes, the third in succession. There are before and after photographs of street corners in which solid things have turned to dust in the blink of an eye, crushed as though a caravan had landed on them from the sky. Nothing lasts, Ariosto, like you said. Nothing lasts.

Later, in town, I find I can't get my head around Trieste. Mainly because it isn't Ferrara. It is heavy with Austro-Hungarian entitlement, a laboured elegance. It seems faintly absurd in its self-importance, not least because, in its wedding-cake main square, people are competing in a walking race, lap after lap, solemnly snaking their hips and pumping their bent elbows, while urgent supporters hand them bottles of water. Otherwise it is another to-and-fro town, another occasional independent state, a nowhere as Jan Morris called it. Full of clever and despairing men washed up like driftwood, searching its streets for something solid to hold on to. Here is Freud at a dissection table, fanatically cutting up eels to solve their mystery of reproduction, eel after eel after eel; and as Ariosto predicted, failing. And here is Mann with his homosexuality buttoned under layer upon layer of wool, balancing his enormous moustaches and scribbling at *Buddenbrooks* in the Hôtel de Ville. Just over there is Stendhal as French consul, and Saba struggling with depression and opium, writing his shadow poetry and selling antiquarian books to James Joyce. And here, round the corner by the canal, is James Joyce himself, taking his daily walk in prickly Irish suitings, peering at Trieste through milk-bottle-bottom glasses. I feel too hot just looking at him but we decide to follow him anyhow, to see where he might go.

We trail him, away from the sea, along streets that are humming with traffic and we end up at a little glass-fronted coffee shop, Joyce's favourite. We have coffee and delicious tiny pastries, standing up at the counter, while he and Svevo take a table and have red wine and ideas for breakfast. I don't have the stomach for wine but I eavesdrop on their conversation. What was it they'd been discussing? Oh, just friendship, women, prostitution, diet… Then, exposed Corporation emergency dustbuckets, then the Roman Catholic Church, ecclesiastical celibacy, the Irish nation, Jesuit education, the study of medicine…

'We were talking about races and nationalities.'

'But do you know what a nation means?' says Joyce.

'A nation?' Svevo answers. 'A nation is the same people living in the same place.'

'By God then,' Joyce says, knocking back his breakfast wine, 'if that's so, I'm a nation for I'm living in the same place for the past five years.'

Yes, I think to myself, brilliant! That's probably about as certain as you can get. 'I am a nation.' Nothing is ever as precise as nonsense. There is something towering about Joyce that makes me afraid – his extravagance, with all the wandering, outsider status that extravagance at its most literal contains. Extravagant revolt, extravagant language and ideas, extravagant filth. I don't know what would happen if those bottle-bottom glasses turned their beam on me. So I don't address him directly. I just hope. Say something, I think, ducking my head over my coffee – say something to me about those big words that make us so unhappy: the nets of language, nationality and religion that you try to fly. Neither man says anything.

They just sit in rare silence, staring into their glasses of wine. 'Then, it isn't a race that makes a Jew,' says Svevo finally, 'it's life.'

Above the bar inside, rows of glass jars filled with coloured sweets stand hip to hip. Everything is made of wood or sugar. All the decorations, all the packaging, is from another time, Leone pastiglie, fine fruit jellies, absinthe. When exactly are we now? I have lost my bearings in the fourth dimension. I am disoriented but Joyce and Svevo, once started again, are not stopping. From the lesbianism of Sylvia Beach, to Joyce's love of Victorian drawing-room ballads, they have ricocheted towards d'Annunzio. His politics, they say, are unsympathetic but as a novelist Joyce rates him as high as Tolstoy. I don't want to join in. I couldn't even if I tried, and I don't agree about d'Annunzio. His novels have the same effect on me as eating all of the coloured contents of the café's glass jars at once. We leave the authors to their discussion.

I wonder about him as we pick our way back to the city centre. Joyce lived and died abroad, and in the thirty-seven years of his exile he returned home only three times. Why is it that all his writing is set in the country of his birth, its geography so precise that you can take a tour of his novels street by street? Why, having so comprehensively revolted against the tie of nationality, is it Joyce we think of when we think of Ireland? I press where I think my nationality might be located, like looking for a bruise. Do I feel more English for being abroad?

We do everything a tourist should. We go all the weary way up to the lovely cathedral on the city's heights, with its view and its stonework and its great rose window. We put money in the slot that illuminates the Byzantine mosaics so that the Apostles, who have stood there quietly for millennia, leap to life. They have carefully differentiated hair and beard styles, and they stand in sandals, amid flowers and date palms, against a gold ground. They look solemn despite their surroundings, holding up their fingers in coded gestures. Their job is dissemination, though their mouths are closed. I am trying to read their names so as to be able to address them, while beside us an English family, in pale, intolerable jerseys and with a guide, ask questions that are not connected to curiosity. 'We are getting information,' their faces shout in concentration. 'Look at how much we are improving ourselves.' The guide begins an answer but the English people are shouting too much internally to hear. 'The more information we have, the better we will be,' they shout. 'Don't ask us what we will do with it. We will display it in some form. Perhaps we will wear it, instead of our jerseys sometimes.'

Immediately I stop pressing for my Englishness. Rupert and I file out.

Is that all I am doing? Have I too improved? My tolerance levels certainly haven't. Have I got any information to wear instead of my own jersey? I would run some checks if I only knew how. Any information at all, any kind of enlightenment? What is there to pin all this to, that I might build something of my own, something bigger than a one-man nation perhaps, or something that I might share without prejudice with my compatriots, or with my race as a whole? If Ariosto were here I would ask him; must I accept this too, this conscientious self-improvement? Is this my lesson, that I belong with these people? Instead, Saba with his opium-medicated depression appears kindly at my shoulder. 'Trieste is melancholy. Try elsewhere,' he suggests. 'Trieste is a place where one asks oneself what am I here for? Where am I going? It isn't a place of answers.'

Crawling across the toenail of Slovenia, into Croatia, I push out into cultural ignorance. Now, like the Apostles silent in the dome of the church, I couldn't speak even if I wanted to. The language, like something with a burr in its throat, is a foreign fuzz of s's and z's. I recognize nothing, not even the alphabet, with its digraphs dz and lj and nj, its little hatted letters – its s's and c's in crowns and peaked caps, its curiously crossed d. I look down at the foreign money in my hand; the little notes so brightly coloured they look fake. Does this still work, Rolin? How much of this will it take to build me a hospital?

The coast, as we drive down, is picturesque. Little towns that try as I might I can't crack open for any meaning. In a campsite so vast that one man came to the shower block on a moped, there is an army of cheerful cleaners, none of them obviously saints, though you never know. They talk and sing loudly, advancing across the already pristine floor pushing ahead of them giant window squeegees. Every syllable alien. I have dropped like a stone into a pool of silence. I don't know how to greet them so I pass in a Tourette's twitch of gestures and smiles and comedy nodding. They stop mopping and their response is kind, restrained, perhaps a little pitying. I bolt myself into a cubicle. I don't feel I need to be any more naked than I already am. If I could, I would shower fully dressed.

Afterwards we lie in the van trying to sleep. Rupert manages. I don't. I listen instead to the mosquito who, in the high-pitched whine of her own language, is politely warning me of her intention. To take my mind off it I look in the dark at the postcards we have stuck on the cupboards, the Vix krater, Rolin's hospital, an illegitimate d'Este with a shaved forehead and an inbred chin, Joan and Mariette and a wood-cut print of Ariosto in profile. These are all information and enlightenment of sorts. This, I tell myself, is what I have taken away from all my looking. I love the postcards. They give me a stupid amount of pleasure. What I don't know is whether they please me for themselves, or for the fact of their appropriation – because we chose them. They are my own magpie nest that I have feathered and when I look at them I feel at home. Am I just looking at a reflection of my edited self? Or a reflection of the improved self I would like? The night advances. It is darker and darker. I can only see the outline of the cupboards now. Instead, the pale jerseys of the English tourists glimmer in my mind and I am found out. They are the postcards I deliberately didn't choose.

I must have dozed off, for when I awake d'Annunzio is lisping at my ear. He is talking about his house, that nightmare junkshop collection of dark clutter under damask ceilings. 'When I ask it a question,' he says, 'it answers in my language. It is me.'

'Don't tell me that. This is different. I don't want to hear,' I hiss back at him, careful not to wake Rupert. But am I caught after all – not even as Joyce saw it, in the nets of nationality or religion, but by something even smaller, even more culturally local – trapped in myself? Like a bird against a pane of glass, beating my brains out against the invisible limitations of personality. I keep thinking I can see outside. I keep thinking outside is where I belong. To come all this way just to find that I'm dressed in a pale jersey, exactly where I was when I started, is one thing, but please, someone, tell me d'Annunzio is not in here too. Tell me he's on the outside.

'I'm lost,' I say to Rupert.

'I know,' he replies. 'I'm trying to help.'

'I mean, I don't know where we are, or where we are going. I seem to have got to the end of what I know.'

'Well,' he says, 'we are going back, like I told you. We are going back to the beginning, via Thrace, which in ancient times was sometimes just called Europe. We'll have a look at its treasure because that's unmissable. And then, I admit, I'm going home.'

'Actual or spiritual?'

'Spiritual, of course.'

'To Greece, then.'

'To Greece. Via the Balkans.'

We scoot across Croatia to get to Bosnia. We stop at Rovinj to look around, to walk up to the campanile in the town built by Italians. It is picture pretty. On the quay fishermen are unloading in a snowstorm of gulls. Small boats stacked with coloured crates, in a more ordered version of the coloured buildings that the town has heaped right to the sea's edge. Four men, whose movements are so smooth they might have mechanized themselves, are unloading. Giant yellow trousers pulled up under their armpits and held up with braces. Faces as if made of stone. They are fishermen but everything here seems to be for show. As if they were part of a performance, a circle of people watch and take photographs. Rupert, shutter clicking, says, 'I love a human chain,' and the men go on as if we were see-through, or not even there.

Some of us make videos because it is impressively smooth and economical, their action, and because, beyond the simple task of unloading, they are performing an important function. They are making this place, which is otherwise just for tourists, into somewhere that is both real and wholesome. They are proof of a quaint and enduring way of life, battling our old enemies the elements, in a way that makes us healthy again, sends us back to our screens and our controlled atmosphere cleansed and rooted. We move off slowly, checking our images are true, stored safely for later, so at any time we can pull them out, see that the umbilical cord is still there, still connected to life, to the place of real and innocent endeavour, where at least in some countries, our relationship with the world we live in is direct and unmediated.

At the top of the town's hill is another cathedral. Huge, smelling of stone and incense. In we go, and out again, among a crowd of Koreans in fancy hats, all of us respectfully looking. In the piazza outside, the Koreans pose for selfies, standing with their backs to the thing they came to see, because as d'Annunzio has told me, what we are looking at is, in the end, only ourselves. And because how else can we know that where we are living is the world?

On the way down again, a sleekly healthy cat is eating its breakfast on a doorstep, one small silver fish at a time. It sits a little apart from the packet, as if out of politeness, removing each fish fastidiously from a white-paper wrapper containing about ten others. It is unhurried, not at all greedy, civilized. 'Good morning,' I say to it, in Italian, because this is a bilingual town. It glances at me but doesn't answer. I go on down the quaint steep cobbled street, past the quaint little houses, painted dolly-mixture colours, with their flowering plants and their shutters. And all this prettiness, which was built for living and working and dying in, is now for spare time, for looking at, to Instagram as proof of our presence in the world. The fishermen have finished unloading and gone home. At the empty quay, a thin man with a grey face, his whiskers stained yellow with nicotine, inches slowly by, sucking at a cigarette and I look at him too. If only Rolin and the carpione were here I would tell them things are different from how they thought. There has been another prepositional shift. We live neither in nor off the world now. We have distanced ourselves even further; mostly these days, in designated places, we also live *at* it.

We stop again at Pula to buy food and I spot Joyce, younger but still teaching English, pacing among the Roman ruins. He is unhappy. He wants to go back to Trieste. The bottle-bottom glasses fix me like headlamps. 'Istria,' he tells me, 'is a long boring place wedged into the Adriatic peopled by ignorant Slavs who wear little red caps and colossal breeches.' As expected I don't know what to say in response. He is so scathing, so prickly in his tweed. I am afraid of his scorn. I open and shut my mouth.

'I'm sorry,' I start to say, intoning it as a question. Behind me Rupert sounds the van's horn – he is impatient to get going.

We pass through Rijeka. We would stop but we can't if we want to reach Bosnia by nightfall. Inching out of the town, in traffic, I see d'Annunzio for the last time, hysterical in uniform, shouting from a platform at a crowd of supporters. He has taken the town in a bloodless coup, claimed it for Italy, and if Italy won't acknowledge it, then he and its part-Italian population will declare themselves independent. The Free State of Fiume; a one-city nation.

'In today's crazy and cowardly world,' he shouts, chin skyward, chest out, 'there is a sign of liberty, in this crazy and cowardly world there is an immaculate thing: Fiume. There is only one truth: and that is Fiume; there is only one love: and that is Fiume! Fiume is the brilliant lighthouse, the light that shines so bright amidst the sea of perfidy.'

'Let's come back some other time,' Rupert says, accelerating away. I smile at him. He never told me he didn't like d'Annunzio either. It's the first time I've heard him position himself somewhere unequivocal.

We reach the border and press on through darkness. There is only one campsite so we head for that, tipping off the road when we find it, into what seems to be a small tussocky field. Below but unseen, the sound of a river rushing its own stones. We put on a lot more clothes and go to sleep.

In the morning there is ice on the inside of the van so we can't see out. I open the door to find we are in a field so steeply sloping that it might be trying to tip us off. A small tin shed with a stick in a metal hoop instead of a lock houses a squatting-loo. To its left a metal draining board, with just a hole where the sink should be, balances itself on scaffolding poles, braced against the field's crazy tilt. It has a garden hose and one tap containing frostbite. Several large reels that once held cable of some kind have been stood on one end as makeshift tables. Otherwise there are willows and apple trees and bare-branched walnuts. In all the fields there are haystacks, poles poking out of their tops, and at the foot of the field, in the valley bottom, a river flashes. We totter down the incline to find, at the riverbank, what might have once been a train carriage, bright yellow and with a little ladder up to a padlocked door at one end. On the door, there is a sign which has Reception written on it in large letters, but there is no one in sight. Reception is not receiving.

Later, as we are brushing our teeth, a small man in wellington boots and a beanie cap arrives with a tray. He is the campsite owner and he has brought us breakfast. Plum brandy in small tumblers and a delicious kind of sweet spiced apple tea with large chunks of cooked apple in the bottom. We drink all the tea and eat up the apple while our friend watches. Rupert refuses the brandy. 'You drink,' our host insists. 'Madam drive.' I drink my brandy and then, for politeness' sake, Rupert's, while our host writes his name and email address on a piece of paper. 'Please tell all your friends,' he says. Then he looks thoughtfully at the paper where he has written his name in capital letters. 'NEDO'. After a while, in front of it, he puts a small 'Mr'.

All the way to Sarajevo, just as I found at Rovinj, I am *at* the world. A river, the Vrbas, propped on one elbow in the mountains mid-country, has lain itself down the length of our journey, extending its waters north, to the Sava, to the Danube, to the Black Sea. It casts its glitter upwards as it unrolls, so that every leaf on every tree flutters to catch it. Everything, even the rooted things, expressing the wish to follow, glinting, glancing. Take us with you to the Black Sea. And looking at it, I too suddenly want to go backwards.

Has there ever been such a river in the world before? Every now and then we get out to look at it, wide and shining, shallow over stones and then tucking itself round in foam, before gathering into apparent stillness in pools. But we resist its siren-call, and go onwards with wooded mountains either side, sometimes steep, impassable crags, sometimes ravines. So thickly and variously wooded; alder, willow, poplar, apple, plum, hazel, field-maple, walnut. Small rounded fields, tethered cows. Vines, fields full of giant cabbages. Washing, wood chopping, maize harvesting. Everywhere, even on balconies, there are wood-stacks. The air smells of wood-smoke. A better place to come for your looking all in all, because here life is lived all year round.

We make slow progress because often ahead of us is a ride-on rotavator, with a trailer attached. Resigned-looking people sit in the back being carried into towns which still, or also, smell of wood-smoke. Holes in the road, dust, shops where it isn't immediately obvious what they are selling, and against the sky, pencil-point, white minarets because, under the Ottomans, the Bosnians gave up the brand of Christianity that was particular only to them and converted to Islam. Several times, in different towns there are people pushing wheelbarrows down the street. Wood-chippings heaped in one. Shopping in another. Then out of town again the far side, still by the river. And all around, the wood-clad hills are hazed with light like the pile on a pelt, as though in a hurry the mountains had thrown a fur cape about their own shoulders on their way to the horizon.

Why is Bosnia so beautiful? Maybe it is the hardship of the night, or the blue-sky, clean-swept light, or the double-plum-brandy breakfast, or the fact that it feels unknown. I can feel myself starting to soar, the purple phrases rising unstoppable. As if out of the corner of my mind's eye I catch sight of Chekhov. I've been reading his collected letters. He has a mild but penetrating look, the same as in the picture on the book's cover. 'Sorry,' I whisper. I know he would disapprove. I damp my enthusiasm. I am trying with pained self-consciousness to avoid the 'deadly dose of lyricism' he criticized in his brother's writing. Beech, hornbeam, acacia. The river, dammed now at intervals for electricity and emerging from a narrow tunnel through rough-cut rock, giant pylons on the heights the other side, and even they look good. Little scratchings of man on this un-man-made place. The river still alongside. Light raking down across the tops of the gorges in long fuzzed shafts. Police sitting motionless at the roadside, smoking out great clouds, and behind them still these long, lit, steeps with every leaf alight.

'I'm sorry, Chekhov. I can't help myself.'

We have been trying to reach some friends of my brother, Bosnians living in Sarajevo, but when we ring, no one answers. 'Better not try again,' I say to Rupert. 'It might not be convenient. We've never met.' And for once he agrees. So we settle instead into an empty campsite on the edge of town and luxuriate in its hot-water taps, trotting back and forth carrying saucepans as buckets, swabbing the tiny spaces of the van. Across the gravel to the stainless steel sinks. Load all the dirty crockery into a bag. Go back for the washing-up brush. On the way back, turn the bag inside out. Load it all into the clean side, having vaguely washed the dirty side first. Stow it. Collapse the collapsible strainer. Put the plates on top. Put the frying pan on top of the plates. Put the saucepan in the frying pan. Put the bowls in the saucepan. Wedge the cups into corners. Everything tightly tessellated.

My brother's friend rings. Bang head on cupboard standing up to answer the phone. A gentle, educated voice that I don't know. He and his wife insist, it says. 'I'm afraid we absolutely insist that you stay with us tonight.'

He comes to fetch us so we don't get lost trying to find his house. He is a tall man in a sheepskin jacket, with a quiet, thoughtful face. 'And another thing,' Chekhov says, 'don't put the names of people you actually know into your stories. It's bad form: first, it's overfamiliar, and second, your friends lose respect for the printed word.'

'Alright, Chekhov, I won't.' My brother's friend.

At Sarajevo, everywhere you look, there are visible reminders of war, buildings still pitted with bullet holes, star-burst shell-marks in the pavement, painted red to indicate fatality. Sarajevo's Roses, as they are known. There are mosques and churches. There is a tram system whose cars have turn-of-the-century polished wood interiors, the Austrian Empire trying out for Vienna. There is a blue glass tower twisting itself skyward, and neon everywhere, on the shot-pitted blocks, on the modern glass.

But it feels like a place that is trying to get up from something, still stunned maybe, a ringing in its ears, held in anxious suspension. Damaged inside and out, as we learn, its three ethnic communities are locked in grim balance: Bosniak, Bosnian Serb and Croat, now culturally defined as Muslim, Orthodox Christian and Catholic respectively. The beautiful mix of the city, which looks the product of tolerance, is, since the war, a desperate stasis. Nothing, not even the design of the flag it should fly, can be agreed on; what one group suggests the others will resist or veto. So the UN High Representative decides. 'Here, if you can't agree. Use this one.'

This is explained to us over supper by my brother's friend. He was seventeen when war broke out. On the threshold of life, hoping to travel, to go to university. He refused at first to believe it – someone surely would not allow this to happen, that a country should turn in on itself, eat itself from the inside out. He waited. And it happened.

Sarajevo, where he lived, as he still does, was subjected to the longest siege in the history of modern warfare, 1,425 days. Surrounded by the Serb army, the city was a sitting duck for the artillery trained on it on all sides, raining down from the encircling mountains. There was continual shelling. Snipers covering some of the main thoroughfares and crossroads daily killed both military and civilians. Water, electricity, food and medical supplies were cut off and the river was poisoned.

So, imagine, these precious years, the ones that we love to waste in posturing and experimentation, snatched from you, and instead the scar of permanent change stitched into your centre. Imagine the senseless anger forced on you, as if your insides had been swapped for something burning, some permanent hot coals that are not you but that you can't get rid of because what *was* you is lost, and they are now all that you have. Imagine struggling afterwards for tolerance, for rationality. Imagine the distance between those who have had to act and those who haven't.

I almost daren't open my mouth.

My brother's friend has a quietness about him, an authority of experience. He is not sanguine. 'Europe,' he says, 'is a noble idea that was built on the premise of peace, which would grow naturally out of economic interdependence.' He speaks with great urgency. 'Peace is its goal. What will happen if it comes apart? I can tell you,' he says, 'if there was war in Europe, or globally, on Wednesday, there would be war here on Tuesday. That's a fact.'

Hear that, you Eustaces? It is war we should keep in mind, not economic prosperity. 'On the contrary,' Eustace, materializing briefly, says, 'they are

chicken and egg.' He reaches across me to help himself to a piece of burek. 'Good luck deciding which came first.'

Whether Eustace is right or not, it is also a fact that war, which we spend so much time and effort commemorating, is impossible to keep really in mind. Or rather it is easy to keep in mind, easy to remember or horrify ourselves with imagining, but in the end impossible to believe in. It is always never going to happen to us. It is too stupid, too wasteful, too nonsensical. We are always too liberal, too civilized to make that mistake. So we do nothing and then, again, it comes ravening upon us. What casual, self-indulgent, empty asses we are.

At our friend's recommendation we go into the city the following morning with a list of sights to see. We visit the tunnel that kept Sarajevo alive, dug round the clock from both ends in eight-hour shifts and along which, at first on doubled backs and later in carts on a railway track, supplies could be brought in and refugees could make their way out, often waist deep in water. We meet our friend for a traditional cebap lunch in the market. He has taken the afternoon off to show us round. 'They say it tastes better if you eat it with your fingers,' he says, 'but I've tried both and it tastes no different.'

We walk along by the river. We look. We walk by the bridges. We stand at the street corner where the open-topped car stalled, having taken a wrong turn, the driver looking down at the wheel in the embarrassment of doing his job badly, grinding at the gears and inwardly cursing. And on the opposite pavement the educated son of impoverished peasant parents, short, barely more than a boy, with nationalist ideals burning in his eyes, steps up to the car and coldly shoots its occupants almost point-blank.

What have you done, Gavrilo Princip?

But he doesn't either care or hear. He is sure someone is to blame, for his father's untenable poverty, a third of his little income gulped down by the landowner every year, because economic prosperity hadn't been kept in mind, or hadn't been kept in mind for all. Someone is to blame for Austro-Hungarian oppression, for his own shortness of stature, for his sickliness. Someone must be to blame for all this.

So, after he was expelled from school for demonstrating against the Empire, he crossed into Serbia to volunteer for the Black Hand Gang, but he was told he was too weak. He was too small. He was sent away. He crossed back again and took himself to Vranje where he trained in the use of bombs and guns and blades. Radicalized. And he stood in the throng with his gang members, lining the streets when the Archduke Franz Ferdinand passed, and although he missed his first opportunity because of the crowds and the speed of the passing car, he didn't miss his second.

'I am a Yugoslav nationalist, aiming for the unification of all Yugoslavs, and I do not care what form of state, but it must be free from Austria.'

'But what have you done?' I scream in his face; for the unthinking desperation of the violent act; for all violent acts; for my brother's friend whose youth was taken, for all the youths gone, all the waste and misery and for the stain of remembered suffering which won't go away. 'What have you done? This could never be an answer. Look, you have started the First World War. You have tipped everything into chaos. Can't you see? Have you any idea of the figures, the casualties? In your own country alone fifty-seven per cent of the male population will die, in terrible conditions. You raise your hand like that, you squeeze the cold metal trigger, and what comes out of that tiny barrel is not a bullet but a little metal egg which will hatch a monster that will gorge on men for the next four years without stopping.' I look round for support. 'Tell him, Dunant, Christine. Tell him, Ariosto, tell him what war is.' I don't know where to turn in this moment of convulsion, when everything seems to hold its breath and the man in the car jerks with the impact because something has entered his neck with such force that his life is gurgling out of him faster than he can think, as he puts his surprised hand to the place, too late. 'Tell him, Ariosto!'

But Ariosto, who has written such violence it might be a modern film, can't tell him because he himself has dressed it up in armour and in ironic glamour. Ariosto accepts. He shrugs. He is sorry for me. This is how we are, his deep eyes say as he turns to go back to his garden. This is how we all are, and now in the flat fields of France, already the grass is puckering, spouting mud and village boys and stones up into the patient sky. And even if Ariosto could tell him, Princip wouldn't hear. He has swallowed a cyanide pill that won't work and he's trying to turn the pistol on himself. He has done what he came to do and now he is ready to die. And if a man is ready to sacrifice the only thing he has, then how despairing is he of change by other means? What can you really do?

Sarajevo inside its ring of mountains, like the eye of something; a storm perhaps, a whirlpool. I have the brief impression I am looking into the heart of the matter, and the matter is bitter and conflicted, in particular when it looks most beautiful.

We haven't finished looking. We look at the library which was burned to the ground together with all its contents, perhaps on purpose, in the Bosnian war. We look at the place in the middle of the market where Austria-Hungary and the Ottoman Empire meet like a confluence of rivers, a church visible in one direction, a mosque in the other, and which looks, whatever the reality, such an attractive, such a possible mingling. We walk all the way down to the archaeological museum and we look at the classical remains and we look in the falling dusk at the curious stećci, the medieval tombs and standing stones of Bosnian Christianity, the fat crescent moons and ball stars, the deer, the vine leaves, the men on horseback with hands raised to the sky. I don't know what any of it means.

'Are you still hoping for meaning?' Rupert asks in the museum's courtyard garden, among the tombs, but he asks it gently. 'Even after all I've shown you, all you've seen?' He gestures widely, sweeping his open palm so that it gleams, silvery, under the moon. I can't answer. I just look at him dumbly in the moonlight. 'Look how lovely it is,' he says. 'Look at these stones we don't understand. They are lovely in their mystery. They mean something – everything – for a while, and then they pass and something else takes their place. Isn't that enough?'

'So things will never get better?'

'How can they?' Rupert says. He takes me softly in his arms. I think he means it both ways.

We walk back and buy supper and drink tea in the Han, and we buy a piece of carpet to hang in the van, mainly because Sarajevo is a strong place that leaves its mark on you and, if things are all there is, we want to have something to take with us.

We are going to Višegrad for the night, before crossing Serbia into Bulgaria. Saying goodbye to our friend and his family, his eleven-year-old daughter, an intelligent, self-possessed, trilingual child, invites me to walk her rabbit round the garden. We put it into a little blue harness and take it out. Her parents built this house, she tells me, to their own design. The process was an intolerable boredom. I would like to build myself a house, I tell her. She shakes her head. That would be a mistake. She had despaired of her parents at the time. It was as if they had gone mad.

Instead I show her our van. She wouldn't mind living in a van but it would have to have everything her house has, including her bedroom. Above us, further up the hill, is the house of her great-grandfather and, to one side, the house of her great-uncle. The rabbit hops about. I know she went to school in Spain for a while but how does she speak such perfect English? 'I learned it off YouTube.' She is solemn and confiding. She would like to go to America. She would like to go to London because it has patterned Sellotape. She would like us not to leave. Why don't we stay one more night? I explain we are heading for a boat that only goes once a week. If we delay we will miss it. We need to be across Serbia by the day after tomorrow. The girl looks up at me. She says in a whisper of inherited fear, shaking her head, 'Don't stay there.' She has no first-hand experience of war, she only knows that there was once an enemy.

For a long time afterwards I could hear her hushed little voice, while her rabbit hopped about on its string, innocent on the grass.

It is raining. The Drina, unlike the Vrbas, is opaque, wide, green-grey and sliding. It looks treacherous, its surface boiled with currents that are fast even though it looks slow. As if it had something to hide, or as if separate things had been forced into combination: a solution, in every sense.

I have mixed everything up in my waters, it might say. You can't tell things apart any more. You can't tell nationality, or religion. You can't tell what belongs to whom or who belongs to what. You can't tell what came first, or why. I am carrying it all away, swirled together, to spill it out into the Sava, which will spill into the Danube, which will spill into the Black Sea. Just like the Vrbas. It is better that way.

Rivers don't actually say anything, of course, so I look instead at the bridge. Such a perfect design, each one of its eleven arches completing itself in reflection, its triangle points making diamonds; a slight raise at its centre, where there is a stone sofa projecting above the water. This is where the characters in Ivo Andrić's novel of the bridge, through all its ages, sit and talk. Today, since it is raining, no one is sitting. Instead, little umbrellas are crossing quickly, back and forth, angled against the drops. There are ducks on the flats below and mist on the heights. On the far bank, the rubble and clutter of modern houses tips down the slope and gathers in a heap at the shore; undistinguished-looking, painted stucco or thin modern brick, built for speed and economy. Trash when you compare it with this bridge, which has stood in the flow for six hundred years and which, when you look down at the insistence and the weight of the water against it, has such strength and, when you look at it from afar, has such airy elegance. It is an anomaly, something of such grandeur for an apparently out of the way place.

But if you do look down at these opaque and tricky waters, you can see, balanced in a basket on the back of a donkey, the child whose idea the bridge originally was, being ferried across in similar weather. Taken by the Ottomans for a Janissary, the elite corps of the Sultan's army, he is a little piece of flotsam in the great tide of an empire's will. As the ferry swings in the current, his mother, who has nothing to do with empires, turns her agonized voice into a rasp, and files herself pointlessly and exhaustively down until there is only dust on the bank he is leaving behind.

In Turkey, when he gets there, the child, along with other Christians similarly taken, is forced to convert to Islam. He is made to change his language. He is deprived of family, of country, of context, but he is educated; he is given a chance, which he is quick to take. At the end of his life, as Grand Vizier, he controls the whole of the Ottoman Empire himself. So was the taking of him bad, or good?

Either way, it was he, the Grand Vizier, who, with everything at his fingertips and money beyond the dreams of avarice, remembered that a nowhere place could use a bridge and had the leading architect of the day design one. 'Start it there. On the far bank, just by that heap of dust,' he would have ordered, suddenly remembering his mother. His own people can be used, as forced labour, to build it because to these kind of men, where progress is concerned or the building of everlasting monuments, human life, like his own for instance, counts for nothing. It is just materials, like the stone. 'Use it, I say. I don't care how. I won't be there to see. Just get the job done.'

Or did he say, 'Treat them properly. Pay them their wage,' which whatever petty official was put in charge, didn't, pocketing the money and starving and beating the workers? Whose fault is it when things go wrong? I will ask this man, Radisav, from Andrić's novel *The Bridge on the Drina*, which version is correct. Only, when he turns stiffly round, I see that he can't. He has been impaled for insurrection on a sharpened stake, driven in through his anus and out through the top of his back at the corrupt official's request. His body has been made to accommodate a tree; and if so, who dreamed it up: the Empire, or the individual, or the novelist? Because these things happen over and over again, and I am wondering what button I would have to press to flick myself into base brutality. I mean, is the monster outside, in the place, or the culture, or the particular oppressive circumstance, or is it inborn? Ariosto? Someone? So I know?

Because listen on this bank for a moment and you'll hear, not even that long ago, another woman, not the Vizier's mother this time, sobbing in the scrubland for her son, buried hastily among the bushes.

'Oh. Oh. Oh. You don't deserve to lie here. In all these thorns. Oh my son. I didn't want this to happen to you.'

She is scrabbling weeds away from a makeshift grave with muddied fingers. And, at the same time as her boy was killed, her husband, a bony and exhausted man, in a column of others like himself, was on the run in his own country. Did he stop for some reason? Caught short, maybe, or to tie up his shoe, so he lost the others? Because he got taken, and now he stands gulping, dry-mouthed with the enemy's hand on his shoulder. And now, at the enemy's insistence he puts his own hand to his mouth, to call his younger son down from hiding.

'Come down,' he calls. 'I'm here. You don't have to be afraid.' He calls his name again and again and I can't hear in the call whether there is some coded desperation that warns the boy off. I hope there is but I can't tell. Some terror that the boy flat in the undergrowth higher up can hear. 'Come down.' (Don't come.) 'Don't be afraid.' (They will slit your throat. They will tie your hands with wire, young as you are, and shoot you in the back. They will bulldoze you into a mass grave and call themselves war heroes.)

I can't tell whether the bony and exhausted father knows or not what will happen. And a person with fine features passes, a civilian in late middle age, whose dignity prints briefly and eradicably as he is hustled by a gunman into a truck. 'Are you afraid?' they ask him. He doesn't answer at first and then he half turns, in a soft voice.

'Of course I am afraid.'

Someone will stop this before it happens, I think, just as my brother's friend did when it first broke out, because there is all that history from which we are supposed to have learned. We have all these mechanisms in place now, the UN, the EU, the Council of Europe, Amnesty, NATO. It isn't the Middle Ages. We have documented our most recent brutalities, Stalin's purges, the Armenian genocide, the Roma, the Holocaust, Pol Pot, Rwanda. We have frozen them into the neutrality and objectivity of history so that we can look carefully at what happened, so that we can move on.

So tell me, as time goes forward, why is there never on? Why is there always only back?

No one puts a stop to it. In Srebrenica, the besieged town from which these men were escaping, people are now starving. The enemy is pressing closer. Don't worry, the UN has said, you are protected by us. You are our first created safe zone so we will not let you suffer. Only it isn't happening. There is no evidence of protection. 'Help us,' the commander wires to central control, whatever that is. 'We need airstrikes. We need reinforcements.' Altogether elsewhere, people, highly qualified, in offices with the acronyms printed across their letterheads, haver over the right thing to do. They are caught in the tragedy of the measured response to imminent brutality. 'Oh no, they wouldn't,' they say, in answer to their dread. 'They couldn't do that. That won't happen.' The requests for help are ignored or denied. 'Play for time,' they say to each other. 'Until we know.'

'I'm afraid the wrong piece of paper has been used to file the request,' someone who doesn't want to be held responsible answers, in the desperate hope that the right thing to do will suddenly become clear. Meanwhile, anxious boys in blue berets, whose war it isn't, gulp at their Adam's apples on the front line, and hope and practise ducking.

Finally news reaches the town. Central Control have decided to help. They will strike. It will happen between six and eight in the morning. But at six in the morning there is thick cloud. 'Nothing,' the starving victims of the siege say to each other in the world's first UN safe area. 'Nothing. There can be no help with this cloud cover.' By seven it has lifted and with it hope. Perhaps now. They strain to hear. Forty thousand people look up at the sky and wait for the planes. They are waiting in silence. They are listening with their ears, with their eyes, their minds, their whole bodies for the thrum of an engine, but there is only birdsong pouring itself over the town as though it were an ordinary morning. The planes, so far airborne for over an hour, are out of fuel. They have had to return.

So the enemy just walks in, with its tanks of course, against a starving and unarmed populace. And the town, as it was always going to be, is under occupation. The invading army parades its strength down the main street. On either side, as they pass, there is uneasy silence. Eyes registering exhaustion both of body and of any kind of hope. And here is a brutal man, like there always is, Ratko Mladić, who makes promises and breaks them and whose face is like a plate of cold meat, telling a camera that now revenge for some previous, distant, suffering will be enacted, now it is someone else's turn; authorizing massacre and turning up to watch.

'I had a house with roses, tall beautiful roses. We both had jobs. We had a good life, like normal people. Here, if you look at the picture, that is me with my husband. I won the prize that night for the best hairdo.' A lovely woman from Srebrenica is talking to an interviewer, long after the event. Her voice is measured.

But at the time, as it all unfolded, as the enemy passes between the lines of assembled townspeople, the lady with roses among them, the plate of meat tells a news camera, 'They will all be put on buses and taken somewhere they will be safe.' He moves his hands about as he speaks, to emphasize his truth. 'Here is a can of coke for your kids. Here is some candy.' They should proceed to the first buses.

So the people head over to the buses, some of them running in their haste to get out and then, inexplicably, it seems that almost as their foot is on the step up, the men are being separated from the women. What is happening? Everyone is so desperate, so tired. Everyone is so afraid because they know in their hearts that the hatred between themselves and these people is huge. It is limitless. What is going on?

'Put the women only on the buses. You, move that way. Even the boys, the boys as well. You, not her. Go on that side.'

'My husband had his hand on my shoulder and his hand was trembling.' The woman who had the tall roses puts her own hand to her shoulder to indicate. 'I feel it always on my left shoulder, that hand trembling. I feel it in my whole body. And that hot whisper at my ear. He told me, everything will be alright. Everything will be alright. And I just left. I just left silently. I didn't look back.'

Afterwards everything went silent, as if the world's tongue had been cut out. Nothing. No news. 'Where is my husband?' Where is the man with the strong but trembling hand?

'Where is my bony exhausted husband and his younger son? We have none of us heard anything. We know what happened but we need to be told. We can't stop hoping until we are told. We are standing in that place in the past; ghosts in our own lives because we can't move on. We have heard nothing. For four years.'

And it is true, on the internet in documentaries, time stands still at that spot, just as it does in their own lives. I can watch them, over and over – the ragged lines of prisoners in the news footage, the dead-eyed interviews, the repeated pleas for closure.

Or, it is peace-time, for instance, and the women are getting out of a tourist bus. They wear headscarves and they have flowers in their hands, some of them, and they help each other out, the mothers hobbling on thickened ankles, the wives looking baffled, as though something is lost but no one quite knows what. Out of the bus, they pass down a little run of steps into a long building that is partly underground. One or two baulk and turn away at the last minute. When it comes to it, even having waited so long, they find they can't do it.

And now, if you follow those who can, in the half dark of the building, what are these white crumpled-looking bags, sagged at the knees on shelves? What is there in these bags? Stacked like sacks of flour, all the same, all yellow-white, on slatted shelves in this long tunnel here. Is there anything important in these white-yellow paper bags? Has someone lost something, kept here all this time under the ground? Tell me.

The men were ended. They were taken to warehouses or schools or gymnasia or just open fields, where they were beaten to death, or shot, or beaten and shot, or shovelled wounded but still living, by bulldozers into mass graves. The women who were not ended themselves but who left, had something else ended, something to do with time, and to do with life. They were no longer the 'normal people' they had been, who had holidays and roses and jobs and husbands. They were people who had somehow slipped through one of time's holes to get caught forever in the silence of leaving. And they go on leaving, some of them, for the rest of their lives, from that one still point, but doing it over and over, doing it differently.

Yesterday, for instance, the woman with the roses turned for the last look at her husband that she never took. Today she resists, strikes the guards. Tomorrow she will try pleading, the day after sobbing, the day after that arguing. And the year after clinging. And the year after that dying instead of surviving. All the many, many options there were, that have to be lived through just because they weren't lived through, and none of which would, in the end, have changed anything.

What we have to do sometimes, in order to accept.

On the other side, the side of the perpetrators, something similar happens sometimes. Someone slips through time's holes, getting stuck forever, so that his whispered confession to some doctor or other leaks out, like Midas's secret, onto YouTube. Sit round, everyone, and have a look, so we can point at him, this monster, whose face barely out of its teens has the look of a plucked crow. His eyes as if shrunk inwards in avoidance and his hands extended, dangling far below bony wrists, as though in some subconscious effort to distance himself from them, because something must be to blame. 'My hands did it by themselves. I am still me. I am a person too.' Somebody's tormented son, chain-smoking, haunted by himself, in a plastic chair. 'I'm not at peace when I sleep. Not at all. I see pictures. I see ten pictures.' Such a precise number. Because some superior suggested that he give free rein to the basest imaginings he could muster. Someone trained him on pigs. Someone carefully moulded him, as if out of window putty, into this sweating, brutal, bag of nerves, at war with himself. Who, then, is to blame? Because this too is a casualty. This death-in-life is murder of a particular kind.

I'm looking at the water under the bridge, passing, trying its best to carry it all away. Is it working? Because water is just time made manifest; and time is one of the kindest things we have.

On our way out of Bosnia, we go to visit the Dobrun monastery, established in the fourteenth century. To my surprise it is brand new – the Germans, having used it as a weapons store, blew it up when they retreated in 1945. There is nothing much left to show what it once was, just one little white church with frescoes on its front and a gypsy woman inside the porch, disconsolately sorting empty bottles. Behind it, in rows, there is a little town of neat beehives. Everything else in the valley looks forgotten. The once large and comfortable farmhouses stand, dilapidated, among lichen-hung orchards. What a lost place. Though the houses in fact are still lived in somehow, some ghost-life, some scrabble for subsistence among memory and dust and cobwebs. Stucco peeling. Brick and timber exposed. Doors hanging off their hinges. And in the yard of one house, silent guard dogs, chained in the falling rain.

At the Serbian border, when we reach it, there is a tailback. Huge logging trucks queuing. We have to pay a one euro tourist tax and then we are through, in the country the little girl with the rabbit was afraid of. Everything is immediately different. Everything is made of wood for a start, long wooden tiles on all the houses, wooden churches, Cyrillic script on all the signs.

The landscape opens out into a plateau of tawny-coloured grass. Small hillocks dotted with drenched haystacks and little wooden witch's-hat houses, like in a fairy tale, with dormer windows that look like flaps raised in the roof. Sheep and the first scatterings of snow. On the slopes, there are woods of beech and pine. We aren't stopping, not because of the little girl with the rabbit's instruction but because if we are to catch our boat there isn't time. We do all our looking through the van windows.

At the roadside, at intervals, life-size wooden sculptures are offered for sale. What for, I wonder, and how would you get one bought on impulse into a normal car? They are rough-looking figures, as if carved in a rage of drunkenness with a hand-axe, although one or two have smiles or a hand raised, waving an everlasting greeting.

It is a day of unrelenting, comedy rain. After a while the water seems to be coming upwards as much as down. The road is narrow and there is a permanent tail of traffic which processes slowly in and out of brimming potholes. And now instead of the wooden figures there are the corpses of dead dogs, about every mile or so, as regular as bus stops, always just one lying patiently decomposing in the rain. Otherwise the landscape is quiet and open. There are fields of maize and spotted cows, and front gardens full of giant cabbages. On one side, as we crawl past, a cat is sitting, intent, in tall grass. And on the other, for a long time a woman in a black working-man's cap pedals her bike meditatively across a field parallel to the road. The rain is still pouring but she cycles on without either apparent discomfort or inconvenience.

We coast through a village and out again. Two men having an argument underwater without noticing it gesticulate and shout. And down the main street someone else bicycling, with a cardboard box roped on the back with elastic. The box has split in the wet and is sagging hopelessly on either side of the back wheel.

By early afternoon we are desperate to stop. We fill up with petrol and walk back and forth across the sheltered forecourt, trying to stretch out our legs. 'Let's just find somewhere to have lunch,' Rupert says when he reaches the end of his third turn. It is more like dinner time but I agree. We choose a small wooden building on the next town's high street because we think it looks like the sort of place that might serve national dishes. Or that is what we hope.

It is like entering a sponge. The room is hot and full of steam and covered, for the most part, by an enormous rug that, when it runs out of floor-space, has simply been nailed up the wall. Everything that isn't carpeted seems to be wet, the little red-check tablecloths, the walls, the windows, the cutlery, and even the face of the waiter who arrives to take our order from the menu that we can make neither head nor tail of. We have been looking at it nonplussed for quite a while. The waiter stands, waiting, with his streaming face. He is kind but he doesn't speak English. 'Let's just have some things that look like they might be starters,' I suggest, so we order a selection of small dishes that, at a guess, sound like they might be vegetable-based.

In due course three different types of meat arrive, with accompanying bowls of cabbage that has been reduced to sodden ribbons. Steam pours up at us. We're immediately sopping. 'I don't know how much of this I can manage,' I hiss at Rupert when the waiter leaves. 'It isn't at all what I thought it would be.'

Rupert, who is phlegmatic when it comes to food, has already lowered his head and is forking kebab into his mouth. 'Just do your best,' he tells me, as if I were a child. I choose not to. I look around instead. Not many others are dining here. A stolid woman, alone by a window, spoons up soup. On the other side a man with a papery face is telling his companion about being in jail. I lean in a little to listen. 'It was at Maribor. I read Kierkegaard there, you know. It was like a small university. Really so many interesting people.' He blinks. He is having trouble with his glasses. He keeps taking them off and wiping them with his handkerchief. He has – or am I imagining it? – the delicate frame of the tubercular sufferer, the wide shoulders of his overcoat suggesting emptiness. I'm not sure who he is but he looks familiar.

The men talk on in lowered voices. 'So you were taken by the Austro-Hungarians?'

'Of course.' He takes off his glasses again. He was imprisoned because of his political sympathies, as a friend of Gavrilo Princip. 'Only then,' he goes on, 'after Princip, did it begin – the real persecution of the Serbs and all those connected with them.' He blinks at his interlocutor through newly cleaned spectacles. This is important to him I can see, more important than it is to his friend who is busy making inroads on a mound of something with his fork. 'There were reprisals, you see. Very brutal reprisals by the Bosnian Muslims.' The friend lowers his fork.

'Ready?' Rupert asks, leaning back having finished the meat. 'Shall we?'

I shush him with one hand. 'But this is so interesting. I think that man is Ivo Andrić, you know, who wrote the bridge book.'

'Where?' says Rupert, turning round. 'Oh I see, yes, I think you're right.' Andrić glances up, noticing he has been recognized. He lowers his voice. Now I can hear almost nothing.

'He was talking about his past,' I tell Rupert in an urgent undertone. 'He actually chose Serb nationality after Princip, even though he was born in Bosnia – out of solidarity.' But Rupert doesn't seem impressed, or perhaps for once he is not giving it his full attention. 'He *chose* another nationality, out of sympathy – you see?'

'Yes, I see,' he says, standing up. 'That's good but I think we should go.'

Andrić is explaining something else now. His voice rises again, unconcerned. He is describing the wild beast that lives in man, waiting for the barriers of law and custom to be removed. His friend is not asking the right questions – what wild beast? I am thinking. And is it in me? I don't want to go yet.

'What about coffee?' I say hopefully to Rupert who is now paying our waiter.

'We can take it with us.'

I get up slowly. 'That wild beast,' Andrić is saying, 'was now set free. Many Serbs were butchered after this. At Višegrad.' I take a long time putting on my coat, so as to listen. I hear something about changing principles and systems; something about men of power being stupid and the world of learning being weak. 'However much I looked, listened and wondered,' Andrić says, leaning across the table and punching out his words, 'I found neither meaning, nor plan, nor aim in any of it. But I came to one negative conclusion: that our individual ideas, for all their intensity, do not mean much and cannot achieve anything; and to one positive one…' but in the movement of chairs and the rustling of coats I miss the positive. I hear something about legends, something about disparate ethnic groups, something about Yugoslavia '… harmonized and overcome by a knowledge of history.' Really? I think, disappointed. I must have got it wrong; surely history, of all things, has been proven not to work. I would stay and argue the point but Rupert has gone out ahead of me into the rain, so I give it up and follow.

'One thing I did find out,' I tell Rupert as we pull out onto the road again. 'Although I couldn't completely hear it, Andrić came to one positive conclusion. So the project isn't hopeless.'

Rupert smiles. '… yet.'

By the time we reach the far side of the country, the rain has drowned the border guards in their boxes. We sit in a queue of three cars, watching their motionless bodies. Their eyes are open but they don't seem to see. Occasionally one or other shows a sign of life, raises a hand without altering the position of his head, puts a cigarette to drowned lips and inhales. Motionless again.

After a while, in silence, another guard arrives and relieves the dead man in the box. We look up in hope, switch on the engine to indicate purpose if not impatience, but the new guard sits heavily down as if nothing but water were before him. So this is how it feels, I think, to dissolve.

Bulgaria when, against all hope, we are finally allowed through, is raining at motorway speed. Great sheets of surfable spray curl to either side of the van. There is the combined roar of water and traffic. The red tail-lights of cars and lorries blur into the distance, their colours have run. Eventually, at long last, we arrive at Motel 80, a campsite and service station rigged out in heavy-metal memorabilia. Rock explodes as we push open the swing door. It is very warm. There isn't an inch of space on the walls for photographs and vinyl – Metallica, Megadeth, Slayer, Judas Priest. The people behind the bar have multiple piercings and black clothes and very white faces. They look terrifying but they speak with oddly gentle voices. This is so surreal. We are shown round the campsite, which is still under construction. We are offered electricity from a little power-output at the corner of the pitch. We plug in and sit looking at our devices. Nothing happens. It turns out that the electricity hasn't yet been connected. We trudge over to the shower block. We undress and stand shivering under the shower heads, clutching our little bars of soap. No water comes out of the tap.

The Serbian rain, like a second Flood, seems to have washed the world away. In the morning the clouds pull back as if they were roller blinds to reveal an unending empty plain of great width and flatness. Everything looks strange as if it were a new start. One huge mountain appears crisp in outline, peaked like a child might draw and suspended in silhouette as if it belonged not to the land but to a country of the sky. We drive towards it, which now that we are dissolved, drifting in solution with all that has gone before and belonging nowhere, seems as sensible as anything else.

Where in fact are we?

Back at the beginning of European time, that's where. We have fallen, as Rupert promised, to the floor of our travelling, down as deep as you can go, at the edge of our historical vision, the almost undifferentiated gloom where it all began. Between 10,000 and 5000 BC on the plains of Bulgaria where the first people in Europe stopped moving as they always had done so far, and instead pitched a camp that became home, and didn't leave until they were driven out. Where for the first time instead of following their food they sowed it into the ground and waited for it to multiply and then, while they were waiting, made things out of what they found around them on the ground or in the rivers, stone or clay or, in this place, gold.

Here, in Plovdiv, among the findings from the Dolnoslav cult complex in the town museum, is a woman, for instance, made out of clay, wearing some clinging white garment round her waist, like a sarong decorated with scrolls, and with tendrils of hair falling down her back, swept as if by a breeze across her bottom. Here is a long-legged clay man, arms raised, head missing, wearing a belt. Here are some people who are pregnant, some people who are halfway to being birds. Some figures in white stone that you would swear were Cycladic but that are millennia too early. Here are some useful things: vessels decorated with rhythmic and complex designs in white paint on clay. Vessels with lovely practical handles. A little salt cellar in the shape of a sheep.

It's an incomprehensible mystery. 6000 to 4000 BC. These are among the oldest things I have ever seen. The museum flyer suggests they were made by the Stone Copper people. I never knew such a people existed – unless Stone Copper is just the cold, unvisualizable Chalcolithic, in translation. I want to ask the little statuettes who on earth they are. I want to know how they manage life, what they believe. Some say they worship the moon. Is that why so many of them seem to be sleeping? The clay heads have shield-shaped faces with closed eyes and little incised eyelashes. They look very peaceful. The ones who are awake have slightly surprised expressions and sharp noses and long slant eyes of great beauty. One has inlaid eyes of palest blue and tiny, painted, lips. Their mouths are so small, so closed, as if there weren't any point in speaking, or as if words hadn't yet bagged out their mouths with overuse. What could you do with a mouth so small, pursed in millennia of sleep; would a word even fit in that delicate slit?

By itself, in a case, is a wide and lovely cup, with white decoration and a handle. It looks just patterned to begin with but after a while I see, or I imagine I see, what its pattern is saying. Either way, these complex triangles with dark openings look like tents or wigwams pitched in a line. Some have whorls of what might be smoke coming out of the top. One or two are taller than the others, and all are ranged along the bank of a river. Suddenly I can see who these people are.

They are moving about in the great Bulgarian plain, on the banks of the river that lazes through it, wearing these fish-shaped pins as ornaments. Their arms are decorated with these spiral armlets that end in leaves. Someone sitting at the entrance to their tent is using this beautiful bowl with the two-eyed snake, painted in red, coiled carefully round the inside. Someone else is using this feathered owl-shaped jug. Obviously they are just people. Obviously they are no less chaotically human, no better perhaps than their messy, confused descendants, including ourselves, today. And obviously, despite the tiny perfection of their mouths, they speak, but in my mind, they are moving about their newly fixed landscape in watchful silence. Their slant and beautiful eyes are extra wide for looking and their mouths are closed. They are just observing, just accepting, no doubt. They haven't yet made a mess. They haven't yet ruined anything. They are fishing and growing their corn and keeping sheep and making things.

And yet, what happened? They disappeared. Some say it was climate change and others that horsemen of great savagery, tall men with grey eyes and red or fairish hair, whirled down on them from the Steppe and wiped them out. The Eustaces, perhaps, arrived to commandeer the gold and make either relentless war, or finer and finer, uglier and uglier artefacts, or both.

Once you've reached the bottom you have to come up. That's the rule. If I had a choice I would like to stay here, with the Stone Copper people from Dolnoslav. I am trying to shrink my wind-sock mouth. I am stretching out my eyes. But there is all the Eustaces' gold to be waded through in the museum's next-door rooms. There are still towns and countries and politics and the nonsense of nationality, and there is still all that water-weight of time above, where technically I belong. And anyway the Stone Copper people have gone – they have gone, with their tight-shut mouths and with all their observations, their looking and thinking, down under the ground that they stopped to till, taking with them, in silence, all their wishes, all their thoughts and beliefs, whatever on earth they were.

As I said, there are still towns; there is still, everywhere, the bizarre rubble of towns. This one has pylons, great big pylons, for instance, marching up the middle of the dual carriageway into its centre. It has a little rill there, on the right, and a nice-looking fallen-down house on the left. It has wrought-iron gates and weeds and rubbish and a half-ruined villa standing quietly in its own garden. Further in, it has giant churches, golden domes, trams, statues of crazed-looking kings with exceptional hair. It even dares to look permanent. It is populated as though it is certain to stay. It has people, even noticeably individual people: this lady, for instance, in a pale pink flat-cap and dark glasses. She is clutching a bunch of chrysanthemums to her chest, her jaws working while she waits at the traffic lights. Or this handsome old man, rooting with frank interest through the rubbish containers by the roadside, who finds a black umbrella and tries it out and looks pleased.

But these things, even these domes and the absurdly scaled civic buildings built to fit the ideology of Communism rather than its people, all of these things, however individual or distinct, are nothing more than grit bowled along in time; accreting by chance here or there, catching in nooks and crannies but like us, just passing, not truly belonging. Everything is on the move.

This is some of what I understand at last, as we mount the steps of another museum. Our fight for durability, for locality, for relevance as we are rolled, resistless, in the tide. These stupendous shallow steps, these serried windows and blocky chandeliers and echoing halls, they are the vast see-through boxes for belongings where we carefully gather together and preserve all that we think we are, where we fold our hands and pray desperately to our innermost selves, please let this be permanent. Please let this not be carried away and please let its placing be significant. Please let this be me, my culture, my country, my very importance. And we lay our things out under lights, in lines, as methodically as fishing, and we hope thereby to hook ourselves to a place in time, to a time in a certain place. A belonging.

And while it says one thing under its breath like a mantra, this museum just by its cavernous existence affirms its opposite. All of this, although it is unquestionably here, has gone. Nothing lasts, nothing at all.

Which is a relief as I pass through these rooms, wading through the brashness of their Thracian contents, case after case of it, kicking aside these zoographically precise deer's head rhytons, these drinking cups with fur and veins and antlers, with eyes so real they might be actually looking at you, all made out of gold. Up to my knees in platters and urns, trying to get at what might be underneath. But there is so much of it to shift, plates and cups and crowns and little statuettes of charioteers in microscopic detail, and shields and helmets and greaves. The Panagyurishte hoard that Rupert wanted to see. It belongs to one of the men with exceptional hair, Sevt III, King of the Odrysians in the fourth century BC. Impossibly decadent, impossibly technically proficient, his treasure looks like something Edward VII might have used for state occasions. And heaped around it is treasure from other places I've never heard of, belonging to other kings with exotic names, to Teres I, to Cotys. I squint at giant boards that tell me the names and extents of ancient tribes. The Odrysae, the Bessoi, the Getae, the Daci, the Triballi. I am none the wiser. I look across at Rupert who is photographing illegally. He will be no help. Then I look again at the artefacts and suddenly, despite their names, they look contradictorily familiar. They look Greek, or sometimes Celtic. I may not recognize their owners' tribes, or their territories, or their kings, but I recognize these things. I even recognize the stories on them. They seem to speak some communal language of decoration and myth, something more lasting than the people who made, or wore, or used these things. I lean in as if to listen but all I can hear is Rupert's shutter click, click, down the other end of the gallery.

Then in the far case, among treasure from Mogilanska Mogila, there is a single greave, an ornate shin guard not designed to be worn for fighting, but designed for death; a funerary offering. It is fourth century BC, silver ornamented with gold and, for the second time, as with the Dolnoslav cup, I suddenly see what its pattern is saying. The whole of the knee plate is a face, such a face as might fit all places. Its hair is dressed in tight, stylized Assyrian knots. Across its forehead is a Greek-looking vine wreath. It is divided in two, forehead to chin, under two Assyrian-type eyebrows, curled and feathered like ferns. One half of the face below has elongated Celtic-looking features, the other is striped with gold like the death-mask of an Egyptian pharaoh. The shin is ornamented with dog-headed snakes, standing on their tails, like something from the Vix treasure. The face is silver. Its borrowed ornamentation gold. I look at it for a long time. It is in itself a museum, a collection of artistically or geographically distinctive things, carefully assembled, claimed, and put in one place. Hooking itself into the great civilizations. 'Who are you going to show it to,' I ask the silver face, 'when you are dead? What will it prove you were, and to whom?'

The greave says nothing. 'Or will it just prove how far you got? Is it some kind of boast? Look what I did. Look how rich I was, how powerful – down the empty lengths of eternity.' Still nothing. It just gleams its endurance back at me, art and prosperity and war all seamlessly entwined, surviving. This is what you and I are, it might say, its wearer gone under the ground. This is what it is to be human. All these things, we have developed and borrowed and passed on, culture to culture, always the same tangled cycle. This is what we are: the violence of war and the push for wealth and the unearthly beauty of art. Good luck disentangling all of that.

'Maybe,' I lean in, 'this is what it means to be a man, because you were in control all that time, not me, and because I'm pretty sure there was art before there was war. I saw it at Dolnoslav. I saw what those first settlers made before war swept them away.'

'Who are you talking to?' Rupert has finished photographing the gold.

'No one,' I say pointedly, looking at the impassive little face in the cabinet. 'No one at all.'

We drive slowly away, leaving the town with its unbuilt or half-built outskirts. Towns are neither here nor there. We leave the woman in the purple cardigan sweeping her doorstep and the man in the long blue overall pacing out his vegetable patch in thoughtful strides.

Here are poplars in autumn dress, against a pale blue sky. The van windows are open and my feet are up on the dashboard. All this open space. All this freshness and air on these plains, at history's beginning. It's exhilarating. We are in a country as flat as a pavement. A tractor ploughing in a cloud of dust by the motorway. Seagulls circling. Stubble burning. On one side a herdsman tends a flock of sheep the same colour as the field, on the other a mixed herd of cattle grazes. There are horses and carts on the motorway bridges and, further on, down to a meandering river, a hunting party is strung out across the fields. Then a solar farm next to a ruined factory. Low, low hills at the back of the plain, woods of oak and ash and willow, and on the skyline the tumuli of the men from the Steppe.

War and Money and Art.

Here they come, the ones who made the greave, dressed in all the gold they have snatched, flying across the plain on their horses. I watch them go. They are quite a sight, their horses so fast and so white that even Homer once stopped to admire them. They wear fox-fur caps with the brush hanging down their backs, and long boldly patterned cloaks and boots made of fawnskin. They are going too fast for me to see the size of their mouths but they left no written record, so they too kept a kind of silence. A man with luxuriant hair for his age, softly parted in the middle of a wide forehead and with a long and ringleted

beard, is also watching. His own mouth, which I can see, is a little turned down in disapproval. 'They are a backward people,' he tells me. I tell him about their predecessors whom I prefer, those gentle people with their owl cup, but he isn't interested. He is partisan and he is watching the Thracians. 'They sell their children. They tattoo their aristocracy and allow their daughters to sleep with any man they please. They think they are immortal.' I think of the greave. 'You know,' he says, 'when it thunders and lightnings they shoot arrows into the sky as a threat to the god.'

You have to admire their confidence. But Herodotus doesn't. He shakes his heavy head. 'They only reverence the idlers among them. The tiller of the soil is scorned.' He turns to me. 'The men they honour most among themselves are those who live by war and robbery.'

'Just as I said,' I tell him. 'I knew it. They are the first Eustaces.'

'The Thracians have many names,' he says, raising his eyebrows, 'each tribe according to its region. If they were under one ruler, or united, they would, in my judgement, be invincible and the strongest nation on earth. Since, however, there is no way or means to bring this about, they are weak.'

'I disagree.' I look at Herodotus sadly. 'Now they are very very strong.' The Thracian Eustaces are moving fast in the distance now. 'I know. They are my tribe now. Be careful,' I say under my breath to the riders, 'be careful in your spoiling. The world may not be as endlessly replenishing, or as roomy, as you think.' I stand with Herodotus in the empty plain. 'As a tribe,' I tell him, as if in apology, 'we love to talk. What we never ever do is listen.'

The bleached plain reaches on under its pale blue sky. We cross the Maritsa river, leaving the Thracians with their promiscuous daughters and their gold-hungry, tattooed nobles behind. In the fields by the road, the obligatory rows of pneumatic cabbages and beyond them, on a little church, is a stork on a haystack which it seems to have shifted, piecemeal, onto the bell-tower. A horse and cart trots past us on the hard shoulder, going the wrong way. It must be warm because we pass a herd of cows whose herdsman is stretched out on the ground, full length, asleep. When I look back, Herodotus is walking slowly among them, his clothes fluttering behind him as if he had wings.

By nightfall we have reached Greece. Rupert has reached his spiritual home and we have run out of land – when you get to the sea you can't drive any further. So we stop and get out, gingerly unfolding our legs and backs like rickety picnic furniture that might not hold. The Aegean is lapping, black with night, at the harbour wall and Kavala, dressed for dinner with its necklaces of lights, is looking down at its own reflection. We walk about the town, provisioning ourselves for the trip, waiting for the giant *Nissos Mykonos* ferry with its red funnel to come heeling round the breakwater blaring its foghorn, the whole town shrunk to a huddle of dolls' houses, as it swings itself to stern.

On board, everyone seems to be rushing, ourselves included, clumsy with armfuls of bedding trying to find a space to sleep. We make a nest that the stork on the bell-tower might approve of, only on the floor, between some reclining chairs and a corner wall where it is possible, if you slot your legs carefully between the legs of the chairs, to lie down, more or less, at full length.

We give ourselves up to the boat. When we get off again in the morning, we will have reached the end of our journey – and then what? Will things be different?

All night long with the engine juddering and the swaying feeling of suspense, I try to collect together what I have seen. I clutch at my memories. And then, in my sleep, I have the distracting impression that everything is very far below me. Am I sailing, or flying? It isn't that I'm afraid of falling. I'm afraid of dropping something. I don't know what. Something I must keep hold of. Something I have found or been given, like Gilgamesh's flower, that was the point of the journey we have made. But what exactly? I keep worrying. Is it Ariosto's book, or Rolin's velvet purse, or the Stone Copper silence? Or is it, like the museum greave, all of them rolled together into one? I look down, lacing my fingers, thinking to stop whatever it is from slipping. There are little lumps of something in my hands, like rubble, but soft and dusty. Used paper handkerchiefs? Owl pellets? I wake up just as they are rolling away from me, bouncing out over the ship's rail into the sea. I should have known. We don't, as a race, hold on to anything. Whatever it was that I might have learned is spiralling already, in slow motion, down through the miles of unlit water, to lie on the bottom among the other lost things; the bones, the ships, and all they were carrying, all the knowledge of before. Gone.

Continue. Nothing ends. Things just carry on in different form. In the small hours the ship stops at Lemnos. It seems there is a prison here. Long, low, buildings with an abused look and, inside one of them, a man with the most pointed beard I have ever seen is writing by the light of an ancient oil lamp. Yannis Ritsos, born in the Peloponnese in 1909, now imprisoned for his Communist politics.

'Why don't you use electricity?' I whisper. 'It's been invented.'

'I know,' he says, glancing up with that look of absence that people concentrating hard for long periods have when you interrupt. 'But I'm used to these oil lamps. The guards can't see them. And they're watching me. I must have done something very wrong.' He says it thoughtfully, as if to himself. 'I rejoice in new things but these... these allow me to see amid all the changes, the immutable element.' He is a poet, obviously. Between his fingers he holds a rough cigarette which he is smoking despite tuberculosis. He looks exhausted. He is spending his days in forced labour, stone shifting, and his nights writing. From time to time he looks at his hands, the long fingers tipped with tobacco-stained nails, as if asking them directly how it is that they can have let so much slip through. Sometimes, in his poems, he is just counting his fingers. Sometimes he is angrily tying his own hands. Sometimes he is cutting them off. He uses many tricks to survive in prison but what he can't forgive his hands is their getting used to it.

The thing he doesn't mind losing is his family's wealth, the big house under the ash-grey mountain at Monemvasia, long since sold. He has cast in his lot with the sufferers and the fighters. He is a Communist. But his mother's and his brother's deaths; his father's and his sister's madness; his country's balance; his freedom; his loves; his ability to hope and to believe... He shakes his head. These are things that have put themselves down inside him with the solidity of stones. He trips over them continually.

Later Ritsos will be sent to Makronisos where he will be tortured. His books will be banned, as will his paper. Soon he will not officially be allowed to write at all. He bends his head. For the time being, on anything he can find, the linings of cigarette packs for instance, he goes on writing.

I could ask him if it is worth it, his commitment to Communism, to nationalism, but that would be insensitive. Belief, if you have it, is everything – meaning, where it exists, is both personal and sacred. If I have learned anything on this trip, it is that. 'They are burning my poems at the foot of the Acropolis,' he says as if he has heard me. 'I must be doing something right.'

'I met someone once,' I say. 'He too was a radical and he wrote poetry. I don't know if it was good or not. I don't speak his language but he was very young. He was poor and he was very small. I don't know which thing was more responsible for his anger but he couldn't wait for change. He had to force it, so he stepped forward out of the crowd. He pulled a gun and shot some people in a stalled car at close range. That was for nationalism. It didn't end well. Communism at the beginning of the twentieth century I can understand, but nationalism seems childish – such a wishful construct.' This is just what I said I wouldn't do: question his private meaning. I feel cheap.

'Nationalism, under occupation,' Ritsos says, narrowing his eyes, 'is simply freedom. Freedom to have your own identity, to live the way you wish to live, the way your fathers have lived; freedom not just to come and go but to belong. Freedom is everything. If you cannot see that, then that is because you belong to the oppressors not to the oppressed.' He is stern but I deserved it. I think of the Eustaces, from whom in part I am descended, riding north across Europe. I think about England. In the dark, in the confines of this prison against free speech, with its fences and its mean little concrete yards, I think I can dare to say how England is.

'I come from an island,' I tell him, whispering as if I too were a prisoner. 'Perhaps that makes a difference. It can't help feeling distinct.' He nods slightly. 'And maybe our island culture is more focused on the individual than the collective life. We have suffered invasion in the past, I mean a long time ago, admittedly. We were oppressed, by his own admission, by William the Conqueror but that was in the eleventh century. Long enough to forget, and to uphold the individual. You see, we believe in the effort of the individual to effect change for themselves. That's what drives our society, a kind of DIY approach. That's what we admire, individual strength. Secretly we have no respect for the weak. And you're right, I admit it, that has made us perhaps a bit brutal. We are among the oppressors.' I run out of steam. It feels like a defence and a confession. I don't know what I expected him to offer – absolution perhaps. He looks at me with his penetrating gaze, before bending over his paper again.

I listen to the scratching of his pen. It sounds so loud, perhaps because it is forbidden. It's frightening being in prison. I'm worried someone will hear. But they can't stop him writing without stopping him breathing first. Somehow he manages. Somehow he goes on, in the light of his oil lamp, because he believes in his duty to change, because writing too is freedom and because he is lonely. When he finishes, he rolls up his poem, posts it into a bottle like people stuck on islands are supposed to do. Then he buries it in the stony ground. I can't help looking amazed. I open my mouth to tell him – does he not know we are on an island? There is sea all around us. I can drop the bottle for him over the harbour wall if he thinks it will help – or I can tell someone.

'It isn't a message in a bottle,' he says. 'Messages in bottles are cries for help. This is a seed.'

Again, I feel one step behind. It seems I understand nothing after all. 'I have been listening a lot to Ariosto,' I tell him instead. It comes out like an apology. It was his talk of seeds that reminded me but I am thinking now of a different way. I'm thinking of how someone dedicated to acceptance can make a burrow for themselves inside a system, tunnel out to freedom through a world of words.

'Well,' Ritsos says, lifting up his pointed beard. He looks like someone on a black-figure vase. 'Ariosto and I have similarities. I borrowed his name once, for a late book, because with some shifts you can make it mean airy nothingness, or you can make it mean best. But Ariosto was careful. He stayed one side of a line that I publicly stepped over. We have different tolerance levels and so we favour different solutions. I am not careful, at least of myself. Truly,' he says to me with a fierce look suddenly, 'I sometimes think that only being torn to pieces can keep us whole.'

It seems as if I am in touching distance of something, or maybe it is just getting light. I hesitate. I want to ask more. Ritsos is smoking, looking at the pale square of the window that faces the port. I want to tell him where I have come from, what things are like now, ask him what he makes of the world's many changes, but there isn't the time. I have to go back to Rupert and the ship. The dawn is showing. Not so much a lightening as a thinning, a watering down of night's opaqueness. I am thinking about freedom and loneliness and what Ritsos calls the 'immutable element', when he interrupts.

'I would like to give you something before you go.'

I put a hand to my chest and bow my head slightly. I start on, 'How could I?', 'But there is no need…', 'You have already given me…' and all their various et ceteras.

He waves his hand at me. 'It is nothing. Go aboard. I will find you.'

I hurry away, as he instructs, threading through the crowds at the dock – the running, the whistling of the loading crew, the revving engines in the damp of dawn. I go up to the first deck to wait for Ritsos. When he reappears, coming from the direction of the cabins, he is carrying something huge, fireman's lift, over one shoulder. A crippled mess of a man, Philoctetes.

What?

He lays him at my feet, straightens up with one long-fingered hand easing the small of his back and then walks away without saying anything. 'What am I supposed…?' I shout after him. I am flabbergasted, opening and shutting my mouth in cartoon surprise. At my feet Philoctetes stinks. He has a visibly festering wound which is leaking something indescribable. I feel briefly furious. I am not a doctor. And now the ship is leaving. People not travelling are hurrying ashore. This isn't at all what I expected. This is categorically not a present. I rush to the rail.

'Ritsos! What am I supposed to do with this?' What the fuck, I would like to say but I don't.

Ritsos, already down on the dock, half turns and goes on walking. 'Read the myth,' he shouts over his shoulder. He sounds uncompromising. Then he says something I miss. His voice getting harder to hear. He is walking surprisingly fast, as though he is worried I might give Philoctetes back. 'You won't win the war without him,' is what he says.

What is he talking about? It was going so well and now it's all suddenly stupid. 'But I'm not at war,' I shout down. 'I'm just travelling.' The ship is moving away now, faster and faster. Smoke from its scarlet funnel streams into the beginning day. Philoctetes lies at my feet and Ritsos is dwindling on the quay. He has his hand to his mouth. He is shouting. I lean to listen; his voice floating faint across oily waters. But I can't hear properly.

'Are you sure?' I think he said. What does he mean? What war? Is it a metaphor? I think he was pointing. I can't be sure.

Following the line of where Ritsos was pointing, if he was pointing at all, I look away to where the humps of other islands rise, strung out along the coast of Turkey. Then, bobbing black and in between, I see things I hadn't noticed before. Little overloaded crafts swing crazily between the crests of a wintering sea. Out of them swarm ant-like shapes, one after another, floundering through shallows. They are people. And all the while that we have been talking, it seems, these ragged people have been steadily coming, some of them carrying children, some carrying possessions, out of the east, out of the night sea, boarding the islands as if they too were boats.

Someone watching with me at the rail, following the direction of my gaze, says, 'It has been going on like this for months.'

I know it. For months and months, and now the islands, like the boats that they aren't, are getting fuller, overladen to tipping, and still the people keep on coming.

'It is crazy,' the man says, flicking his cigarette butt over the rail. I watch its little red light until it hits the water.

Is this what Ritsos means? Is this to do with me? Because even if it is, still I don't see how Philoctetes is relevant.

I don't get it, Ritsos. Mainly I am thinking of how fast and how determinedly he walked away. Nevertheless, I hump Philoctetes down to our nest on the lower deck, where Rupert, who is a champion sleeper, is sleeping. On our way down all the people we meet look at us and back away, their lips curling involuntarily in disgust. I feel both angry and implicated. Philoctetes leans very heavily. He complains all the time and he has a slightly whining voice. Nor does it stop when I make room for him in my place in the nest. I sit apart with my knees to my chest, fuming, not sleeping while his wound leaks onto my bedding and he complains.

He is hungry. It isn't comfortable. He is in pain, can't I see? He feels betrayed by his friends. He was the best warrior of all of them, did I know that? Had I heard of him? It is for this reason that he has Herakles' bow; *he*, not anyone else. Not Agamemnon, not Ajax, not hated Odysseus, *he*, Philoctetes. Because he is the best.

Mostly I don't answer, hoping he will stop. He doesn't. His comrades abandoned him. Do I know how long he has been marooned, sick, on that island? Can I imagine what it feels like to be discarded as soon as you are no use, and by the most underhand means? He was left, sleeping in fever, with barely any food, while his friends tiptoed to the shore and set sail. He had to crawl after game on the mountainside. Have I seen what the mountains are made of? Rock. Rock and thorns. He shows me his lacerated arms and legs. He doesn't care for Menelaus. Menelaus is overbearing and weaker than he pretends. He himself had been courting Helen before Menelaus appeared. Helen would have been his. Paris is worse. Ajax is stupid like an ox. 'Ritsos is a bore,' he says after a while, changing tack. 'He's not a warrior. He did nothing but write and talk about collective effort.'

'Shut up!' I tell him. 'Shut up! I don't want to listen to your moaning.' I find him banal, insulting. His voice is irritating, let alone his opinions.

He looks at me. He says suddenly, 'I wasn't like this before.'

We sit in silence and now I feel guilty. I can imagine how bitterness and shame might shrink a person.

'I wanted to go home. In the end,' he says, 'I wanted so badly to go home. Can't you understand that? And I was stuck on this island, with this wound that I could get no treatment for, and people came every now and then, strangers from other countries, with concerned faces. Such pitying faces, wanting to hold my hand and weep with me. I didn't want to weep. I wanted to kill Odysseus who left me here. I wanted – I still want – to slaughter the whole Greek army and heap them like cattle on the shore and leave them for the crows to pick at. I wanted to slit their throats and fuck their wives and burn their houses. And then I wanted to go home and see my father and see everything just as I left it, safe and peaceful.'

I say nothing because honestly I can't think how to respond. He doesn't notice. He just carries on, his sickness both mental and physical, uncontainable. 'These visitors that came,' he says, 'they had compassionate speeches for me. They gave me a little food, or some clothing. But there was one thing no one would do, whenever I mentioned it: take me off the island, or take me home in safety.'

He stops. He is glowering at me. Perhaps he will kill me – he seems unstable. I glance at Rupert, wondering whether I should wake him. But his wound is very bad. It is true he has been ill-treated. Partly out of contrition and partly out of self-interest I decide to clean and dress his foot. Remembering Dunant, I get up and fetch sachets of salt from the cafeteria where, even at this time, people as large as cows sit chewing their way through pastitsio, with glazed eyes. I empty the sachets into a cup and wash the wound with salt solution, trying my best not to retch. Then I dry it and dress it and give Philoctetes water. 'Get some sleep,' I tell him. 'You are off the island now. Stop nursing your grievance and start getting better.' He looks at me startled, but he doesn't answer; instead, he settles into the blankets.

I sit up thinking. Below me, the deep juddering of the ship's engines. Philoctetes is still stinking but at least now he is asleep. I am tired. Nothing, it seems, can be helped. Nothing good can be held on to for long enough to be of use. I think again of the little owl pellets that I let go in my dream. Perhaps it was Ritsos's immutable element that was parcelled up neat inside the regurgitated skin and fur – the one thing, behind all the glittering changes, that stays the same, whatever that might be. Our human template perhaps: the passions that drive us or drag us so blindly, the engine of our necessity. Would knowledge of that have saved everything? If it's immutable then presumably it can't be gone.

Again, continue.

The boat docks briefly at Lesbos. I lean my lack of sleep over the rail, into the wintry sunlight, clouds scudding towards us from the coast of Turkey. Everything is on the move. Little lorries are loading and unloading, cars, bikes, people bustling. The cabs of trucks reverse at speed, up the ramp of the ship, to the frantic accompaniment of whistles. 'Ela! Ela! Pame!' Never has there been such a hurry, so much to do. The trucks re-emerge attached to containers, without any compromise to their speed or manoeuvrability. On the side of one, the giant transfer of a girl in a Barbie-pink bikini eats a matching coloured ice-cream, her bottom provocatively stuck out. A huge crowd of people presses forward to board, while men and women in some kind of uniform open the metal mesh gates a crack, so as to control the flow. Everyone seems to have a whistle in their mouth and everyone is using it.

Something at the back of the press of passengers catches my eye. A single black face. It is a boy in a kingfisher-blue baseball cap. Even at this distance his movements seem odd. Then I realize: he is acting normality. I can see the restlessness, the desperation, that he is pretending isn't there. I can see him, hang back and hang back. I'm in no hurry. I'm relaxed. No, please. You first. And when finally he goes through, in a little rush like someone who gulps their breath and ducks their head in the onrush of a wave, he is motioned, as he knew all along he would be, to one side despite all his carefully schooled nonchalance.

Glancing up, glancing down, shifting, shifting. How is it possible for one body to contain so much visible tension?

One of the officers, trousers tucked into heavy boots, also acting, holds up a piece of paper to the light for an unnecessary time. The moment spins itself out dropping, dropping on its thread, agonizingly weighted, to the inevitable flat refusal. The boy is waved away. He has a moment when something sprung in him rebounds, a half turn back, as though thinking to try pleading, or to ask why maybe. Why can't I go? A soldier raises one hand, flickering his fingers in a gesture of goodbye. It probably isn't meant to be cruel.

The boy is out through the gates. Then he stops one more time, as if to go back. Stands. Turning to go. Stopping, looking back again. And if I had to choreograph despair I would do it like this. Standing, looking, turning. The slow walk. The shoulders. The dark figure so quiet, so unresisting, screaming its silent scream all the way along the quay. He might not yet be twenty. And the jaunty blue of that hat.

The weather changes. At Chios we disembark at a world that is in tatters. Queues of people under a makeshift tarpaulin roof wait for food. Men one side, women the other. Very cold. Everyone has a card for meals, or little sheaves of paper with impenetrable letterheads and official stamps. We are handed high-visibility tabards and lanyards to wear, so as to be identifiable, and we are given jobs which amount to a kind of empathetic herding. Philoctetes refuses. He melts into the camp, limping away among the tents and containers. He seems to be looking for someone. He said something about killing. He looked at the tents on the beach and he asked which direction was Troy, but I let him go. I can't be bothered to explain. It isn't my problem.

Besides, there are other things to do. We enlist as volunteers. Every day, day after day, there is wind blowing strongly from the sea and, before anyone can be fed, we have to unfold these scraps of paper that have been folded so many times before, some in four, some in eight; folded and unfolded three times a day, every day, day after day, until they have split along the lines of the folds, holding only at the corners. Cold hands and the barely contained frustration of the refugee in question, queuing, always queuing; and the bureaucracy, offered in answer to intolerable loss. Meanwhile, the paper itself is struggling, as if infected with the general restlessness, sometimes fluttering away over puddles, somebody's family's food, gone.

Folding, unfolding, peering to see how many portions are allotted to this person, marking the cross in the tiny box for this meal on this day. And the papers flap their tatters in the rain and the wind, to match the tatters of the netting pinned for protection across the back of this shelter, and the tatters of the tents and the tattered people's tattered lives, fleeing from their tattered countries.

Misery. Restive men arguing. Some drunk already, at seven at night, pushing forward in the sleet. Something other than weather is blowing and flexing through the camp. In the evenings particularly I can feel it, some deep-level pressure-system building. Meanwhile, the women wait in quiet lines. Some have remembered the little plastic washing-up tubs in which to carry away their food. Some have not.

Twenty-one portions, no box.

Six portions, with box.

Still it is bitter weather. The people in tabards are muffled to the eyeballs. They stamp their feet and blow on their hands and make game little jumps up and down, companionably cold. The people in the queue are in thin nylon clothes, some of them rub their hands but they do it almost, it seems, to please us. Cold is our form of communication. Mostly we do not speak each other's languages.

'Plus seven.'

'Two no box.'

'Medical papers. Police papers this side.'

It feels intolerably slow – the people the other side of the trestle tables working as fast as they can, under one suspended lamp. Snow coming horizontally through the shelter now and the line of men, always longer than that of the women, pressing forward. There must be a quicker way to do this.

'Hallo my friend. Hallo my friend.'

We are like people looking at each other through cracks in a fence. Prising open tiny chinks of communication. 'Merhaba,' we have learned to say. 'Ah leyn. Gey fah laah. Al hamdulillah,' jostling the syllables round as if they were a mouthful of pebbles, hoping we have remembered it right.

On other nights, when the snow has stopped, while the food queues elbow and shuffle forward, outside, in the dark, to pass the time, other people in tabards dance. They have made a circle of children and they are dancing to unbelievably stupid western music, always the same songs. This is a good, not a bad thing, I tell myself. Look how happy everyone seems to be. Sometimes there is other music, the music of the world that is lost, and the men dance a complex hopping step, their arms linked. Or two will strip to their vests despite the freezing night, so everyone can see the strange, controlled trembling of the muscles in their shoulders which is part of the dancing. Arms out to the side. Quick, quivering, tense, and the rhythmic, halting, step.

Out across the straits now a little cone of light is standing on the waters, moving on, circling, moving on, as if it too were dancing. It is windy. The waves are high. People stop and stand still and look at the distant searchlight. Bitter, bitter cold. No one says anything. Somewhere in the winter sea an overloaded boat has capsized.

On most nights in the camp there are fights. Fights with knives or just with fists and stones. Twice there are riots and the containers belonging to the various NGOs are burned. There are so many men, so much waiting, and the waiting is for nothing. It is impossible to wait for nothing. Philoctetes should know. I see him from time to time. He is still looking at the tents on the shore and asking where Troy is. He is a slow learner. He still wants to fight, to wreck a town, burn it to the ground. His foot is better but his mind is not. I see him standing with little knots of boys and I can feel the thing that is like a building pressure. What are they going to do? They can't wait here, rejected in advance by everywhere else, for very much longer. They have all this energy for life, and all this slowly fermenting hurt, and they have been here nearly a year already, thwarted, doing nothing. 'I will go,' one of them tells me, half whispering, one day.

'How?'

'I will lie under a lorry.' He opens his arms and legs wide, as if being crucified St Andrew style. 'Ten people escape like this last week,' he tells me. 'Ten people.'

Sooner or later, if people are desperate enough to risk their lives, something will happen.

In fact it has happened. It has already happened that refugees huddled in overcrowded boats have splashed ashore at Chios, jittery with horrors, and babbling about what was taking place back home, but this time the horrors happened at Smyrna, two hundred years before. Janissaries, they say, were out in the streets, armed and killing Greeks as if they were animals. You opened your door to go to the market and there they were, crazed, in broad daylight, running them down in a pack, no matter who you were – a woman even, a child. 'What are you talking about?' someone else interrupts. 'Not just one woman, many women, thousands of women and of children, of unarmed men and priests. Anybody.' His eyes are completely round, as if fixed in a permanent state of shock. 'Anybody,' he says again, 'anyone out about their morning business. I saw bodies everywhere. Thousands have been killed,' he keeps on saying it. 'Thousands.'

No one knows why. Only that Smyrna has become restless and that rumours of the Greek spring, the push for independence, come every day. Neither side knows what, or even where, things will happen next. It is 1821 and the failing Ottoman Empire is in a fever of paranoia. Accounts keep arriving of Turkish merchant vessels that have been waylaid and boarded by Greek independence fighters, their crews slaughtered and heaved overboard, their cargo taken. In retaliation the Sultan hangs the Patriarch of Constantinople on Easter Sunday. But it is as if independence were a disease, episodes breed and break out all over the territories it has controlled so effectively for four centuries. It is not for nothing that Turkey is being called the sick man of Europe. On both sides now everyone is nervous.

Still, Chios, so close to the coast of Turkey, goes on in its dream of prosperity. It is busy as it always has been trading citrus and silk. It is the only producer of the world's supply of mastic, indispensable to the Sultan for his harem but also much in demand for cosmetics, for varnish, as a stabilizer in cooking and as a medicine. For this reason, for its mastic groves and its traditional mastic workers, Chios thinks it is protected. It is rich and very cosmopolitan. Its inhabitants have intermarried with their previous conquerors, the Genoese. They have beautified their capital city, the Chora, with Italianate buildings. Thirty thousand people of different extraction live in the city and another hundred thousand or so on the island as a whole. They are known for their luxuriant gardens, their literature and their success in trade. Ask Thomas Gordon, a Scotsman wandering around with two curved pistols thrust into his embroidered belt and a great, striped, turbaned hat. He will tell you that of all the Greeks, the Chiots have a delicacy about them. They are soft like their climate. They are mild, gay, lively, acute, industrious and proverbially timid.

When the Greek spring rises, first in the Balkans and then on the mainland, in the Peloponnese, the Chiots take little or no notice. They have no interest in changing their status. Things are fine as they are. But they are important to Turkey because they are rich, because of the mastic, so whether they like it or not, they are necessary to the independence. Their secession would be a financial loss to the Empire and a financial prop for the war. Complicated to-ing and fro-ing ensues. A first ship, sent by the revolutionaries to enlist Chios, fails. The Chiots reaffirm their allegiance to the Ottomans. Even so, forty of their leaders are held as hostages to their own word by the Turks. And so it goes on.

In March, independence fighters from Samos, down the coast, land and demand support. The Chiots, many of them, barricade themselves into their country estates and wait. There is fighting and looting, much of it indiscriminate and against the Chiot Greeks, and when it is over the Samians seem to have won. Cautiously the Chiots emerge. Uneasy quiet.

Three weeks later, the Turkish fleet appears, hurrying towards Chios under full sail. The Sultan has ordered that the island be retaken and brutally re-subjected. It is too valuable to lose. All Christians are to be killed or impaled. All men and boys over twelve, all women over forty, and for good measure, all two-year-old children. Everyone else is to be taken and sold in the slave markets of Constantinople. The women are to be raped and the town torched. Only the mastic villages are to remain unharmed.

When it is over, of a population that previously numbered a hundred and twenty thousand, only just under two thousand finally remain. Most have been killed, or sold into slavery. In the high mountains of the island's interior, those whose villages were surrounded jump to their death in the ravines, with their children in their arms, rather than be taken. Around twenty-one thousand hiding in the hills and caves and waiting for rescue by boats from nearby Psara escape onto the sea, heading first for the Cyclades, for Mykonos, Tinos, Andros and Syros.

So Chios has seen it all before. I don't know if it is my imagination, or the conditions in the camp, but sometimes, looking up at its mountain outline in the middle of the day, it can feel as though a shadow has settled over the island. The stark heights, snow covered now. The abandoned villages, where the crows flap with their heads on one side, listening to the sound of the wind. Or the places where tree-stumps and whole blackened hillsides show traces of recent wildfire – so that the island feels scarred and ghosted.

This bottleneck place where more and more people keep arriving and fewer and fewer leave. There are no more pitches in this camp. Look, on the pebbled beach by the sea shore, almost at the water's edge, they've put down these broken-backed tents. There are whole families in these useless little humps, already lopsided with wind. Eight people in a four-man tent lie listening to the pebbles grinding. A tiny child sitting in the open doorway. The constant sound of snapping canvas, and the tarpaulins over the tents flapping in high wind.

Weeks of abominable weather.

Someone's feet are sticking out into the rain.

One terrible night two boats arrive, just short of a hundred people, forty of whom are wading through freezing water because the engine on one of the boats has cut out. And a young man, carrying his cousin's child, stumbles and drops the girl in the water. She is four and she can't swim. Someone pulls her out safely and, in the hut where they wait for dawn, she is wrapped up in dry clothes but for the rest of the night the young man cries. He is so cold. He can't cope any more. He is worried he will die. He didn't mean to drop the child. It is four in the morning.

Throughout the day, when it finally comes, the new arrivals are found accommodation in tents and given papers. One of the families is Afghani. They have seven children. By eight at night the wind is blowing hard and they have been moved across the island to another camp but they still haven't been allocated a pitch. They stand motionless, by a bundle of possessions, in streaming rain. The baby wrapped against the mother's chest is screaming. They speak no English.

Why are they standing in the wind and the rain?

We are well practised by now. We pull our scarves down from our mouths and smile reassuringly. We show them to the distribution place, so that at least they can rest, so the children can have at least the partial shelter of a tarpaulin roof, hurrying them across to sit where the one lantern swings as if possessed and the rain and wind blow in through the open sides. The men put their hands to their chests, bend their heads in a graceful language of gesture. 'Thank you. Thank you.'

Why are they grateful when we aren't doing anything; when what we are doing is so small, so temporary, and is taking so long?

The woman sits on the wooden bench I have shown her, rocking her still crying child. When I bend to offer help, under the headscarf not a face at all but a statue someone has carved, a study of waiting. All angles and planes in some ancient ratio of patience. She is quiet. Only the pale eyes – are they green or just strained? – look at me suddenly soul to soul, while the baby goes on screaming.

I do what I can. I walk away.

We need a break. 'Let's just take a weekend or so,' Rupert says. 'Let's go down to the Cyclades and just take some time out.' And we can. We can go, after all, wherever we want. So we head down to the port and buy tickets and because our faces look white and western no one says we may not. No one needs our passports or ID cards. No one asks any questions. Many of the boys from the camp are here, milling about, looking edgy and without tickets, watching maybe how you could lie under a lorry. It doesn't look very possible. Everywhere, people in uniform are blowing whistles. A police woman in boots is sweeping very carefully under all the lorries with the beam of a huge torch. It's dark and the sea looks rough. We are headed for Syros.

And so are many others. Leaning out over the rail I see them bucking through the waves of a different time, on smaller wooden ships. Tens of thousands of refugees whose lives have been reduced to rubble; among them, a twenty-year-old who has been hiding in a cave in the mountains ever since the Turkish massacre: Loukas Zifos. He has seen such horrors. And he was lucky to get passage, wading out through the water to the dinghy, along with a crowd of others, and the boat from nearby Psara anchored in the bay so bravely in view of the Turks. 'Quick! Quick! Before we are stopped.' Trying not to look back at people he'd known all his life still floundering in the shallows, shouting, as the oarsmen pulled away. They couldn't take everyone.

The Turks saw the ship and fired on it, and those left on the beach to wait for the next load ran instead into the water, hoping to swim out or drown in the attempt. Two women who were nearest pitifully raised their hands and Loukas, on desperate impulse, reached down and held on so they could be towed behind. 'Let go! Let go!' people shout at him. 'You are slowing the rowers. We'll capsize.' But he holds on. When they reach the ship the women are hauled aboard. At least he has done something, one small thing, to right the wrongs, he thinks, trying to rally. But many people are crying, including men. Many people sit, as he does, unmoving on the deck, staring at nothing.

He is wet and the journey is long and very cold. He is given something, he doesn't notice what, to eat. He keeps making a nodding motion with his head as if to dislodge something. He keeps passing one hand over the lower half of his face, his rounded cheeks, the full, almost pouting lower lip. He shivers, however many blankets are put round him.

The following day we dock at Syros. I think of him as I step off into the harbour. It's so elegant this town – the capital of the Cyclades – a testament to the energy and resilience of the Chiot refugees. Because when Loukas arrived it didn't exist. At the water's edge there were just a few warehouses for wine and a little Catholic chapel. There was a town but it stood back from the sea, tipped out like the contents of a child's brick-box down the side of the conical hill above the harbour, out of reach of pirates. Its houses were tiny, primitive almost, many of them just little boxes, unornamented save for a jumble of shutters and washing lines, runs of narrow stairs connecting them instead of streets. It was more like a fishing village. Nothing to compare with Chios, with its lost mansions and its libraries, its country estates and its solid Genoese castle; nothing to its bustling cosmopolitan port, offices, law courts, market place, gardens. Standing on this shore for the first time Loukas would have found himself utterly at a loss. What could he do here? Turning his head instinctively back to where he'd come from, suddenly angry. This is the sticks. There is absolutely nothing here. Nothing.

But Syros had a neutrality that even the Turks acknowledged, and a deep and protected harbour. It was a safe place. And because it was the only harbour deep enough, all the big vessels docked here rather than at its larger neighbouring islands, Tinos or Andros or Mykonos. If you had to start again then this was a place where a start might be possible.

I can see Loukas silhouetted against the sea looking at the empty strand before him. 'Don't let it be for nothing, that you have survived,' he says to himself under his breath. And after that he never stops, because everything has to be built again from scratch.

He is given refuge, like the other Chiots, by people in the nothing fishing town, Ano Syros, as it is now called. He spends his time at the harbour, such as it is, and at night he sleeps on a bench in the shabby little café at the quay, waiting for the ships to arrive. Waking in the night and shifting his stiffened bones one way or the other he often feels something like a trapped bird batter its wings against his ribcage. He listens to the rasp of his breath and he gulps at the dark as if it were water. He can't tell if what he is feeling is panic over what has happened or haste about what is to come. The sound of the sea is the same as it was at home. 'Come on, man.' It takes such a long time, starting over.

When the ships dock he scurries aboard and buys whatever they have for sale. From a Russian boat, for instance, he buys dried fish. He takes it straight on another boat to Tinos, where he sells it in the market at a twenty per cent profit. Then he goes back to Syros. He buys olive oil and crosses back to Tinos again. Eight per cent this time. Back to Syros. The Russian ship is still there. He buys two barrels of red caviar and this time he hires a man to sell it for him so he can turn straight round for Syros without wasting any time.

Everyone is at it, scrabbling back their livelihoods after the massacre. Everyone is trying to make something. Two other Chiots approach him at Tinos. Why don't they band together, make a company buying and selling? It would save Loukas going back and forth. And that is what they do. Everywhere businesses are being started, buildings are being built, on the Chiot model, but grander; town houses in the neo-classical style, set around squares joined by wide streets, all of it made of marble. By the end of the century a whole new city has sprung up, on the opposite hill to the old one. Great houses, with staircases and painted ceilings and candelabra ordered from Paris, a gracious main square with a bandstand, a huge neo-classical town hall, a little opera house with red plush boxes, the first in Greece. Soon it is a rich and thriving capital city, the biggest port, for the time being, on the Aegean. Its growth is astoundingly rapid and it is all built by the refugees.

Ano Syros at first wants nothing to do with it. They refuse to acknowledge themselves to be one municipality. They stay on their hill, as they've always done, staring out at the glittering buildings going up on the other side of the valley. The refugees' town was separate. They must find themselves another name. They call it Ermoupolis, the city of Hermes.

'This is good,' I say to Rupert as we sit in one of the many cafés. We have coffee and little plates of complimentary cake in front of us. 'I'm feeling much more positive.'

He is looking at listings for that evening's theatre performance. 'There's an Athenian mime troupe that looks interesting – or there's cinema, or some kind of contemporary dance somewhere else. What do you think?' We slip so easily back into our comforts. It takes us no time at all to forget. We choose the mime.

But after our two days' rest we are back on Chios to finish our agreed stint. We burrow our way back to our lodgings from the port, through streets that double back on themselves, or come suddenly to an end. It is so confusing even Rupert mistakes his way – a town that lost itself, that put itself back together as best it could. I compare it to Ermoupolis in my mind. We drop our bags and go straight to our first shift. It is evening, black dark and still raining.

I don't know whether it is the calm of our two days on Syros but things seem more disordered. At the camp the NGOs are fighting among themselves. There are arguments over the setting up of a lending library. One organization has a venue but no books. Another has no venue but boxes and boxes of books, none of which they will hand over unless they are allowed to help with the running of the library. They are not allowed. They may not even come into the building. They must hand over the books at the threshold. 'So what's happened?' I ask a colleague while we manage the shifting food queues.

She shrugs at me, 'They refused. They took them all away.'

'To where?'

'The warehouse.' We exchange looks. We have both seen the warehouse. I had to visit it once to find boots for two girls from Eritrea shod only in sodden pumps. I don't have much hope for the books. The warehouse is like a task out of a fairy tale, a vast and windowless room, staffed by a single patient volunteer who sits by a chaos of possessions, as if a hurricane had taken place inside; her job: slowly sorting its damage into piles. Around her steady effort, cardboard boxes rise in towers.

The food queue shuffles forward. Outside the usual dancing is taking place. A blonde Danish girl is leading the Birdie Song while her father films with a small video camera. She looks about sixteen. 'This is such a great learning experience,' her mother tells me. 'We have been weeping in the tents all afternoon. Terrible stories. It's really humanizing for the children.' No doubt. But it's too confusing. I don't know how to answer so again I walk away. I go to find Rupert.

Further into the camp itself a group of people have lit a fire and are cooking spaghetti. 'Eat,' they say to us as we pass. It sounds like an order, so we do. They have tipped it out, sauce and all, into a washing-up bowl. We dip our hands and drop it into our mouths, heads tilted backwards. Rain and pasta mixed together. 'What do you think of African food?' Am I imagining a challenge?

'Excellent,' we say, although to me it has a sour taste.

Over the next days things steadily worsen. An American volunteer gets drunk and starts a fight with the police. One of our organizers resigns with immediate effect. The rest of us play Chinese Whispers with the news. Hard eyes glitter in the food queues and the atmosphere seems volatile. And, in case anything else were needed to guarantee misery, the rain continues. Water has bellied the tarpaulins, lashed above our heads in the distribution centre. Every now and then it forces a crack where the plastic overlaps and a drowning chute finds its way through onto whoever is underneath. We move about with head-torches, the one overhead lamp swinging wildly in the wind.

In the melee for food, under the leaking shelter, I see Philoctetes and the young men gathered in a knot of concentration round someone new. Their heads are bent inwards listening. A man in an old-fashioned trench-coat and a trilby, who looks odd, out of place. Perhaps he arrived while we were away. I haven't seen him before and for a moment I wonder whether he is an official of some kind, someone organizing onward migration. He must have felt my gaze because he turns suddenly, and when he does so, I see that his face, under the hat, is covered by a skin-tight mask. The black symmetry of a Rorschach test somehow sealed over his features like a second skin. He is looking straight at me. Oh no, I think. Not you. My lips keep moving but no noise comes out. Not you. Not you. Nothing comes out above a whisper. I try again, this time out loud.

'What are you doing here?'

He turns back again. He has no apparent interest in my question. No one else has noticed – or no one else seems to know who he is. But we must get rid of him. I look round. I think I need help. He is a frightening man, a very frightening man. I know who he is: one of Alan Moore's Watchmen. He is Rorschach, a kind of incarnation of apocalypse, and he has got the attention of the men around him, including the war-hungry Philoctetes. When he opens his mouth to continue, he speaks in the staccato phrases of extreme lucidity, which is the same thing, in the end, as madness.

'I felt the dark planet turn under my feet,' he says in an odd voice, strained, damaged, the sound of a prisoner filing at an iron bar. 'Looked at sky through smoke heavy with human fat,' he says, 'and God was not there. The cold suffocating dark goes on forever, and we are alone.'

The men around him shift. They have been bred to another creed. Many of them are religious but experience and hopelessness have made them suggestible, and they recognize Rorschach's emotion.

'Existence is random,' he tells them, the patterns that cover his face flexing as he speaks. 'Has no pattern save what we imagine after staring at it for too long. No meaning save what we choose to impose.'

This is the dark side of Rupert's creed. I don't want to believe what Rorschach is saying, or rather I don't want to believe it that way. Most of all

I don't want them to believe it. I shout into the little knot of men. 'It doesn't have to be like that. You can live – we can live differently. We can change. Everyone says so – Andrić, D.H. Lawrence, Ariosto.' But I am absurd, the wrong gender, the wrong privileged nationality. No one is listening.

'It is not God who kills the children,' Rorschach goes on, unstoppable, leaking his message like the roof leaks the rain, while the men who are so desperate, so parched of purpose, so confused and angered and shiftless, drink it up. 'Not fate who butchers them or destiny that feeds them to the dogs. It's us. Only us. Streets stank of fire.' He raises one arm, not in fever like d'Annunzio but almost laconic, lets it drop. 'Was reborn then,' he says while in his audience's eyes I can see the bitter bomb-dust ruins of their native places. 'Was free to scrawl own design on this morally blank world.' He turns again, to face me. 'Does that answer your questions?'

'No! No! It doesn't.' I clutch my hands to the sides of my head in urgency. Something is going to burst. 'It doesn't answer my questions. And it doesn't answer theirs either, although they think it does. You can build a beautiful city – I've seen it. You can make new lives. You can choose your answers. There isn't only one, and anyway, that isn't what Watchmen means,' I shout.

'Isn't it?' My one self, quiet for so long, asks my other.

'I don't know,' I say inside. I don't know. It's all so hopeless. No one is listening. I saw Alan Moore once, in the post office, in Northampton, like someone escaped out of his own text, fantastic and other-worldly in rings and long hair and with a wizard's stick. I was too shy to ask. So I'm asking now. 'Is it this hopeless, Alan? If it is, then why did you make what looks like good so attractive, so right? And why did you then undermine it? Because my one self is starting to believe you, although it very much doesn't want to.'

Rorschach watches me as I stand hesitating. 'Open eyes. Look at evidence,' the flexing mask instructs me, with its weird syntax and its rasping voice. 'All sides are the same. Walked through the streets of Tripolitsa myself, in 1821. Saw the fires where Greeks were roasting Turks on spits like pigs, saw the piles of arms and legs cut off, the pregnant women cut open and dogs heads thrust between their legs. Three days I walked, up to my knees in blood and corpses, screams so loud and so constant, thought they were inside my own head. Tried to number bodies. Lost count after eight thousand. Realized then that dark is inside us all. You too,' he tells me, 'if you listen. That noise you hear. Something battering against the wall of ribs, not your heart. That is the beast you keep waiting to be unleashed.'

Instinctively I put my hands over my ears. I walk away. I remember the wild beast that Andrić said lives in man, waiting for law and custom to break down, and I don't want this to be true. 'When the time comes,' Rorschach says to my back, 'you too will let it out.'

'You are wrong,' I say, stopping and facing him again. I say it with spaces between each of the words. 'You. Are. Wrong.' And while I say it, something in my chest hurls itself repeatedly against my ribcage. 'The only monster I have inside me is my own fear.'

'That is the one I'm talking about,' Rorschach says.

I think of my friend whose child was dropped in the water. She lives with her two little daughters, one called Moon and the other called Light, and her husband, and with them, in the same space, live her cousins and their husbands and wives, eight people in all, one of the better shelters. They are the only survivors of a family party that started out double the size. She has only one functioning kidney; she has escaped from Syria; and she is always optimistic, always laughing. She speaks English and German and, any time we visit, one of her cousins puts her head, beautiful as a giraffe, over the blanket partition between their quarters to watch.

They offer hope. They are determinedly constructive, although in moments of rest the man's eyes show deep mourning, for people undoubtedly but also for his country, which he might never see again. When he moves about in the tent he moves gingerly as though his body hurt. But these people seem to have survived horror and are kind to each other. They are open and they are very positive. I would like to ask her candidly, do you think you have a monster inside you? She doesn't seem afraid of anything. She is grateful for her escape. She could build, I think. She will work. If she can get out of here. She is brave and accepting and resilient. She will raise, if not a city, then a new life out of the rubble of her old one. She will speak a new language and manage her old religion and love her family, and although she will never, however she tries, feel at home again, this won't be the case for her children. So there is – there must be – hope.

Rorschach is watching me closely.

'Is it as bad as you say, Ritsos? Alan?'

'I don't know,' Alan Moore tells my one self, gnomic, with his wizard rings and his wizard's white hair. 'Read more closely.'

There is little time and I see I have to make my own decision. I think of the London I left. There must be something, some thread I can pull, that will unravel all this before it is too late – some charm, some key, as promised, to unpick the pattern of destruction. And in a flash I think perhaps that Joan of Arc was right. Perhaps I did walk out on my country. Perhaps, in my fear of its systems and my hurry to distance myself from its mistakes, I gave up when I should have stood my ground. I do so now, in this place of lostness, instead.

If I have cast myself adrift, I do still have a home after all. I could turn round. I could quiet my fear because Rorschach is right in this alone: that fear is the thing that makes us dangerous, to ourselves as much as to others. Why else do we war and hoard and divide ourselves so destructively from our own kind – if not in anticipation of diminishment, or hunger, or pain; if not in fear of difference, whether national or cultural or social? Then, when we've worried and legislated with only our own interests in mind, we scrabble together the barriers and borders between us, to sit down in the chill of their shadow, and wait for the conflict whose conditions for existence we have just created.

So against this at least, I could flip my fear like a coin. I could watch it spin in the light and see its opposite side come down. And the opposite of fear is faith. In faith I could perhaps go back. I could, in the camaraderie of belonging, try for change or, if change doesn't come, just companionably wait. I could accept the difficulty, the shame of short-sighted muddle and self-interest, the occasionally brutal parochiality, because, whether I like it or not, it is also mine. And because there is much that is lovely there.

The eyes of the men who are watching me glitter. They are waiting. Away beyond them stretch the tents, the miserable streets of the camp whose many potholes, brimming with water, gleam like eye-shine, as if they too were watching, waiting for me to decide. Everything, the brokenness, the endless, shifting, restless feeling of the camp seems suspended, the whole whirling cycle momentarily stopped, caught into my indecision.

I look at the Watchman. 'There is nothing hiding inside me any more,' I say. I open my hands wide. 'I am giving up Fear.' A wind has sprung up and from somewhere in the darkness, at the far end of the camp, a desolate cry carries. The black blotches on Rorschach's mask stretch and slide upwards. I have the feeling he is laughing at me.

After

Loukas, the Chiot refugee, had he known it, is a lesson in homesickness. There is much he could teach me. I think of him as I lean over the ship's rail, leaving Chios at the start of our journey onward, how he never stopped missing his island. It is a luxury after all, open only to those not in exile, not to miss your country. Loukas stayed on Syros for three years and then in impatience took himself elsewhere, his restlessness as much an index of his pain as it was of his determination, his faith in the future. He didn't wait to see Ermoupolis, that substitute city, built. He went instead in the opposite direction to me, to England, because if things were going to be different they might as well be truly different – and because, in England, the canvas was bigger.

He started a cotton business in Manchester and he died, rewarded, a grand Victorian, in a thick English suit, in a wedding-cake house in Bayswater. Every day, if he wanted, he could walk out from his house in Leinster Square, to the park with its new formal garden and its fountains, and its giant planes and limes standing quiet, in grass, beyond. He didn't know quite what he was looking for. Light perhaps. He lived among an enclave of Greek refugees, all in shipping or banking or trade of some kind. He was successful. He died leaving enough money for his sons to make a contribution to the building of Hagia Sophia, the Greek Orthodox cathedral on Moscow Road, in his memory. But sometimes when he sat over his coffee, staring into the distance, his sons noticed a habit he had of nodding his head, as though shaking something loose, of passing one, successful, hand repeatedly over the lower half of his face.

There was the horror of the massacre, the trauma of losing one's loved ones, but that wasn't the only thing. You could madden yourself with remembering that, or you could put it behind you, close it into silence, and make a new life. But even if you did, something else was lost, a way of living, a place grown a certain way, bedded in its own particular customs and memories. He couldn't help remembering Chios, its sea and its stately harbour front, the terrible tragedy of its destruction. He couldn't help remembering the gold stone villas at Kambos, the heron standing on one leg by the water-filled sterna, or the stillness in the roads between the high estate walls, and the scent of the citrus orchards, heavy on the afternoon. Nothing in London or Manchester was like that. None of the money he made could buy that back for him. Places can die, just like people. When they are lost, they are truly lost and he wanted so much sometimes to go home. 'I am Greek, after all,' he would say to himself, looking out at the English rain.

Arriving on Syros once more, I feel so sorry for Loukas. We are following in his footsteps: Chios to Syros, Syros to England – or that's as much plan as we have made so far. If fear was the reason I left in the first place then giving it up means going home. This is a certainty – the first I have felt since leaving London. Even so, I guard my remaining freedom. However certain I am, I don't want to go. There is a little time yet, I tell myself, looking at the marble streets under morning light. We walk around in winter sun, and we rest, in Ermoupolis – the city of Hermes.

'Why Hermes?' I ask when we run into him one afternoon, climbing the steep and slippery marble avenues of his town. It's confusing; he looks so like Rupert. I almost can't tell which is which.

'Because Hermes is the god of tricksters, thieves, roads, boundaries, travel and success in commerce,' Rupert says.

I look from one to the other. 'I didn't know that. You never told me. You didn't say any of those things when I asked, at the beginning, on the station platform.' My mouth is hanging. 'You're the god of the Eustaces.' The real Hermes smiles.

'Why make such a fuss, and anyway you never asked,' Rupert says, photographing us together. Hermes' city is ruining already, less than a century after its beginning. Greece is teetering on the brink. The grand houses are empty and collapsing into the street, doors onto painted hallways swing loose in the wind. I run to catch up. Either side of us, stray cats howl and breed in the fallen rubble. Hermes doesn't seem to mind. Rupert points his camera at the sweep of a shattered staircase, photographs it for the record. 'Look what the Eustaces did. It wasn't all bad.'

'Wait,' I say, tripping on a piece of broken pavement. I snatch at Rupert to steady myself. 'I'm so confused. Are you saying the refugees were Eustaces?' I am incredulous.

'It's your categorization, not mine,' Rupert says, 'but yes, obviously – if you give them a chance, why wouldn't they be? That's what they were before, isn't it, Loukas and his like – traders, merchants? That's what they knew.' I stand still and look around me. I can feel it almost like a wind, the energy to make good, to forget, that swept this place in the fever of exile, as if this was all we ever do – build, and rubble. Build again.

The following spring, still making our roundabout way home, we find ourselves on Crete, camping in gorges and walking and bathing in the rivers. The Greek for spring is anixi; the opening. And that is what the landscape is doing. The plane trees along the river make a pale mist in the valley bottoms. Out of the parched deadness, out of the rock, everywhere, there are flowers. It is like being caught in a Botticelli painting, iris, anemone, orchids, muscari, little coloured pea flowers like jewels in the light, lavender, pinks, wild tulips, fritillaries, sage, the list is endless, a constantly changing carpet.

By the roadside, as we pass, the figs hold up little green hands, either in expostulation or in veneration. I don't know which. But it is the same gesture as the Minoan clay figures in the Heraklion museum make, their eyes wide for looking, their mouths, like the Stone Copper people's, mostly closed. I have seen them in delicate frescoes painted by themselves in around 2000 BC, their hair tumbling about their shoulders, their mouths in secret smiles. And I've seen them in frescoes painted by the Boulogne Mummy's people, wearing complex and beautifully patterned kilts. They are carrying their complex and beautifully patterned pottery in procession, as a present, to the Egyptians. The Keftiu, as the Egyptians called them. I think of the Boulogne Mummy, as it might have been in life, watching their stately approach. They look pleased with their gifts and I'm not surprised. Their art is so lovely, so lively, so observant. Every pattern that life can make, leaves, scrolls, sprouts, flowers, animals, fish, shells, is caught and celebrated here, on plates, on vases, on little delicate coloured cups with handles. There are statuettes and pictures and tables, jars and vases and board games, tiles, trivets, pots and pans.

The Minoans are extraordinary and restless technicians. They work in stone and clay and wood and shell and ivory. They lived between about 2500 and 1100 BC and they left us writings in a script we can't decipher, so we know almost nothing about them at all. But they did paint. That's how I've seen them, in their paintings. I have seen them bull-leaping, both girls and boys. I have seen them dancing and in procession. And on a black vase I have seen harvesters coming home, their elegant three-pronged pitchforks high on their shoulders. Some of them are singing to a sistrum held aloft. One man is turning round. One man has stumbled. There is a swirl of movement. They seem energetic, joyful, full of life. But they have gone now, melted away, as if they were made of snow.

Crete is a violent place. Anything could have happened. Above it, geographically, is an arc of still active volcanoes. Below it is a tectonic fault. It is a place repeatedly riven and scarred, pinned between possible catastrophes. The Minoans are gone, as are the Mycenaeans who came after them. So too are Crete's other occupiers – the Dorians, the Venetians who took over in 1210 and didn't leave until 1650, the Ottomans who came straight after, and even briefly the Germans – all as if shrugged off, perhaps by the mountains themselves.

The Cretan villages we pass through as we walk are mostly poor. Sometimes they have Ottoman drinking fountains in their quiet squares. Sometimes they have churches, built and decorated to an Italian rather than Greek design. Many have memorials to people killed under German occupation in the Second World War, villages that have been burned and left, great bursts of flowers colonizing what was once inside. Often as we head down into another gorge we come across a marker that tells us the names of all the men and boys, sixty-one here, among all this spring opening, among all this hope and renewal, who were ranged above this river and shot under command, by jittery German troopers probably barely out of their teens, just like the Serbian YouTube boy who'd been trained on pigs. 'Just one more thing, Ariosto,' I say as we pass, 'everything changes but everything also stays the same.'

When we lose our way, we are met by old ladies in headscarves tending little tangled gardens. They smile and put us right, often thinking we are German. 'Bitte,' they sometimes say. 'Allo. Allo.' They offer us things and show us their flowers. Sometimes you shoot us. Sometimes we shoot you. Otherwise, we are friends. They don't say it, but that's how it seems.

'We are not German,' we keep on saying. It seems important. The women take no notice.

'German, German,' they nod and smile. 'Bitte. Peraste.' Please and come in, in a mix of German and Greek.

On the windowsill of the house behind, the spoon used to stir the coffee-grounds lies in its little pool, already found by the ants. And the lizard lies on the hot stone, its neck flickering with a minute pulse. All just the same, just as it was the day they really came. It was just like this. You see, there was no warning. Nothing to tell anyone that the day would be any different, when the trucks arrived and 'Raus! Raus!' The men were separated out and never came back. Life doesn't differentiate like that. It just goes on the same.

The women smile at us, bent over their plants, and wave their knobbled hands at the path we are to take. And I can see that they, the survivors, and we, whom they think obscurely may be implicated but are not – and it doesn't matter now either way – are linked anyway, just as they think. If we didn't do exactly this, in this place, then we did something else, somewhere else, to someone else, some other time; either we to them, or them to us. We won't or can't change, for all our talk. We are all of us woven in and out of the same events, the same behaviours, in different combinations, as if we were all one giant Coventry ribbon. What is there to do except wait your turn and then wait for renewal, cultivate it in your garden?

In all countries, for as long as they are allowed, and in whichever place they find themselves, people bend over the ground in acceptance and wait for renewal, just like Ariosto with his capers. Until one day the ground gets up and tucks itself over them and they're gone. The meaning, if there is one, is in the repeat. And the repeat is life, which just goes on until, of course, it stops.

So the Minoans, delicate in their baseball boots and their belted codpieces, spit on their palms, and measure their moment as the bull comes thundering towards them. They lift up their life as lightly as if it were thistledown, facing the danger. They grasp the terrible lowered horns and feel themselves tossed, upwards… into flight… Arms wide, chest thrust forward…

Leap…

Somersault over the back of the bull, back arched and arms outstretched, not knowing that they will make the whole circle, to land again, miraculously on their feet, thousands of miles, thousands of millennia away, in white, in the Camargue, in modern France.

Nothing's changed. Are you listening, God?

Can you hear me? Everything's the same as it was, as it always was.

God can't hear. He has his fingers rammed in his ears against the coming explosion. Never mind. Let him watch my mouth working.

I accept nothing about life but I do see it now. I see the design, in which we are the flaw. I see our anxiety will always outweigh our interest in good. I see the repeated terrors looping out of the long horizon with the little ornamental flourishes offered by civilization in between. I see the ways that we try to fix ourselves into some kind of permanence, through art, or through power, or through wealth and possessions; the ways we find identity or just keep ourselves safe, huddling into significant groups by class, or politics, religion, or nationality. I think of BritAnnia shifting her bags on her step in London, a one-woman nation. 'Well,' I say to her, 'you've got Joyce on your side. Maybe I shouldn't have been so quick to dismiss you.'

'There's also music,' Rupert says, 'and love.' He must have been reading my thoughts.

'Yes, there are those things. But I'm thinking of how to get rid of fear and quiet anxiety. That, I think, is our problem. Music and love are too fleeting. If we can't change then we need at least to belong to something bigger than just ourselves. So, it's unfashionable among liberals, but I've come back to nationhood. That's a strong and unignorable thing – stronger than we like to allow. And maybe Anne and Joyce are right. Maybe that's how to look at it: that each individual is their nation, not the other way around. That way it makes sense, in terms of belonging, in terms of identity, and it is endlessly and healthily expandable.'

'Your time is almost up,' he says.

'How so?'

We are sitting on the balcony of our room, which looks out over the harbour. The ferry, which we always watch because of the skill of its handbrake turn, is rounding the mole, its foghorn sounding. 'I've been thinking about the hold that a country has over its people, and the stupidity of attributing that to abstract and unchanging qualities,' I say. 'But I can see that England, for instance, is something distinct. I can feel the pull of that, now I'm going home. And I've decided it's made of different things, all of which are the result of random events in particular places and none of which are innate.' I glance at Rupert to see whether I've lost him yet. I haven't. 'It is both the way things looked before and the way things have come to look now. It's the deep print of different people, from very different places, all living their lives in one particular landscape. Some of the ways that the print has been made is the result of tradition and practice and technique imported from elsewhere, and some of it is made by people who, mostly for economic reasons, have never left. And all of it is English simply because it has either grown, or been adapted to fit England's particular conditions of ground or climate.'

Rupert is tipping his chair, his feet on the cast-iron balcony top. He turns his mouth down and gives a nod.

'And then, given these beginnings, things have gone on, have evolved or developed, in that pattern, and with that logic, into how they are now. That's all. The emotional response to a place, which is what nationalism depends on, is private. There's no commonality of experience – or very limited. So my conclusion is that a country is a kind of glacier, solid and always slowly moving and changing, while a nation is just a huge number of individual experiences of the glacier, jumbled together, under the assumption that they are the same. Which they aren't.'

'Aha.'

'What you know of it is just what you see through the keyhole of your own character and circumstance. It's not the whole; just your bit. One man, one nation.' I turn to Rupert who is assembling his possessions. It looks as though he is leaving. 'See?'

'I do, sweetheart,' Rupert says. 'I always did.'

So we get up to go and my troubled one self, which has been listening for once, looks experimentally and at a distance, through its own keyhole, at what it knows. And what it knows is a place made of quietness, of walls either stone, or brick, or flint, of gardens turning under hands, of fruit falling however much it is picked, of graded light, of clouds, of churches. Of words and of woods. 'My woods,' it says quietly under its breath.

I'm coming back, BritAnnia. Maybe, if there's room, I will sit down with you on that step. If change is impossible then companionship is second best. We can watch whatever it is that is coming, together, among our bags of belongings, in the glow of your little lighter.

Amen, God, if you're still there.

I said, Amen.

Translations

p. 79   Moi, Nicolas Rolin, chevalier, citoyen d'Autun, seigneur d'Authume
et chancelier de Bourgogne, en ce jour de dimanche, le 4 du mois
d'août, en l'an de Seigneur 1443…dans l'intérêt de mon salut,
désireux d'échanger contre des biens célestes, les biens temporels…
je fonde, et dote irrévocablement en la ville de Beaune, un hôpital
pour les pauvres malades, avec une chapelle, en l'honneur de Dieu
et de sa glorieuse mère…

I, Nicolas Rolin, citizen and seigneur of Autun and chancellor of
Burgundy, on this day, Sunday 4th August, in the year of our Lord
1443…for my salvation do wish to offer in exchange for heavenly
bliss, certain worldly goods…I found and endow in perpetuity, in
the town of Beaune, a hospital for the poor, together with a chapel
dedicated to God and his glorious mother…

p. 81   Il est bien juste que Rolin, après avoir fait tant de pauvres pendant
sa vie, leur laisse un asile après sa mort.

It is only right that Rolin, having made paupers of so many in his
lifetime, should leave them an asylum when he's dead.

p. 107 …un des cloaques les plus impurs, où s'amasse l'écume de
la Méditerranée… C'est l'empire du péché et de la mort. Ces
quartiers…abandonnés à la canaille, la misère et la honte, quel
moyen de les vider de leur pus et les régénérer?

…one of the filthiest cesspools, where the scum of the
Mediterranean gathers… It is a kingdom of vice and death. In these
quarters given over to the rabble, abandoned to misery and shame,
by what means can we empty them of their pus and revive them?

p. 118 J'ai voué ma vie,' he says solemnly, 'à un idéal: la Provence, et je n'ai embrassé mon métier que pour mieux servir cet idéal, pour me trouver plus près du peuple provençal, pour mieux arriver jusqu'à son coeur et pour mieux l'aider à sauver son passé de gloire, sa langue et ses coutumes.

I have given my life to an ideal: Provence, and I work only in order to better to serve this ideal, to bring myself into closer communion with the people of Provence, to enter into their hearts, to help them to save their glorious past, their language and their customs.

Picture credits

p. 36 The Boulogne Mummy © Mark Andrews Photography

p. 65 Cratère de Vix, VIe siècle av. J.-C., *Musée du Pays Châtillonnais –
Trésor de Vix, Châtillon-sur-Seine, Côte-d'Or* © Mathieu Rabaud –
RMN Grand Palais

p. 117 Folco de Baroncelli-Javon by TONIOJF is used under a CC BY-SA
4.0 license. Modifications to this photo include cropping

p. 125 Aubrey Beardsley by Monsieur Abel © National Portrait Gallery,
London

p. 144 Salmo carpio – Carpione is borrowed from the Freshwater and
Marine Image Bank at the University of Washington. Modifications
to this photo include cropping

p. 196 Gavrilo Princip by Gebruiker: used under a CC BY-SA 3.0 license.
Modifications to this photo include cropping